I0715988

L.A. MCBRIDE

STITCHING THE TALISMAN

A KALI JAMES NOVEL: BOOK THREE

Copyright © 2022 by L.A. McBride

author@lamcbride.com

ALL RIGHTS RESERVED.

This book contains material protected under International and Federal Copyright Laws and Treaties. Any unauthorized reprint or use of this material is prohibited. No part of this book may be reproduced or transmitted in any form or by any means, electronic or mechanical, including photocopying, recording, or by an information storage and retrieval system without express written permission from the author.

Cover Artist: Original Book Cover Designs

Editor: Sara Lundberg

ISBN: 978-1-957445-07-6

This book is a work of fiction. Names, characters, businesses, places, and events are either the product of the author's imagination or used in a fictitious manner. Any resemblance to actual persons, living or dead, businesses, places, or events is entirely coincidental.

NEWSLETTER SIGNUP

Subscribe to my newsletter for updates, announcements, contests, and bonus content: lamcbride.com/newsletter/

No one charged into battle quite like a group of twenty-somethings with too much time on their hands and access to an Army surplus store, as evidenced by the group of men across from us. After a tense few weeks, we were ready for a distraction, which is how we ended up outside the local paintball range waiting to face off with our archnemeses. Other than Janis's visiting niece who was a paintball virgin, we'd all been to this range several times, thanks to our ongoing rivalry with this band of twenty-something jerks who fancied themselves soldiers.

What had started a couple months ago as a fun way to spend a Saturday with Riley's witches quickly escalated into what Bea had dubbed Paintball Wars. So far, we were 0-4. The douche brigade we were up against took paintball very, very seriously. Not only did they show up rain or shine dressed in military fatigues, they brought MREs for snacks like they were actual Army rangers or something. They also came armed with elaborate battle plans.

The only formation we'd managed so far was forward.

Today, we were down three players. Emma was out of town visiting her grandmother who just had surgery, Bennie refused to come back after "the incident," and Alyce's tricky hip was acting up. That left me, Riley, Janis, Bea, Helen, and Janis's twenty-four-year-old niece Olivia. Riley had offered to recruit a couple substitutes, so we'd have the required eight people to go head-to-head with the guys. Knowing Riley, it was hard to say who would show up, but whoever it was, she assured me they'd be here by starting time.

"How do I work this thing?" Olivia shook the paintball gun before looking down the barrel. Olivia was staying with Janis while she looked for a job that would get her out of her tiny South Dakota hometown. She was a wide-eyed strawberry blonde who jumped at her own shadow. I didn't have high hopes for her paintball prowess.

Bea grabbed the paintball gun out of Olivia's hands and demonstrated how to use it again. Today, Bea looked like a Golden Girls meets Rambo mashup. She might have been in her late sixties, but Bea was rocking the camo. Although Riley and Bea had tried to convince me to wear camouflage, there were some fashion lines I refused to cross. That was one of them. I'd settled on cute hiking boots, skinny black jeans, and a forest green sweater with a scoop neck low enough I hoped it would give me a tactical advantage.

Riley scowled at Olivia, who was still fumbling around with her paintball gun. "I think she's going to be a liability." Riley nudged me in the side. "We better not lose."

"We always lose," I countered. Facts were facts, no matter how much I'd like to make those puffed-up jerks eat paint.

"Not this time," Riley smirked. "I've got a plan."

"Me, too," Helen said, clutching her brown paper lunch bag. Only Helen knew what was in it, and she refused to let us peek. She mumbled something about secret weapons and ruining the surprise. The guys on the other team had made one too many old women jokes the last time we faced off, so Helen was out for blood. I just hoped whatever she had in her bag didn't get us arrested.

Riley high-fived Helen before turning back to the parking lot and waving both arms enthusiastically. I turned around to see who she'd talked into joining our rag-tag group. Then, I gawked at the last two people I expected to show up.

"How on earth did you convince them to do this?" I asked Riley.

Craig Ward and Max Volkov were headed our way, and the closer they got, the more annoyed they both looked.

"I told them we needed firepower." Riley fist pumped. "We're so gonna win."

I took in the murderous look Volkov was leveling at Riley. "I don't think he's going to play."

"He'll play." Riley exuded confidence that didn't falter even when Volkov nearly popped a vein.

"Why the fuck are we here, Riley?" Volkov asked.

She grabbed his arm with one hand and Craig's with her other, high-stepping backward as she pulled them onto the range. "Come on. I'll explain while you gear up."

They must have been taken off guard because they followed her despite the seriously irritated expressions they were both wearing. As soon as we were on the range, Riley dropped their arms to dig into our bag of supplies. She pulled out the camo paint she'd swiped from my costume shop and squeezed some out of the tube. Standing on her tiptoes, she smeared it across one of Volkov's cheeks, preparing to do the same to the other until he grabbed her hand to stop her.

He leaned down so the two of them were at eye level. "This

explanation had better be good because you said you needed protection."

Riley used her free hand to swipe the paint off the one he held in a tight grip. Before Volkov could object, she reached up and smeared it on the other side of his face. "We do." She pointed to the benches where the other team was camped out. "Those guys are going to take us all out unless you two help us."

Volkov grabbed her second hand, rendering her temporarily immobile. "You do realize I'm the alpha, right?"

Riley shrugged. "So?"

"So, I have more important things to do than play games with a bunch of witches and wannabe soldiers." Volkov practically snarled in her face.

Helen tried to thump Volkov in the back of his head, but at four foot ten, all she managed was a good thwack between his shoulder blades. "You better watch your tone around me, pup."

Volkov opened his mouth but quickly snapped it shut again. He let go of Riley's hands and took a step away from all of us, presumably to gain control of his rising temper.

I looked at Craig, who telegraphed his annoyance more subtly than Volkov but no less effectively. "Sorry. I had no idea she called you."

Craig scanned me from head to toe, lingering on the neckline of my sweater, before surveying the range with a raised eyebrow. "What are you doing here?"

Bea chose that moment to step into his personal space and plaster herself against his side. She batted her eyelashes at him. "We're here for Paintball Wars, sugar." She grabbed one of his big hands and held it up. "I'll bet with hands like this, you'll be able to handle a paintball gun real good." Bea made the most boring things sound lewd. It was her superpower.

Craig took a deep breath through his nose and stared at a point on the other side of the range.

Volkov rejoined the group, his face slightly less livid than when he'd walked away. "We are not staying."

"Don't be like that," Riley cajoled. "Isn't this what you train for?"

"This," he said, gesturing around the range, disgust evident in his voice, "is most definitely not what I train for." Volkov threw his hands up as if to ward Riley off.

Before he could storm off, the douche brigade started in.

"That's right, pretty boy. You better run back home. Wouldn't want to muss up your hair." The skinny guy sitting next to the one running his mouth laughed loudly and clapped his friend on the back.

Volkov looked incredulous. "Did he just call me a pretty boy?" There was no denying he was attractive with his dark hair and pale blue eyes, but Volkov looked more like he belonged in an NFL huddle than a boy band. I was certain this was the first time anyone had dared call him pretty.

The guy doubled down. "You heard me." He stood up and struck a model pose. Like a pack of hyenas, the rest of the group leaned in, ready for the blood sport to begin. *Idiots.*

But they were far from done. The most athletic guy in their group nudged his buddy before pointing at Craig. "Hey big man, why don't you stay? I haven't had a target that big since your mama."

Craig stiffened, the only tell that he was contemplating ripping the man's limbs off one by one and beating him to death with them. I stepped between them, my back to the group of guys. "They're kind of jackasses. Don't let them get to you."

"You mean the way we got to you, sweet cheeks?"

Craig picked me up and swiveled to the side before setting me back on my feet. He made a move toward the group of loudmouths who had suddenly gone very quiet. With the build of a tank, flinty gray eyes, and a shaved head, Craig was intimidating without trying. And right now, he was trying.

Riley got to Craig before he reached the guy, thrusting a giant paintball gun into his hands. "You ready to nail these assholes?"

Craig smiled and pointed over her head at the heckler. "I'm coming for you."

The guy paled and stumbled back a step, the others closing ranks.

With an exaggerated sigh, Volkov stalked over to our weapons pile and picked through them until he found a gun that passed his inspection. He held out his hand, still looking annoyed to be here. "Paintballs?"

Riley rushed to hand over the ammo without a word.

Alyce cackled and settled herself on the far bench, reaching inside her purse to pull out several mini bottles of alcohol. She collected them from hotel rooms and flights like most people collect soaps and little shampoos. She downed the first one in a single gulp and lined the others up next to her. "Give 'em hell boys!"

Riley rounded everyone up in a circle and stuck her hand out. Helen, Bea, Janis, and I all added our hands to the huddle. Olivia was slower, but she eventually caught on. Riley stared expectantly at the two holdouts until Craig and Volkov caved and added their hands to the pile. "For Bennie!" Riley yelled.

Craig and Volkov both looked at me for an explanation.

"It's a long, painful story and one he'd probably rather I didn't tell you."

The other team crossed the field, taking up positions behind a berm. They dropped to their stomachs, resting their guns on top of the raised ground like they were in the trenches of an actual battlefield. Then, the ridiculous hand signals started.

Riley flipped them the bird before tugging Volkov to the ground with her behind a pile of old tires. The rest of us had to settle for crouching behind a tiny half wall made of cedar pickets.

"What's the plan?" Craig asked, his voice close to my ear.

I laughed. "We shoot."

He frowned. "That's not a plan."

"And that's why we lose."

He caught Volkov's eye and canted his head to the left. Volkov nodded. "Follow my lead," Craig told me.

When the shooting started, Craig and Volkov began systematically moving down field, taking turns covering each other while they picked off the other team every time they raised their stupid heads. Because Craig hadn't specified what follow his lead meant, I was content to hang back and watch them decimate the jerks. I'd call it a win regardless of who did the actual shooting.

Craig hit the skinny kid as he sat up to take a shot. He clutched his stomach and staggered backward before getting to his feet, whining the whole way as he trekked back to our side of the field. I looked up when he finally reached us. He held his shirt up to show me the red splotch mark where he had been hit.

"Is it bad?" he asked with a wince.

"Are you kidding me?" I scoffed.

Helen moved closer to my side. "That's four," she said, pointing a finger in the shape of a gun and pulling the trigger as he passed us. She opened her bag and peered inside. "This is bullshit. If those two keep shooting them so fast, I'm not going to get a chance to use my surprise."

"Fine." I raised my arm to get Craig's attention, pulling it back in time to avoid the paintball that sailed overhead. When he looked at me, I pointed to Helen who waved her brown paper bag in the air and gestured toward the guys still cowering behind the berm.

Neither he nor Volkov looked happy about being asked to stand down, but they both took cover behind a rusted-out car and waited. Riley army-crawled her way to us to find out what was going on.

Helen dumped the remaining paintballs out of her gun and replaced them with ones from her bag. I raised an eyebrow. Helen's smile was positively evil. "Just you wait." She peeked around the wall. "I need to get closer."

"Get behind me," Riley told her. "We're going in."

This is how we usually lost at paintball. Riley had even less patience than I had, and that was saying something. Within a few minutes of starting play, Riley would get antsy and go into full-on assault mode. She rarely made it to midfield before being pelted with paintballs.

She caught Volkov's eye and held three fingers in the air, counting them down. "Three, two, one. Go!" She stood up, shielding Helen, who crowded against her back. "Cover me!" she shouted at Volkov. Then, she zig-zagged across the field while shooting paintballs as fast as she could pump them out.

Volkov hung his head for a second before dutifully laying down cover fire for her. Between him and Craig, they managed to keep the other team off kilter enough Riley made it most of the way across the field before she took a barrage of paintballs to the chest. I grimaced. Those were going to welt. Riley clutched her chest dramatically and fell to the ground, revealing Helen behind her.

Helen didn't waste any time shooting her special paintball stash across the berm. She didn't seem to be aiming at the guys very well, but she peppered the general vicinity with her shots. By the time they returned fire, she'd emptied her gun.

"Ha ha! Who got an old woman beatdown now, you little shits?" It didn't make any sense at first. Helen was out of the game after getting hit in the leg, so it hardly seemed like she'd delivered any kind of beat down.

Then, the gagging started. Two of the remaining guys jumped up and ran for us, forgetting their guns on the ground. They were easy pickings for Craig and Volkov. Helen and Riley ambled their way back to the benches.

I gave them a thumbs up. "What was in those paintballs?" I called.

"Magic!" Helen started laughing. "The kind that smells like day-old farts and rotten meat."

I looked back at the two remaining guys from the other team. One of them sat up to puke, making him an easy target Volkov was more than happy to hit. That left a lone player on their side, and it happened to be the guy who had been running his mouth to Craig earlier. Somehow, I doubted it was accidental.

Although Craig was a large man, years of martial arts meant he was both agile and fast, moving with a practiced ease that said he'd done this before. He alternated between quick bursts of speed and ducking behind obstacles for cover. When he was within striking distance of the last guy, he didn't take the easy shot. Instead, he inched his way closer. He made it all the way around the berm, aiming his gun at the guy at a close enough range the shot was going to hurt.

The guy stood up and scrambled over the berm to make a run for it, aiming the gun over his shoulder and shooting indiscriminately at Craig as he went. Craig dropped to the ground, rolled, and came up on one knee, popping off three shots—two to take out the guy's legs and one to the back of the head. *Damn.* He must have been toying with the guy before.

I met Craig midfield, jumping so I could wrap my arms around his neck in celebration. He caught me and lifted me off my feet.

"That's the single hottest thing I've ever seen," I confessed.

Craig looked amused, but he took full advantage of my bout of hero worship to lean in for a victory kiss. By the time he set me on my feet, I was flushed and breathless.

"You sure we have to wait until tonight for our date?" I asked.

Even though Craig and I had spent plenty of time together, tonight was only our second official date. The first had been months ago, but our relationship had been sidelined by murder attempts and complicated by a demon playing fast and loose with my emotions. Since banishing Zepar a few weeks ago, we'd both been busy wading through the wreckage the demon left in his wake. We'd spent a few afternoons together when Craig helped restore my shop to working order, and he'd made it a point to show up at Krav Maga on the nights I trained. However, other than flirty banter and some hands-on technique correction, we hadn't found the time to explore the attraction that flamed between us.

Craig dropped his voice low enough that it did obscene things to my libido. "I'll make it worth the wait." Then, he tucked me into his body with an arm around my shoulders as we walked back to the others. Seven o'clock couldn't come soon enough.

When we were all back by the benches, I did a quick head count. "Where's Olivia?" When everyone looked around, I cupped my hands and called her name.

Olivia's head popped out of an oversized tire she'd curled up inside. "I'm here." She stood on shaky legs and made her way over to the group. She handed Riley her gun and dropped into a seat beside Alyce. "I don't like paintball."

Janis handed out the juice boxes she'd brought in a small cooler. Alyce swiped Olivia's out of her hand, popped the straw in, and shot a stream of juice toward the other team. They scrambled away from her. Once Alyce made room in the box, she opened her last mini bottle of vodka and trickled a bit into the juice before handing it back to Olivia. "Here, sweetie. This will settle your nerves."

Not surprisingly, Volkov and Craig refused to take juice boxes. Volkov stared at all of us in horror as we sat around sipping 100% fruit juice through children's straws and snacking on the goldfish crackers Janis handed out.

When his cell phone rang, Volkov looked at it like a lifeline. He stepped away from us to take the call. As soon as he hung up, he was back in alpha-mode, his tone clipped as he talked to Craig. "We need to go. There's been an attack."

Our celebratory conversation died as reality reared its ugly head.

CHAPTER 2

After one too many people piled into my Volkswagen Beetle, I made the rounds. Janis and Olivia had driven separately, but that left me to drop off Helen, Bea, and Alyce before heading to my shop with Riley.

"So." Riley waggled her eyebrows. "Where is he taking you?"

Hopefully, the attack Craig and Volkov left to investigate wouldn't be serious enough to derail our date. "We're planning on dinner and a movie." I couldn't help but smile at the promise of an ordinary date. Good food, a little dinner conversation, and a dark movie theater with an oversized tub of popcorn drowning in butter sounded perfect to me. Tonight, we could just be two people getting to know one another better.

"Going for the classic, huh?"

"Yup. We're taking it nice and slow." I parked my car and turned off the engine.

Riley eyed me skeptically. "Slow?"

"Slow."

Riley reached in her pocket and pulled out a bill, waving it in front of me. "Twenty bucks says you don't make it to dessert."

"You're on." A bet with Riley was hard to resist. This time tomorrow, I may be ponying up twenty bucks, but it would be a small price to pay if it meant getting naked with Craig. Even without the demon influence amping up my sex drive, our chemistry was palpable.

While I dug my keys out of my purse to open the door, Riley pulled down a flyer taped to the window of my shop.

"Sweet!" Riley handed me the sheet of paper.

I scanned the flyer, which was for a new tattoo place opening in West Bottoms. No prices were listed, but the flyer advertised a limited-time offer for a one-of-a-kind tattoo. I flipped it over, but there wasn't a name or address listed, just a phone number. Not wanting to leave it on the street, I folded it up and stuck it in my purse.

As soon as I got my key in the door, my phone vibrated. My nerves kicked in as I stared at Craig's number. Maybe the attack had been a minor incident, I reasoned, and he was calling to solidify our plans.

When I answered the phone, I hoped for the relaxed Craig I'd come to know in the past few drama-free weeks. What I got was enforcer Craig.

"Do you know the old textile factory off Liberty?" he asked.

"Yeah." It was a few blocks away. "Why?" I felt dread pooling in my stomach.

There was a pause, but I could tell he hadn't hung up from the background noise. Whatever was going on, the person barking orders in the background didn't seem happy about it. "How soon can you get here?"

"Ten minutes. What's going on, Craig?"

He exhaled. "It's best if I fill you in once you get here. The Tribunal is calling in a favor."

If the Tribunal was turning to me for a favor, whatever it was, it was bad. "Okay. I'll be right there."

"I'll meet you outside." He paused. "Don't go in without me."

My dread intensified. With Craig's warning ringing in my ears, I explained what was going on to Riley. I offered her my apartment keys. "Do you want to hang out at my place?"

"Nah. I'll catch a bus." She waved me off. "But call me later, okay?"

"I will."

I didn't have to pause at a single intersection to wait for cars, since the streets were mostly empty, which meant I made it there in record time. From the grim expression on Craig's face when I reached him, I knew that was as good as my luck was going to get today.

"What happened?" I asked once I reached him.

Most people paced and fidgeted when they were stressed. Craig went statue still. His unmoving stance signaled our brief interlude of normalcy was about to come to an abrupt end. "We've got a dead witch."

My heart sped up. "Who?" The only local witches I was on friendly terms with were Helen, Bea, Alyce, Janis, and now Olivia, but they had all been with us when the call came in.

"Her name is Anne Edwards. Do you know her?"

I shook my head, relieved her name wasn't familiar.

Craig glanced at the closed door as if he could see the crime scene from where we stood. "Whoever got to her, it's not pretty." He turned back to me, assessing my reaction.

By now, we'd spent enough time on crime scenes together

that he should have known I wouldn't fall apart. But I appreciated his concern just the same. "How can I help?"

I already knew what they were going to ask of me. There was only one reason the Tribunal would call me here, but asking the question bought me a few more minutes before I had to face whatever was behind that door.

"We need you to call her so we can find out who did this."

I noted what Craig didn't say. He didn't say they needed help to find out what happened. That, they must already know from the scene.

"All right."

I knew the sight would be gruesome as soon as he pushed the door open and led the way inside. Craig might look like a street thug with his shaved head and bodybuilder bulk, but he wore chivalry like he was born to it. He always held doors for me, so him going in first meant he wanted to shield me from the view as long as he could. He stopped a few feet inside the door, and I stepped up next to him, giving his arm a reassuring squeeze as I moved past him.

I sucked in a breath as I took in the room. Someone had painted a ten-foot circle on the concrete floor with red spray paint, ringing it with salt and sigils, some of which I recognized. I felt the scar tissue from Zepar's mark itch, the memory of a similar circle still fresh in my mind. I forced myself to step closer, ignoring the cold sweat beading on the back of my neck.

It wasn't the sigils or the lit candles or even the salt circle that drew my attention though. I stared at the witch in the center of it, her arms and legs extended in an X. There were no bindings I could see, just her limbs arranged like a doll's so her hands and feet touched the inner bounds of the circle.

"A summoning circle," I said out loud, even though everyone in this room knew exactly what we were looking at.

No one answered me, but everyone was watching for my reaction. There were several people here, along with Craig, who remained standing next to me. As the local alpha and high-ranking Tribunal member, Max Volkov was the man in charge. He circled the room along with several of his shifters, presumably searching for clues that might indicate who had done this. Volkov crossed to where I stood staring at the scene before me.

"Thank you for coming." Volkov said.

Max Volkov and I were not friends, even if he had helped us win a paintball game. Volkov had voted twice against outright killing me for accidentally summoning a demon, so he got brownie points for that at least. He was still a dick most of the time—to me anyway. For him to pull out good manners on my account reflected the gravity of the situation. This wasn't merely a dead witch, and we both knew it. Two attempted demon summonings in Kansas City within months of each other warranted every fear I felt warring inside me.

"Of course." My voice was equally cordial, but I couldn't pull my gaze away from the woman in the circle. "What do you know about the victim? Anything you can tell me might help me communicate with her."

"Her name is Anne Edwards. Twenty-nine. She was a member of a local coven. She moved here three years ago from Portland." Volkov stared down at the dead witch. "From what I know, she was well-liked and kept to herself, for the most part."

"Have you talked to the witches' council?" I asked.

I was stalling, but Volkov answered anyway. "They will be my next stop. Right now, we need you to communicate with her. Perhaps she knows who did this to her." He didn't sound optimistic though. He swept his arm out, gesturing to the circle. "At the very least, she can recount what happened and hopefully give us something that leads us to the practitioner responsible for this."

"I'll do my best." I wasn't talking about the summoning. That part was easy—at least for me.

"Do you need anything?" Volkov asked.

Most necromancers needed all the ritual trappings to summon a spirit. All I needed was something metal connected to the deceased to serve as the conduit. "Just some space to work." I watched the shifters milling around in the background. "Could you clear out the room? Anyone who doesn't have to be present that is." I swallowed past the lump forming in my throat. "This is going to be traumatic enough for Anne. I don't want a room full of strangers making it any harder than it has to be."

Volkov nodded curtly before directing everyone besides Craig to wait outside. The shifters left quietly, a few of them eyeing me with trepidation as they left. The more I exercised my powers, the more I got used to how uncomfortable talking to the dead made most people. I tried not to take it personally.

Before I could move closer to Anne, Craig caught my hand, his warm fingers threading through mine. His touch was reassuring, and for a second, I closed my eyes and let it ground me. "Thanks," I whispered before letting go of his hand and dropping to the floor next to the dead woman.

Other than the summoning circle she died in, Anne Edwards didn't look like a witch. She looked like a kindergarten teacher. Her dark hair was pulled back in a low ponytail that remained neat despite the manner of her death. She was wearing a floral dress, a soft yellow cardigan, and a delicate gold necklace with an infinity symbol nestled against her collarbone. She would have looked peaceful if not for the skirt that was stained dark red and the blood pooling around her body.

"Whoever killed her cut the femoral artery," Craig said when he noticed where I was staring. "Her death would have been fast."

It was little consolation. I forced myself to look at her face, noting the soft laugh lines at the corners of her eyes, the freckles dotting her nose, and the unblinking glassy eyes I was sure would haunt me in my sleep.

I reached for Anne's hand, trembling as I wrapped my fingers around her wrist where she wore a silver charm bracelet. With practice, tapping into the spiritual plane had become easier, but I still had to work at it. Normally, it would take me a few minutes for the spiritual plane to snap into focus and longer for me to locate the soul I was searching for. Even with a good conduit—silver was one of the best—and a fresh soul, connecting had always taken my full concentration and effort. Today, however, the call was easier. All it took was several seconds thinking about touching Anne's soul, and I could see the wisps floating around her body. A quick tug, and Anne was standing before me.

I gave Anne a minute to acclimate. This was the worst part of what I did—watching a new ghost come to terms with their own death. Anne looked at Volkov first, then Craig, her gaze settling on me last. When she saw her own body on the floor, she took a step back, her hand flying to her mouth. Eyes wide, she looked desperately around the room. I didn't move, keeping my face carefully neutral until she looked back at me for answers.

"Hi, Anne. My name is Kali." I waited for her to acknowledge me with a nod before continuing. "I know this is a shock, but I'm here to help find out who did this to you."

Anne stared down at the blood covering her lower body and sobbed. I stood up slowly, moving closer to her spirit. Now that she was here, I had no need to touch the bracelet anymore. Since the bond between us had been forged, I'd be able to communicate, and even call her again, if necessary, without a conduit.

"Anne. I need you to focus on me, okay?" I kept a bit of distance between us, looking into her eyes when I spoke. "Good. Can you tell me who did this to you?"

She'd stopped sobbing, but her grief continued to permeate the room. She shook her head. "I couldn't see them."

"Them?"

"Yes. I heard two of them."

"Men or women?" I asked.

"I don't know." Her voice cracked.

I took another step toward her, but I didn't try to touch her. No matter how much I might want to comfort a ghost, experience had taught me I wouldn't be able to touch her. "Were they wearing masks?" When she shook her head no, I tried again. "Disguises maybe?"

"Not the kind you're thinking of," she said. "I think their voices and features were disguised with a distortion spell. I could make out two distinct voices, even though only the one performing the spell was within my line of sight."

At least one of them was a witch then. If they went to the trouble to distort their appearances and voices, it was possible Anne knew one or both of them. She was distraught enough without thinking someone she trusted could do this to her, but I had to ask.

"Do you have any idea who could have done this?"

Anne shook her head. "No one." She stared down at her vacant expression. "Who would do something like this?"

I didn't have an answer for her. "Is there anything you can tell me that might help us identify them? Height, weight, clothing?" Anne's frown grew with each thing I listed. "Anything?"

"I'm sorry, but no. When I woke up, my mind was fuzzy. At first, I thought I was at home in my bed, that I drank too much the night before and was hungover."

"Did you? Drink I mean?"

"No." She took a deep breath. "When I finally got my bearings, I could see someone standing over there." Anne pointed to a spot near Volkov. "It was the one who was chanting an incantation."

She didn't have to tell me it had been a summoning ritual. The sigils beneath our feet confirmed that much. I examined the way her body was arranged in the circle. "Were you bound here?"

"Compelled." She gritted her teeth. "I couldn't move, no matter how hard I tried. Not even when one of them sliced open my artery and watched as I bled out." Anne balled her hands into fists, her body stiff with rage.

I understood exactly how powerless she felt because I'd been in the same situation myself a few short weeks ago. Except in my case, I'd survived. Anne hadn't been so lucky. I turned to Craig and repeated what Anne told me. "One of them must have been a vampire."

Craig nodded.

Although they were forced to work together on the Tribunal to govern, it was unusual for a vampire and witch to willingly work together. I had gotten the distinct impression there was little love between the two factions.

"Is there anything else you can tell us that could help us hunt down whoever did this and make them pay?" I was struggling to keep my voice neutral, the memory of what Zepar and Naomi had done to me too raw.

"I'm sorry, but everything was so hazy. I can't remember anything else." Anne dropped her head into her hands, rubbing her temples as if she had a headache. If only a migraine was her problem. Anne's head snapped up. "Wait. There is something."

From the look on her face, I knew it was going to be bad. I wasn't wrong.

"Here." She tapped the front of her shirt, an angry flush on her cheeks. "One of them cut a demon mark into my skin."

I couldn't help it. I took a step away from her, my hand flying to my own chest. Craig didn't miss my reaction.

"What is it?" Craig asked.

I held up a hand when he moved toward me. "I'm all right," I assured him. I repeated what Anne said. Craig leaned down and peeled Anne's shirt back, being careful to protect whatever modesty he could. Seeing the raised red lines left by a demon claw made me sick to my stomach.

Craig pulled his cell phone out of his pocket and took several photos of the mark. "It's different."

We both knew he meant different than mine. I knelt to take a better look. The sigil on Anne looked like a puzzle piece with a small cross at the top and two dots in the upper corners. The longer I stared at it, the more certain I was I'd seen it before. Chances were I had stumbled across it while searching for Zepar's sigil, but I couldn't help the shiver of unease that ran through me at the sight of it.

Craig continued examining the demon mark. "Ask her if

she noticed anything odd in the weeks before her death. Did she notice anyone following her or watching her?"

Anne's brow furrowed. I didn't have to repeat his questions. Ghosts could hear and see everyone around them. It just didn't work both ways unless I helped matters along. I motioned for Craig to come closer and reached for his hand. As soon as we made contact, his quick inhale let me know he could see Anne as well as I could.

His usual stoic expression was replaced by shock, but he recovered quickly, his face once again settling into an impassive mask. "I can see her." He looked down at where our hands were joined.

Anne was watching the two of us. "He couldn't see me?"

I turned my attention back to her. "No. Only I could see and hear you."

"You're that necromancer."

I couldn't help but flinch at the judgment in her voice. Craig felt it and squeezed my hand.

"I'm sorry," Anne said. "I didn't mean it like that."

She had, but I let it go. "Did you see anything odd before your death?"

"I didn't see anything, but I did get the feeling I was being watched in the weeks before..." She trailed off, looking down at her own body. "You'll find who did this?"

"We will," I said, not knowing if it was a promise I'd be able to make good on.

"Thank you," Anne said before disappearing.

Her gratitude was premature, but I knew I was going to be neck deep in this one. It was hard to walk away when someone counted on you for justice. The fact that my experience with Zepar and Naomi had been so similar made this feel personal. I wasn't a big believer in coincidence. Whoever killed Anne was connected to what had happened to me. And I needed to know the how and why.

After Anne left, the headache and dizziness hit. When I swayed on my feet, Craig braced his hands on my upper arms. "Woah. Are you okay?"

"I just need a second to regroup." Although it had gotten easier to call spirits, the post graveside-chat hangover hadn't lessened at all. I dug around in my purse until I found my bottle of extra-strength painkillers and swallowed a couple.

While I was regaining my equilibrium, Volkov called his shifters back in. They quickly returned to canvasing the room, using their sense of smell like bloodhounds to trace the room. Volkov's phone rang, and he turned his back to us as he answered it.

Once my head cleared, I stepped away from Craig and refocused on the takeaways from my conversation with Anne. "It looks like a witch and a vamp, but that's all we've got to go on. It's not much."

"It's something," Craig countered.

Volkov ended his phone call and joined us. "That's all the time I can buy us. The cops are on their way."

With supernaturals embedded in every emergency response branch including the police, the Tribunal was frequently able to pull strings. It was a necessity to keep supernaturals hidden. Often it meant routing calls to the supernatural community instead of human law enforcement. But sometimes, like this, they let the human authorities do the legwork: things like collecting DNA, analyzing samples, and running background checks. They kept tabs on everything, of course. If it turned up anything that pointed to a supernatural, they sent in the vamps to alter memories and destroy evidence, the Tribunal to run interference, and Craig to clean up the mess. In this case, we already knew the perpetrator was supernatural, so the two investigations would run simultaneously.

"Come on," Craig said. "You can go out the back. We'll handle the police."

With one last look at Anne, I followed Craig across the room. Before I could step outside, he rested a hand on my shoulder.

"I'll stop by when I'm done here," he said.

Tonight wouldn't be our first date discussing a dead body and, given Craig's job and my penchant for collecting the ghosts of murder victims, it probably wouldn't be our last. I took a steadying breath. "I'll order takeout." Movies were overrated anyway.

CHAPTER 3

Normally, the smell of smoked meat was a surefire way to make me forget my troubles. But I'd had precious few normal days in the last few months, and it was going to take more than brisket to distract me from Anne's image. Even so, I clutched the takeout bags filled with enough brisket, pulled pork, and sides to feed a pack of shifters. I juggled the bags in one hand while digging for my keys with the other as I came around the corner of the building to the front of my shop. I had a costume order that had to ship in the morning, and I needed to package it up before meeting Craig.

Distracted as I was, I didn't notice the workers until I almost ran one of them over. I stopped in the middle of the sidewalk to gawk at the construction truck parked in front of the building. Three men wearing shirts with logos that matched the truck were carting drywall out of the back of the truck and into the building next to The Costume Shoppe. Except for a brief occupancy by a taxidermist who cleared out like a thief in the middle of the night, the storefront next door had been empty as long as I'd been in West Bottoms. I watched the men cart in sheet after sheet of drywall followed by big buckets of drywall mud and the tools needed to apply it.

"Hey," I called to one of the workers as he headed back to the building. "What's going in there?"

He shrugged. "I'm just the hired help." The guy bent down and picked up a sheet of paper on the sidewalk and handed it to me. "You dropped this."

"That's not mine."

He flipped the paper over to show another flyer for the tattoo place. He gave me the once-over followed by a sly grin. "Nah. You don't seem the type to get a tattoo."

I frowned, not quite sure what type that would be.

The guy sniffed the air, then tipped his chin at me, smiling. "You need some company to eat all that?"

I couldn't tell whether he was flirting with me or the brisket. "Sorry. I only got enough for two."

He eyed the bulging bags and laughed. "Two, huh? I'm only seeing one of you."

"Stop slacking off, man," one of the other guys grumbled.

"Yeah, yeah. I'm coming." He winked at me. "If you change your mind, I'll be finished unloading this in ten minutes and ready for a break. I'll even bring the drinks."

"She won't."

I didn't have to turn around to know Craig was behind me because the guy made a quick one-eighty and hustled into the building. When I turned to face Craig, he was scowling and staring at the door the guy just walked through.

"Who's the tool?"

"You can't blame him for trying." I laughed, waving a bag under his nose. "I'd fight you for barbecue this good."

He smiled. "Is that so?"

"You know it." I let Craig take the bags of food and moved to unlock the front door. "Do you want to go on up?" I asked over my shoulder. "I'll just be a minute."

Craig looked at the workers who continued unloading the truck. "I'll wait."

It didn't take me long to wrap the package and put it on the counter for the FedEx guy who stopped by first thing in the morning.

Upstairs in my apartment, I grabbed plates, laid out the food, and snagged two bottles of pop out of the fridge. I handed one to Craig.

"Thanks." He sat down, scrubbing a hand over the stubble on his jaw. "I'm sorry I had to call you in—sorry you had to see that."

"I know."

The bite I'd taken sat like lead in my stomach as the image of Anne's body flashed in my head. I set the half-eaten sandwich on my plate, no longer hungry.

"What happens next?" I asked.

Considering the recent body count around here, I should have a better grasp of how an official supernatural investigation worked. Although this wasn't the first murder victim I'd interrogated—thank you, Jack Gates—it was the first time it had been at the Tribunal's request. While I knew Craig was the enforcer for the Interior Territory, an area that included much of the Midwest, I didn't know what that meant for a case like this. Was he the investigator, or did he just mete out justice once the killer was identified?

Craig took a drink before answering, probably weighing how much to tell me. "Now the human police will run the evidence through their systems to check for prints and DNA.

Our people will monitor and report back anything of interest to the Tribunal, so we stay one step ahead of them."

Let the human establishments do the grunt work, freeing up Craig to follow supernatural leads. It was smart, actually.

"Even with the police running evidence, how can you run an investigation on your own?" Murder investigations were not a one-man job, regardless of how capable the man was. "And what about other crimes that occur during the investigation? Who handles those?"

Craig finished his pop and stood to dispose of the can. "Most small crimes are handled by the factions—vampires, shifters, witches, and necromancers. I only need to step in on cases that require Tribunal intervention. Even then, I pull together a team of whoever I need working the case—shifters like today or witches if necessary."

Or a necromancer like me. "And you?" I asked. "What will you be doing while everyone else is digging up evidence?" Craig wasn't a waiting around kind of guy.

He met my eyes. "Whatever is necessary."

I'd come to terms with what that meant, so I didn't flinch. "How can I help?"

"You already did." Craig softened his tone. "Kali, this isn't your problem."

"Maybe not." I tugged my shirt off my shoulder and traced the scar Zepar left me. "But what are the chances two supernaturals get impromptu demon marks, and they're not connected?"

From the tightening of his jaw, he agreed. "I'll find whoever is responsible." His gray eyes were intense as he held my gaze. "And when I do, I will get answers."

"There's not a lot to go on though." I tried to read him, see if he knew any information beyond what Anne had given us, but his expression was closed down. If he ever tired of this enforcer gig, the man could make some serious money on the poker circuit. I continued undeterred. "Here's what we know. Two demon summonings within a month of each other, both atypical because the demon mark was carved into the host body." My mouth went dry at the reminder of what Zepar had tried to reduce me to. "Both Anne and I are supernaturals. In my case, the demon tried to convince me to welcome him in with open arms, and when that didn't work, he tried to force his way in. But with Anne, they went straight for the blood drain, presumably to turn her into a vampire."

"Different demons though," Craig pointed out. He was right. The mark on Anne hadn't been Zepar's.

I stood up and walked into the living room where books were still stacked on my end table from the last time I identified a demon. A few I'd acquired while hunting for the summoning ritual that had brought Zepar here. Others, I'd found after scouring eBay. I had no way of knowing which books were authentic and which books were crap, but I'd bought them all anyway, convinced my encounter with Zepar wouldn't be my last run-in with a demon. I hadn't thought it would be quite this soon, however. I grabbed a book that chronicled the who's who of the demon world. Craig followed me, and we both sat on the couch.

"Can I see the pic you took of Anne's mark?" I asked.

He pulled it up and held his phone where I could see it. I flipped through the pages of the book until I found a match. "Malthus. According to this, he is a prince of hell who sends his legions of demons into battle for his commanders." Someone was playing with powerful magic to attempt to summon a demon that dangerous. *To what end, though?*

Craig frowned, scanning the rest of the entry over my

shoulder. "Two different demons, but neither of them sounds like your run-of-the-mill demon looking for a vampire makeover."

"No. They don't." I set the book down and twisted to face him. "According to Meira, the only reason a powerful demon would allow himself to become a vampire would be to get more power. What kind of power boost could a witch offer a prince of hell?"

"That's a good question. In Zepar's case, he wanted your ability to call demons forward—a definite power boost. When I talked to the local witches, they all described Anne as a quiet, keep-to-herself kind of witch. None of them mentioned anything extraordinary about her."

"No one thought Naomi was powerful either," I reasoned. "And look at what she was capable of." I'd been in her house, and she'd fooled me. I'd had no idea she was the witch working with Zepar. No one else had realized how powerful she was either.

Craig tensed. "Good point. I'll dig deeper tomorrow."

I leaned back against the couch cushion, resting my head against Craig's arm where it stretched across the back of the seat. I should let this go, turn on the TV, turn the lights down, and put in a movie—try to salvage what was left of our night. But I couldn't shake the dread that had me by the throat, my mind spinning as it tried to find the connection between what happened to me and what just happened to Anne. The only thing I was sure of was that there was a connection. If we could uncover it, the connection could lead us straight to her killer.

Craig dropped his hand and stroked my upper arm. "You okay?"

"Not really." There wasn't much point in lying and even

less point in dwelling on my unease. "Let's assume for now Anne was more powerful than your typical witch. Do you think the vampires are trying to strengthen their ranks by luring stronger demons with the promise of supernatural hosts?"

"It's possible, but not likely. Demon hordes are even more hierarchical than shifter packs. In hell, lessor demons are little more than cannon fodder. As vampires, those same demons are more powerful than the human population and on par with most supernaturals. I can't see them inviting stronger demons to this plane willingly."

I thought about the pair Anne described—a vampire and a witch. "What about the witches? Could they be the ones driving this?"

"Maybe," Craig said, but he didn't sound convinced. He turned me to face him. "I'll check into it, but you did your part. This is my job. I need you to let me handle this."

I sighed. "I know." I leaned against his chest, his broken-in t-shirt soft against my cheek. "But this is going to eat me alive," I admitted. "Keep me posted, okay?"

"Done."

After Craig left, the temptation to do a little investigating of my own was hard to resist. Thankfully, Riley showed up with a bottle of tequila, giving me the distraction I needed to leave it alone. For the time being, at least.

CHAPTER 4

The more brilliant my ideas seemed after a few shots of tequila, the worse they were come morning. Suggesting to Riley we get tattoos from a guy who advertised via a homemade flyer was my latest bad idea. But here we were, waiting outside the rickety bay door of a dilapidated warehouse.

In the harsh light of day, I was having serious second thoughts. "I don't know about this." I glanced around the nearly empty street. It was early on a Saturday, and the crowds wouldn't roll into West Bottoms for a couple hours. The only person in the vicinity was a nerdy guy in a Stray Cats band t-shirt we passed on our way here.

Riley set up the appointments last night for both of us to get tattoos, insisting early this morning was the only time the guy could fit us in. Knowing Riley, the fact she had been so gung-ho about this plan should've worried me more.

"Are you sure this is the right address?" I asked.

"Positive." Riley had called the number last night and talked to the owner, jotting down the address we were now standing in front of. Riley put her whole arm into knocking on the door.

I cringed. "Do you have to be so loud?"

She didn't dignify my complaint with an answer. *It must be nice to never have a hangover thanks to her shifter metabolism.*

Riley knocked again. "Dingo, I know you're in there!"

"Wait, Dingo?" I tugged her shirt. "I'm getting a tattoo from a guy named Dingo?"

Riley stopped banging on the door long enough to roll her eyes at me. "Would you relax?"

I eyed the broken bottles and empty condom wrapper on the sidewalk next to us. "Maybe we should just go to the tattoo place by the mall instead. It looked nice and clean."

"The mall?" Riley snorted.

Riley wasn't judgy about a lot of things, but tattoos were one of them. Before I could object further, the bay door rolled up to reveal the man of the hour.

Dingo had soft brown hair that curled around his ears and beady little eyes that darted around the street before settling on Riley, ignoring me completely. "You're early." He didn't sound happy about it. With one last look at the empty street, he ducked back inside.

Riley grabbed my arm and propelled me into the building before my common sense had time to kick in. She pushed me forward. "This is my friend, Kali, who I was telling you about last night."

Dingo didn't acknowledge me. He scooted around us to close the bay door, then motioned for us to follow him. "This way," he said over his shoulder as he led us through dusty crates that looked like they'd been here for decades. The first floor of the warehouse was one cavernous room with only a few old fluorescent fixtures lighting the depressing space.

Dingo paused at a door on the other side of the room and waited for us to catch up. "I've set up my tools upstairs."

He opened the door, revealing steep stairs carved with insults and crude declarations of love. Seeing my hesitation, Dingo finally met my gaze. His eyes were so dark, they appeared black, and I found it impossible to look away. "I'll do yours first. You'll need it before the day is through." He pivoted and ran up the stairs.

How on earth did someone need a tattoo? And how would he know what I needed?

When I looked at Riley, she shrugged. "He's an artist."

Against my better judgment, I trailed up the stairs after Dingo, watching where I stepped. With my luck, I'd step on a board rotten enough for my leg to bust through. I tested each stair before putting my full weight on it, which meant by the time I reached the top, both Riley and Dingo had disappeared into one of the rooms branching off the landing. I paused until I caught Riley's voice, following her chatter into the room on the right. Unlike the downstairs, this room had ample natural light pouring in the bank of windows facing the street below.

Dingo had set up shop under the windows, but seeing his workspace left me more nervous than I had been downstairs. I'd expected to walk into a business, with seating areas and binders filled with numbered tattoo designs to choose from. Instead, there was a lone barber chair with duct tape on the seat. Beside it sat a rolling cart with a rusted-out red toolbox with a padlock on it. Unphased by Dingo's scary little setup, Riley peered over his shoulder as he prepped.

Dingo pointed a bony finger at me. "You're first."

Reluctantly, I sat on the barber chair. Dingo had his back

to me while he disinfected his tray of tools. *At least he follows safety guidelines.* Maybe I was overreacting.

Dingo wore a short-sleeved button-down shirt over a plain white tank top, and the skin I could see was covered with beautiful but mismatched tattoos. His arms had full sleeves, a snake's hypnotic eyes peering out from behind a tangle of brambles on one arm and intricate scrollwork winding around the other arm. A string of skulls was tattooed at the base of his neck, buoyed by an undulating wave peeking from the collar of his shirt. Everything was done in black ink, which tied the art on his body together in a cohesive design. I wondered who had done his tattoos. *Maybe I should go there.*

Dingo turned to face me, bending down to stare into my eyes for several seconds. I shifted under his scrutiny. Finally, he broke the uncomfortable staring match. "Where do you want your tattoo?"

"Umm, on my chest." My hands shook a little as I untied the wrap-around shirt I'd worn for this purpose, revealing the plain black demi bra I wore underneath.

His eyes dropped to the scar where Zepar had carved his mark above my heart. Dingo's eyes flared. "That's a demon mark," he accused.

"How do you know that?" Given he'd set up shop in West Bottoms and recognized a demon mark when he saw one, it was probably safe to assume Dingo wasn't human.

Dingo glanced away, frowning. "You're not the first person I've seen wearing a demon's mark."

I bristled under his judgmental tone that implied I'd acquired this mark willingly. "It's been neutralized. You don't have to worry about attracting unwanted demon attention if that's what you are afraid of."

"Neutralized. How?" He sounded curious.

Riley nodded toward me. "Kali severed the bond and kicked his demon ass back to hell, that's how."

Dingo slowly relaxed and turned his attention back to me. "You want to hide it?"

"I do." It wouldn't be easy to hide the mark because its lines burrowed deeply into my chest. Even weeks after getting it, the skin around it was an irritated red. I counted myself lucky I hadn't gotten an infection. Maybe the hellfire Zepar was born in had sterilized his claws.

Dingo stepped forward and ran his finger across my scar. I jumped when his warm finger made contact, his touch featherlight. "Yes." He stepped back and held his hands up to frame the scar as if taking a wide-angle photograph. "You're worthy of my gift."

I grimaced at the awe with which he referred to himself. *At least he isn't talking about himself in third person. Yet.* I glanced at Riley, but she'd already lost interest in our conversation and had started playing a game on her phone.

"Great," I said brightly. "I have some ideas." I'd spent an hour last night browsing tattoo designs online to find ones with the shape and complexity necessary to disguise Zepar's mark.

"You have some ideas," he repeated. Dingo's eyes narrowed, his magnanimous tone gone.

I dug my phone out of my purse and scrolled to the images I'd saved. "I was thinking something like this." I held up the screen, so he could see the garden gate with ivy growing around it. When his only reaction was a scowl, I scrolled to the next one. "Or this one is nice." I pointed at the brightly feathered masquerade mask. It seemed like a logical choice for a costume shop owner.

Dingo scrambled back, staring at my phone in disgust. "No."

"No?" I studied the style of tattoos he was sporting. Maybe I needed to go with something less pretty. "Okay, I'm sure I can find something else." I squinted at my phone.

"No," he repeated, more forcefully this time, before taking the phone out of my hand and tossing it on my lap. "I do not take requests."

"What does that even mean?"

He leaned in until his eyes were level with mine. "It means I am not some run-of-the-mill tattoo parlor. You do not choose the design."

"What do you have in mind, then?"

"No." He shook his head. "That's not how this works. I don't randomly pick a design." He looked appalled at the thought of choosing the design himself.

"If I can't pick it, and you don't pick it…" I trailed off, raising my eyebrow. "Then who does?" I sure as shit wasn't going to let Riley pick it. I loved the girl, but our tastes weren't even in the same decade. She was black leather and combat boots, and I was all about pretty retro accessories.

Dingo dropped his voice and leaned in as if imparting a great secret. "The ink gives you the tattoo you need."

"Riiiight." As a costume designer, I'd spent a fair bit of time surrounded by eccentric artists, but this guy was taking it to a whole new level.

I considered my options. I could leave and go to someone less weird, but I was already here. Plus, this tattoo was dirt cheap—some kind of grand opening promo. My bank account wasn't exactly flush with cash. And weird or not, Dingo had the tools and the time to cover up this scar for me now. I didn't want to spend another day looking at Zepar's little souvenir.

Do I even care what kind of tattoo I get if it obliterates this scar? No. I did not.

"Fine," I agreed. "Let's see what the ink decides I need."

Dingo smiled and rubbed his hands together. "Wonderful."

He pulled a key from where it dangled on a long gold chain under his shirt and reached for the rusty toolbox on his cart. Unlocking the toolbox, he lifted out a small antique bottle, cradling it like a delicacy in his palm. The bottle was square, its glass cloudy with age and wrapped with a fading label identifying it simply as ink. Dingo held the bottle reverently for a second before pulling the stopper and breathing in deeply as if to draw the scent of the ink into his lungs. Then he set the bottle on the cart he'd wheeled closer to me and reached for one of the needles I'd watched him sterilize earlier.

I eyed the cart suspiciously. "Aren't you going to use a tattoo gun?"

Dingo huffed. "Don't be ridiculous." He held up his implement of choice—an extra-long needle affixed to what looked like an antique bronzed key. Dingo held it out for my inspection.

"Where does the ink go?" I asked, seeing nothing but handle and needle.

He frowned. "On the needle, of course. It takes what it needs."

Okay then. And here I thought he couldn't get weirder.

Dingo demonstrated, dipping the tip of the needle into the bottle. Riley ambled over to get a closer look, her game forgotten. As we watched, the ink travelled up the needle and into the handle, turning it from antique bronze to black.

Riley whistled. "Wicked." She leaned over me to examine the needle. "Can I watch?" she asked Dingo.

He pushed her back a step. "Suit yourself, but don't get in my way."

Riley quickly grabbed a chair from the side of the room and positioned herself behind Dingo, making sure she was on the side away from the windows, so she didn't block his light. He looked from the blackened needle to me. "Ready?"

I nodded. "Ready as I'll ever be."

Dingo settled himself on a stool, scooting close enough I could smell the mint toothpaste on his breath. He ran one finger along the ridges of my scar before bringing the needle to my chest. "How are you with pain?" he asked.

"Old friends," I assured him, steeling myself for the feeling of metal tunneling into my skin.

"Excellent. Now, don't move."

He didn't bother sketching the tattoo first, just tapped the tip of the needle into my skin with firm pokes. The first few minutes were uncomfortable as he worked, but it was far from reaching my pain threshold. Soon enough, I relaxed into my seat and watched Dingo work. I expected him to have to stop repeatedly to refill the ink, but as the minutes ticked by, he kept tapping a design into my skin, the ink seemingly limitless.

"Look at that," he breathed, watching as the design began to take shape. He acted like he really had no idea what design he was tattooing into my skin.

Riley met my eyes, her face flushed with excitement. "It's going to be a real stunner."

After twenty minutes, I stopped watching the clock. As the endorphins kicked in, I found myself lulled into the rhythm of

Dingo's work. Riley and I passed the time alternating between idle conversation and comfortable silence.

"What do you say we celebrate your new ink at Grinders?" Riley asked.

"I thought alcohol was a no-go right after getting a tattoo."

Riley grinned. "It is, but karaoke isn't."

I laughed until Dingo pinched my leg with an admonishment to hold still.

"Ouch! Stop that."

Unrepentant, Dingo pinched me again before going back to his design.

I looked back at Riley. "Thanks, but I'll pass."

Riley huffed but let it go as we both watched the tattoo take form. Although I was peering at the design upside down, and it was smeared with ink, I could make out the tips of wings and beaks. A few minutes later, Dingo finished, resting the needle that was no longer black on his tray.

"What is it?" I asked.

"Let's find out." Dingo acted like he really had no idea what design the ink had chosen. He reached for folded gauze, wetting it and carefully wiping away the excess ink. Passing me a small hand mirror, he stepped back and surveyed his design.

The tattoo was a definite work of art. Zepar's mark had been swallowed up by the dark bodies of crows, their wings a deep, silky black and their eyes sharp and watchful. One crow was larger than the others and seemed to be peering at me. Around it, several smaller crows perched on branches and spread their wings in flight. It was beautiful.

"Death," Dingo whispered, a note of awe in his voice as he studied the birds.

I sputtered, but Dingo continued oblivious to my reaction.

"The ink has chosen a symbol of death for you." He met my eyes. "A murder of crows."

Of course, it did. But despite the macabre symbolism, I had to admit it felt perfect. The crows were so realistic, it almost looked like their feathers were ruffling in the breeze. As I admired it, I felt a tendril of magic winding its way across my skin. My eyes widened, and I gingerly touched the tattoo.

"Woah." I jerked my fingers back. "I felt it move."

I looked up, expecting Riley and Dingo to scoff at my overactive imagination. They were both watching me carefully.

"I should hope so." Dingo's gaze was assessing. "It's the magic bonding to you."

"Huh. Magic?" I didn't think he was talking metaphorically because I felt the warmth of the magic settling into my chest. "What does the magic do?"

Dingo went back to his cart and began sterilizing everything again. "No idea." He laid the bronze-handled needle on his tray.

"How can you have no idea? It's your magic."

"No. It's not my magic." He tapped the bottle of ink. "I already told you. The ink decides what you need." He continued wiping down the barber chair before indicating Riley could sit down.

"But you're the witch," I objected. "Wouldn't you have to, I don't know, direct it or something?"

"That's not witch magic, girl. The ink itself is magical."

Riley settled herself in the chair I'd just vacated and bared the inside of her wrist.

Dingo ran his fingers along her vein before measuring the width of her wrist with his fingers. "Not everyone can use the ink, of course." He reached for a new needle—this one affixed to a tarnished silver key. He bypassed the antique bottle of black ink he had used for me to reach for another bottle, this one with ink the color of sepia. "Only someone worthy of its magic can use it to create a talisman, and only those worthy of its gifts can receive it."

As the flutter of unfamiliar wings beat against my heart, I felt a shiver of unease. And I remembered Dingo's warning. Somehow, before this day was done, I would need the talisman now stitched into my skin.

CHAPTER 5

To put the warning out of my head, I buried myself in yards of brightly colored tulle back at my shop. With the Kansas City Renaissance Festival fast approaching, I had been concentrating my time and talent on bar maids, ornate gowns, and fairy costumes. The latter was what I was working on at the moment. I was finishing up the skirt, so I could move on to the wings. Tulle was my least favorite material to work with, but nothing crafted whimsy quite like the airy fabric, so tulle it was.

I had just put a piece of clear tape on the bottom of my sewing machine's presser foot to avoid snagging the delicate fabric when Craig knocked on the glass door. The shop wasn't open today, so it was just me. I flipped the sewing light off and left the half-finished skirt for another day.

"Hey," I said nervously, opening the door. We didn't have plans, and I hadn't expected to see him today. As much as I loved spending time with him, surprise visits from Craig didn't usually come with good news. The shuttered expression and tension he carried told me today wasn't going to break that streak. "What's wrong?"

He paused inside the room, waiting for me to relock the door and face him before he answered. "There's been another murder."

The faces of every witch I knew flashed through my mind. "Who?"

"No one we know," he assured me. "I put out some feelers to see if there had been anything similar in recent weeks."

"And you found something?" I guessed.

"I did. A couple other territories reported an uptick in missing persons the last couple of months. At least one of them was a witch."

I dropped into a chair, and Craig sat next to me. "You think they're related?"

"I don't know yet. But one of those contacts called back to report a dead witch who was just found. Same M.O. right down to a demon mark carved into the witch's skin."

I flinched. One dead witch was a crime, two was a pattern. I didn't like the implications, and judging from Craig's clenched fists, neither did he. "Same mark?" I asked.

"No." He pulled out his cell phone, scrolling through texts until he hit one with a photo. He handed it to me. The mark didn't match the one we'd found on Anne's body, and it didn't match the one Zepar had carved on me. Even so, I felt like I'd seen it before. I just couldn't remember where.

I zoomed in and studied the swirls and lines that felt so familiar. "Do you know which demon the mark belongs to?"

"Not yet. I sent it to the Celeste to research, but I haven't heard back."

"Do you mind if I send a copy to my phone? I can look in the books I have to see if I can turn up a match."

"Go ahead."

As he waited for me to hand his phone back, I got the feeling there was more to Craig's visit than a report of an unidentified demon mark. I didn't have to wait long to find out what it was.

"It just happened this morning," Craig said.

"The murder?"

Craig nodded. "The local witches' council managed to quarantine the body until I have a chance to examine it, but they can only buy me a day or two before it has to go to the morgue." He rubbed the back of his neck before meeting my eyes. "I hate asking you to do it again."

I knew what he was asking and how hard it was for him, so I covered his hand with my own. "I'll do it."

"Are you able to call a spirit again so soon?" Craig had witnessed the aftermath of my powers, so he knew how draining they could be.

"I'm back to normal." Between the recent summoning and the generous shots of tequila, I was feeling far better than I had a right to be.

Craig looked relieved. "How soon can you be ready? There's a flight leaving for Chicago tonight."

My smile faltered. "Chicago?"

He nodded. "I figured you might want to see your family, so I cleared my schedule this weekend. We can stay an extra day." When I didn't respond right away, he looked at me curiously. "How long has it been since you've been home?"

It had been almost two years since I left Chicago, packing every crevice of my Volkswagen Beetle before making the trek to Kansas City. I hadn't looked back, and I hadn't kept in close contact. "Since I moved here."

If Craig was surprised, he hid it well. "Do you want to see them?"

My relationship with my family was complicated, but in addition to seeing them, this was an opportunity to do what I'd been putting off for weeks now. "It's definitely time."

I thought about the letter from my grandmother. I'd been carrying it around since I discovered it, rereading and analyzing every word she had written. Instead of finding answers, I came up with more questions on every pass. I couldn't keep stewing over this. I needed to talk to the two people who might be able to give me answers—my dad and my grandmother. It said a lot about my deteriorating relationship with my family that I'd rather call my grandmother back from the dead than broach the subject with my father.

"There's something I need to do first. How soon do we need to leave for the airport?"

Craig checked his watch. "I'll grab a bag, book the flights, and pick you up in three hours."

I packed on autopilot, throwing enough clothes and toiletries in a duffle bag to get me through the weekend. I tossed in a couple books on demonology for in-flight reading.

It took me ten more minutes before I gathered the courage to call my father. I wasn't avoiding him because of animosity. There hadn't been some big falling out or words hurled in anger. Just the opposite actually. When it came to my dad, we'd spent years drifting through the same house together after Claire died. By the time I moved, we'd grown so good at the silence, the goodbye was hardly a fracture. He'd called a few times, of course, and we'd made the appropriate small talk. But it had been years since we'd had a conversation about anything that mattered.

Now as I sat on my bed, folding and unfolding the letter

my grandmother left for me, this trip felt inevitable. It was long past time we talked about what happened to Claire, even though the conversation would rip open wounds that had never quite healed.

"Hey, Dad?" My greeting was shaky when he answered the phone. "It's Kali. I'm going to be in Chicago this weekend for business." I took creative license with the purpose for the trip because telling my father—who had been on the police force all my life—I was coming home to visit the crime scene of a murder was out of the question.

"You're coming home?"

Hearing my dad's gruff voice put a lump in my throat. I swallowed past it and faked cheerfulness. "I am but just for a couple days. I'd like to see you and Drew if he's not busy."

"Of course, we want to see you! When will you be here? I'll change the sheets in your room."

I hadn't anticipated that. "Dad, I'm bringing someone. We rented a hotel room."

"I see." There was a pause, the sound of the television in the background filling the void. "How about supper tomorrow night then?" he asked. "Bring your friend."

Even though I wasn't sure I wanted Craig and my father in the same room, I didn't argue. Add Drew to the mix, and they'd either be bonding or brawling by dessert. "Perfect. I'll let you know when we land."

After saying our goodbyes, I stashed my grandmother's letter back in my purse and called Meira. While she wasn't enthusiastic about the idea of summoning my grandmother's spirit, she agreed to help me. I didn't want to do it alone.

I took my time choosing an outfit suitable for the occasion, finally settling on a flowy A-line dress with a dainty floral pattern. The dress wasn't my typical style. It was the kind of dress you wore to church or to an old-fashioned picnic, sweet and feminine. Because it was the last dress my grandmother had bought me, I'd carted it around with me all these years even though I hadn't worn it since her death. I put the dress on and checked my reflection in the full-length mirror on the back of my bedroom door, satisfied that I resembled the young granddaughter she'd left behind.

Rifling through my jewelry box, I found the silver pendant she'd given me for my twelfth birthday. It was half of a broken heart, the type of friendship jewelry abundant in childhood. The other half of the necklace was buried with my twin sister Claire. I hooked it around my neck, the once-familiar weight feeling hollow against my chest.

One last mirror check assured my tattoo was completely hidden beneath my dress. My grandmother wasn't the sort to object to a tattoo. If she'd lived longer, she probably would've taken me to get it herself. But seeing it would invite questions, and the last thing I wanted to talk to her about was the scar beneath it.

When I got to Old World Occult & Curiosities, Meira was ready for me. She eyed my floral dress with a furrowed brow. "Don't you look lovely."

"Grandma Dottie bought it," I explained.

"Ah, I see."

I followed Meira into the back, where she had two cups of tea steeping and some incense burning. I'd learned better than to wave off her offer of tea. It was easier to smile and accept it, taking a token sip or two to make her happy. When I tilted it to my lips, the smell of peppermint settled my nervous stomach, and I was grateful for it.

We both took our time finishing our tea, neither of us

bothering to make small talk. Although things were not as tense between us as they had been, I wasn't totally comfortable around Meira either. Despite taking her up on her offer of mentorship, there was only a fragile sort of peace between us.

I took a couple deep breaths to steady myself before reaching for the silver necklace around my throat. "I guess we should get started."

By now, I'd had a lot of practice summoning ghosts, but calling my grandmother was going to be the hardest. I was both desperate to see her and anxious for answers. Underpinning it all was the fear that had been eating me since Claire's death, a fear that my sister's killer would never be caught. Although my grandmother had gone to Romania to track down a suspicious man who had been watching Claire before her death, I had no idea if my grandmother had discovered anything more about him before she'd been killed. There was only one way to find out.

I sat on the floor, my legs crossed beneath me, and settled my breathing. I stroked the necklace and envisioned my grandmother's face. The tattoo on my chest warmed and the spiritual plane snapped into focus effortlessly. I took my time sifting through the souls surrounding me, but none of them felt familiar. None of them belonged to my grandmother. I stroked the necklace she had given me and concentrated harder. Still nothing.

"I can't find her," I whispered.

When I looked at Meira, she was frowning. "Because you two have a familial bond, it should be easier for you to locate her and call her to you."

"It should, but it's not." I tried to keep the sharp desperation out of my voice.

"Maybe you should try again, this time with the letter she left for you since there's a strong emotional connection to it."

My shoulders relaxed. "That's a good idea." I rummaged around in my purse, coming up with the folded letter my grandmother had left in the car she'd gifted me all those years ago. This time, I held the letter in one hand and the necklace in the other. I tried to find her for half an hour, but nothing happened.

"Kali, I think you need to stop for today."

Frustrated, I opened my eyes, blinking against the light. The first thing I saw was Meira, her expression pinched. "Not yet."

"You know the cost of overdoing it—the headaches and fatigue." She stepped closer to me, studying me. "Are you okay?"

"I'm fine." I wasn't lying. I felt the flutter of wings against my breast and wondered if I could thank my new magical tattoo for my lack of headache. Not willing to have a long discussion on the merits of getting a magical back-alley tattoo, I didn't mention it. "Why can't I reach her?"

"I don't know," Meira said. "Perhaps your feelings are too tumultuous to focus enough to locate her."

"No," I insisted. "I can see other souls, just not hers. Even with this letter, all I see when I look for her is emptiness. There's not a trace of her."

Meira frowned. "Perhaps she doesn't want to be called."

I wanted to argue, insist my grandmother would always come when I called, but too many people I had counted on disappeared on me to be sure. "Could she even do that?" When I was first exploring my power, Meira had insisted I held the strings, that I was the one who forged the bond with the souls I called. Why would my grandmother be different?

Meira smiled. "Your grandmother had a will of iron. If she didn't want to do something, there's no one on this earth who could force her." Meira's gaze was unfocused, as if she were reliving memories of earlier times.

"But why? Why wouldn't she want to come when I call her?"

Meira must have sensed the crushing grief that was weighing on me because she touched my arm, trying to comfort me. "She loved you."

"I know." I had no doubt whatsoever my grandmother loved me fiercely. But loving someone and showing up when that person needed you were two distinct things.

"Knowing Dottie," Meira said, "the only thing that would keep her away when you call would be a need to protect you."

"From what?"

Meira's gaze dropped to the letter I still clutched like I was afraid to let it go. "Whatever got her killed."

CHAPTER 6

By the time the plane landed at O'Hare in Chicago, it was well past dark. Because the flights had been booked last minute, Craig hadn't been able to get two seats next to each other. I spent the hour and a half in the air battling for an armrest with a sweaty forty-year-old who had roaming elbows and a snore capable of waking the dead. My tattoo might protect against summoning-induced headaches, but it was useless against headaches caused by close-proximity snoring.

On the bright side, I didn't have to worry about my seat mate noticing my odd reading material. It hadn't taken me long to locate the newest sigil Craig had shown me. This one belonged to a demon named Shax who had a particular talent for finding lost objects and detecting lies. Both would be handy skills to wield, but Shax was a big step down on the power scale compared to both Zepar and Malthus.

As soon as the plane landed, I climbed over the slumbering man to get my carry-on bag. Once I was off the plane, I waited for Craig who was seated further back on the flight. Because

Craig was well over six foot tall, it was easy to spot him in the crowd shuffling down the ramp.

"Hey," he said when he joined me. "Rough flight? I heard the guy next to you from where I was sitting."

"Yeah. I'll be stocking up on industrial-strength earplugs for the flight home."

Craig reached for my bag, sliding it off my shoulder and adding it to his smaller one. When your entire wardrobe consisted of faded denim jeans and black t-shirts, it probably made packing light easy. I relinquished my bag gratefully and stretched my stiff muscles. After we navigated the airport and hailed a cab, I closed my eyes and settled in for the ride to the hotel. Craig nudged me awake when we arrived.

While Craig checked us in, I made a pitstop at the vending machine for a much-needed shot of carbonated caffeine. It wasn't coffee, but it would have to do. Our rooms were on the third floor at the end of the hall. Craig opened my door first, depositing my bag on the bed and checking the room.

The room was spacious with a king-sized bed, a small side chair, and a well-equipped bathroom. With the last-minute nature of our trip, I was expecting a run-down motel along the interstate, so this room was downright luxurious by comparison.

"I hope you don't mind," he said as he opened the door that joined our rooms. "I got a suite. Given the reason we are here, I didn't want you in a room alone."

"No, it's great. Thank you."

While I doubted I was in any danger, I was still happy to have him close. Under different circumstances, we might have even shared a room, but other people's tragedies had a way of putting a damper on any romantic notions.

I followed Craig through the door he left open into his

room. His room was identical except for the small sofa in place of a side chair. "What's the plan?"

Craig tossed his bag and walked over to the windows, opening the curtains and taking stock of the surroundings. "We're meeting the witches in the morning to see the body. After that, I have a few leads to follow up on before dinner at your dad's. Our flight isn't until the next morning."

I joined him at the window. "You don't have to come to dinner, you know."

He turned back to me and frowned. "You don't want me to go?"

If I hadn't been around Craig as much as I had, I would have missed the undercurrent of hurt in his question. I wrapped one arm around him and leaning into his solid strength. "It's not that. But I realize how awkward it is to meet my family under these circumstances." I gave him a little hip bump and a wink. "Normally, family dinners come after the second date."

He relaxed. "To hell with normal. I want to meet them."

"All right," I agreed, "but don't say I didn't warn you. My dad and brother can be obnoxious." I hadn't brought a guy home since my high school prom date.

"Oh?" He didn't seem concerned.

"You'll see soon enough." I gazed out the window at the city skyline, my mood souring as I weighed the chances of my upcoming conversation with my father ending well.

"This is really your first time back?" Craig interrupted my thoughts.

"Yeah." I dropped my forehead against the window, the glass cool from the air conditioning unit below it. In the fading daylight, the lights beyond the window could have been any city. It was both familiar and anonymous, and I lost myself in the view.

Craig nudged my shoulder. "You hungry?"

"Starving. Do you want to go out or order in?"

"Definitely out," he said.

I suspected his choice was more about avoiding strangers coming to our rooms than it was due to a genuine desire to explore the city. But it gave me the opportunity to suggest my favorite local dive bar, which served a wide selection of beer on tap and the best chili fries in the Midwest.

After a quick shower and a passable continental breakfast the next morning, Craig and I took a cab to meet the local coven. They'd kept the body sequestered where they found it: in the unfinished basement of a house in foreclosure. While the day was sunny and mild, a dense fog surrounded the house, obscuring the sidewalk that led around to the back. The neighborhood itself was quiet, and everyone seemed to keep their curtains closed.

Craig paid the fare, and the cab driver took off as soon as the door was closed, looking at us in his rearview mirror as he sped away. Not that I blamed him. The minute we stepped out of the cab, I felt an overwhelming urge to climb back in and put as much distance between me and this place as I could. I glanced at Craig.

"Magic," he confirmed. He pointed to the fog blanketing the house. "It's a spell meant to repel people."

"Smart." It made sense. To keep a dead body on the premises, the less attention, the better.

Craig opened the gate to the backyard. "Hold on to me."

He waited until I hooked my fingers into the belt loop of his jeans before walking into the backyard. Because we couldn't see more than a foot in front of us, it was slow going to get to the door. When we reached it, Craig knocked. The witch who greeted us didn't waste time on an introduction. She waved us in before pivoting and heading down a set of stairs.

Once inside, we could see again, so I let go of Craig and followed them into the basement. I'd prepared myself for the stench of a day-old dead body, but the only thing I smelled as we descended was the familiar musty smell of a neglected basement.

Before I could comment, the witch leading the way explained. "We've cast a spell to keep the body in stasis, so Fiona is as preserved as she was when we found her, hours after her death." She paused at the base of the stairs, waiting until we'd joined her to flip on the overhead lights.

I clutched Craig's arm as I took in the scene. Fiona looked to be even younger than Anne, barely out of her teens. Like Anne, her arms and legs were stretched out to touch the circle painted on the concrete floor. Unlike Anne, Fiona's face was marred with a bruise across one cheek and dried blood at the corner of a split lip. We didn't have to search for the demon's mark. It was carved into her forehead.

My breakfast threatened to come back up, and although I desperately wanted to look away, I kept my eyes trained on her face. Craig waited until I released his arm to move closer, crouching down to check out the body with a practiced detachment. He pulled out his phone and snapped several photos of her battered face, a tightening of his mouth the only tell it bothered him. He'd seen a lot more dead bodies than I had, but seeing a young woman carved up like this was particularly disturbing.

Craig paused to examine one of her hands that was curled into a partial fist. He grimaced. "Blood under her fingernails."

The witch who accompanied us moved closer, her face pinched in sorrow. "Our Fiona was a fighter."

Craig bent closer. "There's something in her hand." He reached into his jeans pocket and pulled out disposable nitrate gloves. It made sense that in his line of work, he had to come prepared. "Do you have the kit I gave you earlier?" Craig asked me.

I dug around in my purse until I came up with the small evidence collection kit he'd handed me earlier for safekeeping. Despite my desire to get a better look at the mark, I didn't move closer. I watched as Craig pried a wadded-up piece of paper from Fiona's hand before scraping under one of her fingernails. He transferred the dried blood to a container and sealed it.

"Will that work? To preserve the DNA, I mean?" the witch asked.

Craig handed the kit and the sample back to me, and I tucked both in my purse.

"It should. We'll put it in the freezer when we get back to our hotel. Once forensics gets here, they'll take their own samples. We'll get that report as well, but in a city like Chicago, it's hard to say how long it'll take to process the evidence. I can put a rush on this one." He picked up the paper Fiona had been holding and flattened it.

I stepped closer. "What is it?"

Even with its crinkled surface, it was obvious it wasn't ordinary notebook paper. The page looked like it had been torn out of a book and was yellowed with age. However, it wasn't the state it was in that was concerning, but rather what was written on it. "Do you think it's a summoning spell?" I asked.

"Maybe." Craig turned to the witch and held the paper where she could see it. "Could this be Fiona's?"

She shook her head. "That's not her handwriting. And I don't recognize the spell."

Craig handed the paper to me. The handwriting looked familiar, but I couldn't place it. Craig took his time combing through the room, looking for any other evidence that could lead us to the killer.

When he was finished, he turned to me. "Are you ready?"

"I am." I looked at the witch who had kept her gaze on the dingy basement window rather than on the woman sprawled in the middle of the floor. "How well did you know Fiona?" I asked her.

She spoke so softly, I had to lean in to hear her. "All her life."

I glanced at Craig. "Have you explained why I'm here?"

He nodded.

"You're a necromancer," she said, her voice flat. "You're going to question her."

I stepped close enough to make eye contact but not so close it made her uncomfortable. "Yes. My name is Kali. What's your name?"

"Shelly."

"Shelly, when Fiona comes back, it will take her spirit awhile to register she is dead. She'll be very upset. And that's before I ask her to remember what happened to her."

Shelly swallowed and looked at her feet.

"It's up to you," I continued. "But if you don't want to stay for this, it's ok."

She stood still for a minute as if she couldn't decide. Finally, she nodded and went back upstairs.

"I need something metal of Fiona's to call her." I checked her body for jewelry. She didn't wear a necklace or bracelet, but she had a small silver ring on her pinky finger and earrings shaped like teardrops in her ears. "The ring is our best bet."

I stepped closer, but Craig held up a gloved hand. "I'll get it." He pulled off her ring and handed it to me.

I closed my fist around the ring, feeling my tattoo flutter as I looked down at Fiona. I offered Craig my other hand, and he took it. The call for Fiona's soul was effortless. One second, I was thinking about her, and the next she was standing before me looking down in horror at her own mutilated body. Despite my initial misgivings about getting a tattoo from a guy named Dingo, the magical boost was proving to be quite useful.

Craig took an involuntary step back dropping my hand. "How did you call her so quickly?"

"It's a long story." Although I had every intention of telling Craig about my tattoo, now didn't seem like the best time to get sidetracked.

I gave Fiona a couple minutes to acclimate. When she straightened her spine, I made the introductions before launching into my questions. "Hi Fiona. My name is Kali, and this is Craig. We're here to find out what happened to you."

When she didn't object, I extended my hand to Craig again. "It'll be easier if you can be part of the conversation." He only hesitated a moment, but his whole body was rigid when he placed his palm against mine.

"Fiona, can you tell us everything you remember about the day you were killed?"

At the reminder of her death, Fiona staggered on her feet. She steadied herself and swiped the tears from her pale cheeks. When she recalled what happened, she described the events in detail. There was enough overlap between her story and Anne's that the two deaths were obviously connected. Fiona told us she had been sitting at a coffee shop working on a paper for her college history class when she started feeling woozy. After that, she couldn't remember anything until she woke up in this room. She paused her retelling and shuddered, her eyes darting to the dark corners of the room as if searching for the perpetrators.

"Could someone have drugged you?" l asked. "The barista, maybe?"

Fiona chewed her fingernail as she considered it. "I guess, but I go there all the time, and I didn't notice anyone new. It could have also been magic. I can't be sure."

"Magic?" Craig's voice came out harsh in the quiet room, and Fiona took an instinctive step away from us. "What makes you think it could have been magic?" He spoke softly now to avoid startling her further.

She shrugged. "My drink didn't taste funny or anything."

Not all drugs altered the taste of a drink as stout as a flavored coffee, so we couldn't rule it out altogether. Looking at the worried expression on Fiona's face, I dropped that line of questioning and moved on to something more productive. "What do you remember after waking up?"

Fiona reached up and touched the bloody demon mark on her forehead. "This. I remember someone carving this." She dropped her hand to her side and looked down at her body.

"Did you see who did this to you?" Craig asked. When she didn't immediately respond, he prodded. "Anything you can tell us could help, Fiona."

She sank to the floor and traced the bloody mark on her forehead with a trembling finger, her face stricken. "I couldn't see the person who did this. His face was obscured—some kind of magic, I think. He took his time carving into me."

I clenched my jaw imagining the horror and the helplessness she must have felt.

"He?" Craig asked.

She nodded slowly. "I don't know how I know, but I'm sure it was a man."

Craig handled the rest of the questions. Like Anne, Fiona had heard two distinct voices. She said the magic felt different than a typical witch. When Craig asked her if it felt like a necromancer's magic, I stiffened.

"Maybe. I haven't been around any necromancers before now." Fiona looked directly at me, frowning.

I tried not to squirm uncomfortably. I didn't like the thought of someone like me being capable of doing this to her. Craig didn't glance at me, keeping his full attention on Fiona as she considered it.

"The magic didn't feel like yours, though," she told me.

"What does my magic feel like?" The question was out before I could help it.

"When you first called me, it felt like a gentle tug. Now, it feels like a cord connecting us together. But there's no malice in it. It feels…" She searched for the right word. "Comforting."

I didn't respond, but some of the tension I'd been holding left my body.

"And the other magic?" Craig asked.

Fiona closed her eyes. "That magic was full of malice—dark, like tar coating my skin as he chanted. And no, I don't remember what he chanted. I was too busy watching myself bleed out."

"You couldn't move?" I asked.

She shook her head. "When I first woke up with someone leaning over me, I could move. I scratched his face. But after that, no." Fiona stiffened. "There must have been a vampire here, too. He compelled me." She deflated and rubbed her eyes with the back of her hand. "But I couldn't see him clearly, either."

I grabbed the paper that had been wadded up in her hand. "Do you recognize this?"

Fiona scanned the paper. "No. But it looks like some kind of ritual."

Craig reached for the paper, bringing it closer to Fiona. "Are you sure? I found it clutched in your hand."

Fiona stared down at her prone body and the hand still curled as if it held something. "I don't remember having that in my hand. I don't think I've ever seen it before."

He handed it back to me, and I folded the paper in half before tucking it into my purse with the rest of our confiscated evidence.

Although we questioned Fiona for another half an hour, we didn't get much useful information. Like Anne, she couldn't think of anyone who would wish her harm, and she didn't recall anything out of the ordinary in the days leading up to her murder.

After releasing Fiona with a promise that whoever did this to her would be held accountable, we found Shelly upstairs where she paced the kitchen. As soon as she spotted us, she sank into one of the nearby chairs in the breakfast nook. Craig and I joined her, sitting on either side of the table. Craig recapped our conversation with Fiona, watching Shelly's reactions closely. It was his job to suspect everyone, but I couldn't help but wince as I watched the emotions overwhelm her.

"Can you think of any reason why Fiona might have been targeted?" Craig asked her.

"No. She was a sweet girl. She wanted to be a nurse, you know?" Shelly's voice broke. She stared out the window. "Fiona volunteered at the hospital every week. She wanted to work with burn and trauma victims, help with their rehabilitation. Even though Fiona would never hurt a fly, she felt a duty to help because of what she was. She said it was a calling."

I beat Craig to the question. "What she was?"

Shelly looked up. "Fiona was a fire elemental."

Craig's interest sharpened. "How powerful was she?"

"Very. She was the strongest elemental I've met," Shelly said, clearly proud of the young witch.

"What's a fire elemental?" Although my knowledge of the supernatural community had grown considerably in the last year, there was a lot I didn't know. At Shelly's look of confusion, I explained. "I didn't grow up around supernaturals. This is all new to me."

Shelly studied me skeptically. I imagined she was trying to reconcile my ability to call Fiona so easily with my utter lack of knowledge.

"It's true," Craig said. "Meira is mentoring her."

Whether Shelly knew Meira in person or from reputation, Craig's assurance was enough to placate her. "What do you know about witches' magic?" she asked.

I recalled Meira's explanation. "Just that they draw their magic from the earth."

"That's a simplification but yes. Witches draw from the elements, all of which are based on earth magic."

"By elements, you mean earth, wind, water, and fire?" I asked.

"Yes. Most of us can channel small amounts of magic from multiple elements. Each element fuels a different type of magic. We tap into earth magic for potions and spell work, air magic for incantations, water for cleansing, and fire to focus intention." Shelly checked to make sure I was following her so far. At my nod, she continued. "Rarer are the witches with concentrated power drawn from a single element. These elementals can tap into deep magic in their respective elements, allowing them to manipulate those elements to a degree. Earth elementals are not uncommon, but there are far fewer air and water elementals. And fire elementals like Fiona are the rarest."

"Exactly how rare are they?" Craig asked. If Craig had to ask, the witches must be tight-lipped about the distribution of power.

Shelly's expression became guarded. "Only the governing witches' council knows the number, but Fiona is the only fire elemental I know."

CHAPTER 7

We hadn't made it two blocks from the crime scene before I asked the obvious. "Was Anne also a fire elemental?"

"I don't know," Craig said. "But I'll find out."

Once we were back in our hotel rooms, Craig punched in a number and put his phone on speaker.

Celeste got right down to business when she answered. "What did you find, Ward?" As both the witches' representative on the Tribunal and a powerful member of the governing witches' council, Celeste had been briefed on the murders and what we'd found so far.

Craig ticked off our latest discoveries, including our conversation with Shelly. "Do you think Fiona was a target because she was a fire elemental?"

The line went silent as Celeste considered it. "Maybe. Hold on a sec. I need to check on something." Although Celeste covered the phone, we could hear her asking someone in the background whether Anne was an elemental. Whoever she was speaking to was far enough away I didn't catch the response until Celeste repeated it. "Both witches were fire elementals." Her voice was grim.

If they were as rare as rare as Shelly claimed, there was no way that could be coincidental. "Do you have any idea why someone would be targeting them?" Craig asked.

"None."

"I need a list of the remaining fire elementals, Celeste." Craig glared at his phone as if he knew her answer before she gave it.

"I can't do that."

He clenched his jaw. "Then their deaths will be on your head."

Celeste was quiet so long, I was afraid she'd disconnected. "I'll try to persuade the council. But Ward, I'm not sure they'll be willing to make the information public."

"So, don't make it public," he snapped. "In case you hadn't noticed, I'm not the public."

"I'll do my best. I have to go, but I'll be in touch." Celeste disconnected the call before we had a chance to ask her about the page we'd found in Fiona's hand. Craig paced to the window, the phone clutched so tightly in his hand, I expected the screen to shatter any second from the pressure.

I was so used to the unshakable version of Craig, I wasn't sure how to approach him agitated. "Are you okay?"

"Fine." He stared out the window for a long time. "I need to clear my head. Stay inside, and keep the door locked." Craig didn't look at me as he crossed the room. "I'll be back in time for dinner."

I didn't argue, and I didn't push for answers. "Okay."

From his closed-down expression, I could tell he was fighting for control. Celeste may have triggered whatever he was battling, but she hadn't caused it. I suspected whatever had him shaken went far deeper than the two dead witches we were investigating.

No matter how many years had passed since Claire's death, stepping foot into my childhood home made it feel like I just lost her. Even with her gone, her presence overwhelmed the space. Fragments of Claire were in the dining room photo shrine of her life and in the soccer medals framed in the living room. She lingered in the threadbare chair my dad wouldn't get rid of but wasn't comfortable sitting in because it had been her favorite. As I stood in the entryway awkwardly hugging my dad, who looked like he'd aged a decade in the two years I'd been gone, the weight of her memories suffocated me. Maybe it took two years away from Chicago to realize how stifling my childhood home had become.

I stepped out of my dad's loose embrace to introduce Craig. "Dad, this is Craig."

Craig extended a hand. "It's nice to meet you, sir."

Dad's attention shifted from me to Craig, his body stiffening as he took in the man standing behind me. After decades on the police force in a city where too many men modeled themselves as the next Al Capone, my father knew dangerous when he saw it. Craig had surprised me by dressing in something other than his wardrobe staples of jeans and a tight black t-shirt, but it would take more than a pair of khakis and a button-down shirt to make him look like anything other than what he was—a man who dealt in intimidation and violence.

The longer my dad studied Craig, the more pronounced

his frown became. "Mark James." Dad finally shook Craig's hand, but there was nothing friendly in his greeting.

If my dad's scrutiny made him uncomfortable, Craig didn't show it.

I looked around Dad. "Drew's not here?"

"He's running late," he said, still eyeing Craig. "Drew's working vice now."

"So I heard." When Dad didn't make a move to invite us in, I wrapped my hand around Craig's arm and guided him toward the living room.

Dad followed, sitting on the couch across from us. "I thought you were here on business." He looked pointedly to where I was still holding onto Craig's arm

I stiffened. "Craig is, actually. I tagged along." He'd jump to the conclusion that I only came to see him and Drew, which was better than explaining that I came to talk to a dead witch. My dad had no idea real witches—or any supernaturals for that matter—existed.

Before Dad could grill Craig further, the back door opened, and Drew strolled in. At one time, my brother Drew and I were close, but the camaraderie we shared growing up had evaporated abruptly. The easy-going big brother who liked practical jokes and teasing me died right along with Claire. In his place was a man who saw the world in black and white and who had little time for the frivolities he saw as my life. One glance at my brother's hard eyes and rigid jaw told me little had changed in the time I'd been away. Still, I crossed the room to where he stood.

For a second, I caught sight of the old Drew as he wrapped me in a bear hug and rubbed his knuckles on the top of my head. "Hey, shorty."

I batted his hand away, relaxing as some of the tension

bled out of the room. "Come on, I'll introduce you. Craig, this is my brother Andrew." I smiled up at Drew, but he didn't smile back. By the time Craig stood to shake his hand, Drew's mask was firmly back in place. I hated this version of my brother.

"Craig was about to tell me what kind of work he does," Dad said.

Drew dropped to the couch beside Dad and crossed his arms. Drew had been hitting the weights hard since he'd turned seventeen, and he looked like a younger, bulkier version of my father.

Craig relaxed back into the couch. "Security."

Dad snorted. "What kind of security job lets you bring a date?"

Drew's eyebrows raised as he looked between us. "Date?"

"Private security, sir." Craig didn't mirror the hostility Dad and Drew were throwing his way. "I'm here as a consultant."

Drew leaned forward. "And who exactly is paying that consultant fee?"

Craig met his eyes. "I'm afraid I can't disclose client information."

"Sounds familiar," Drew said, the implication Craig was here on shady business clear. Maybe when you spent day after day dealing with the seedy underbelly of a city with a homicide rate as high as Chicago, you became jaded. But I didn't appreciate the sneer he aimed at Craig.

"What the hell, Drew?" I moved to stand up, but Craig's hand circled my wrist, keeping me on the couch.

"It's okay. I'm sure your family just wants to make sure you are safe."

Most men would take the olive branch Craig was extending, but not my brother. "My sister seems to gravitate toward trouble."

If he'd meant to offend Craig, he'd have to try a lot harder. Craig ignored Drew to smile at me. "That she does."

I cleared my throat. "Okay, then. I'm starving. Are we ordering in or going out?" Neither my brother nor dad could cook anything more complex than a pot of spaghetti with canned pasta sauce.

When it was clear Craig wasn't going to flinch no matter how much either of them postured, Dad checked his watch. "I ordered a couple pizzas. They should be here any time."

I followed Dad into the kitchen, leaving Drew and Craig to their stare down. The testosterone was thick enough to choke on, and my nerves were already on edge.

Dad grabbed the plates and drinks, while I tossed a packaged salad from the fridge. We'd done this so many times since Mom left that our movements were on autopilot. Before I could take the salad to the dining room, Dad stopped me.

He kept his voice low. "So, this guy?"

"He's not what you think." When he didn't look convinced, I sighed. "Give him a chance. You'll see. He's one of the good ones."

"If you say so."

We made it through dinner without any outright hostilities, with Dad steering the conversation to more neutral topics like the weather and football. Drew didn't say much, but since he was putting away more pizza than the other three of us combined, it wasn't too awkward. After dinner, I cleared the table, and my dad put on a fresh pot of coffee. Without deep dish pizza to distract us, the conversation stuttered.

I grabbed a cup of coffee for myself and one for Craig, letting the men in my family fend for themselves. Blowing on my steaming mug to cool it off enough to sip, I paused in front of the buffet. When I was a kid, my mom would fill the top with decorations for the season—brightly colored leaves and gourds in the fall, Easter figurines and fake grass in the spring. Now, it was a decade-old shrine to my sister. Photos spanning her young life crowded the surface, and while the rest of the house could use a good dusting, not a speck was visible here. I picked up a silver frame. In it, Claire stood between my parents at one of her many awards nights, her smile lighting up the frame.

We may have been twins, but we had been far from identical. She was light to my dark in more ways than one. The hole she left behind was one I could never fill. The room went quiet, and when I turned back to the table, everyone was watching me. I caught my dad's gaze, but he looked away.

"Excuse me." Dad stood and headed down the hall to the bathroom.

I blinked back the sting of tears and took a sip, not caring that the coffee scalded my tongue.

Drew rested his elbows on the table. "I'm surprised you came home. It's been what? Two years?"

"I guess it has." I sat back down. "How have you been, Drew?" It was supposed to be one of those icebreaker questions people who haven't seen each other for years lobbed at each other.

Drew narrowed his eyes. "You'd know that if you bothered to return my calls."

"You didn't leave a message." It was a weak excuse, and we both knew it.

Drew glanced down the hall to make sure Dad was still in the bathroom before dropping his verbal grenade. "It was a real shit thing to do, K. Dad needs you." His eyes flicked to Claire's photo behind me. "You need to come home."

I waved my hand toward him. "And this is why I don't return your calls. Can't we have a normal conversation for once?"

Drew pushed away from the table, his chair scraping against the wood floor. Dad came back, interrupting whatever guilt trip Drew was about to lay on me. Seeing the fight brewing between us, Dad switched topics. "Kali, I saw O'Grady's was hiring."

I took a steadying breath because I knew where this was going—where it always went. "Okay."

"It's an office manager position. You could put your business degree to use, you know. Be closer to home," Dad said.

"I am putting my business degree to use, Dad."

Drew chuckled. "I hardly think making silly little Halloween costumes counts as running a business."

I gritted my teeth and didn't answer.

Craig rested his hand on the back of my chair. "Have you seen any of Kali's costumes lately? She's talented."

My chest lightened a little.

"No one is saying your costumes aren't great." Dad patted my hand. "But this is a good job—stable, with benefits."

"I'm not looking for a job. I'm happy where I am."

"Is that because of him?" Drew jerked his head toward Craig. "Is he paying your bills with the money from his so-called security work?"

I set my cup down on the table hard enough that coffee sloshed out. "I pay my bills with the money I earn from those silly little costumes. And stop insinuating Craig's work is somehow shady. You don't know him."

Drew stood up, his hands gripping the edge of the table.

"Oh, I know guys just like him. I arrest them every damn day." He stared at Craig, who remained sitting, his face neutral despite Drew's accusations. Drew pointed at him. "He's dangerous."

"That's enough, Drew," Dad said, but from his expression, he didn't disagree.

"What the hell is your problem?" I yelled at my brother, standing up to face him. An hour in his presence, and we reverted to childhood screaming matches.

Drew's face turned red. "What's my problem?" he yelled back. "You run off without a care in the world, not giving a shit Dad already lost one daughter." He punctuated his words by jabbing a finger at me.

"What am I supposed to do, Drew? Stay in this house the rest of my life as a stand-in for our dead sister? Do you have any idea what it's like for me here?" I took a couple steps toward the door, needing to get away from him before I said something I couldn't take back.

Drew followed me. "What it's like for you? What about for him?" Drew's face twisted with anger, and he moved to grab me. Before he reached me, Craig was on his feet and between us.

"Drew!" Dad tried to break up the confrontation, but both men ignored him.

Drew stopped abruptly. My brother was used to being the biggest man in the room, but Craig was a solid wall between us. "Get out of my way," Drew bit out.

Craig stayed where he was, his arm a barricade in front of me. "That's not going to happen. No one is putting a hand on her."

"She's my sister." Some of Drew's anger dissipated. "I wouldn't hurt her."

"You already did." Craig's voice was hard.

I saw the flicker of remorse in Drew's eyes, but it was gone as quickly as it appeared. He channeled his anger at Craig. "This conversation doesn't concern you. You're nothing more than the bad boy she brought home to get under our skin. So do us all a favor and crawl back into whatever gutter she found you in."

I'd had enough. "You're wrong."

"He's right about one thing," Craig said softly. "I am dangerous." His admission hung heavy in the room. "But whatever it is you think I do, you're way off base. And Kali's doing fine on her own."

"If Claire were here," Drew started.

My whole body went hot. "Don't you dare finish that fucking sentence, Drew."

Drew shook his head. "Fine. I won't say it." He grabbed the keys he'd dropped on the kitchen counter, slamming the door behind him as he left.

We all sat awkwardly around the table after Drew stormed out. I tried to get my temper under control, while my dad stared at the table. After several painful minutes when it became apparent there was no going back to polite conversation, I brought up the topic I'd been putting off.

"Dad, I need to talk to you about what happened to Claire."

My father's face shuttered. "Let's not start this again."

I moved to the chair next to him, grabbing his hand and holding it in mine even when he tried to pull free. "I know you don't want to talk about this, but I can't let it go."

I tried to think of the right way to phrase the request, so he didn't shut me down like he always did when I brought up Claire's death. As far as Dad was concerned, Claire's death was a simple drunk driving hit-and-run, and he was quick to avoid anything that hinted otherwise.

I kept my voice soft but didn't dance around the topic. Not this time. "Claire's death was not an accident. I know it, and if you're honest with yourself, you know it, too." When he opened his mouth to object, I barreled on. "Dad, I can't move on without this."

My dad slumped in his chair, pulling his hand from mine. He glared at the door as if it would bring Drew back again to be a buffer between us. I waited for Dad to avoid this conversation like he had every other time I'd attempted it. After a minute of strained silence, he surprised me. "What do you want to know?"

I took a deep breath. "Everything."

For the first time since Claire died, my father shared all the details and inconsistencies that had kept him up at night after she was killed. He mentioned the reports of the car speeding up before swerving to hit Claire and the lack of skid marks to show any braking. Dad told me about the crime scene photos that had disappeared out of her case file as if they had never been there. His voice broke when he told me about the eyewitnesses who recanted their statements, claiming to have no memory of the event they had described in vivid detail during initial interviews. By the time he was finished, my dad's shoulders were slumped, and he held his head in his hands. "It almost got me fired, you know." He lifted his head, his eyes begging for understanding. "I had to let it go."

I wrapped him in a hug as big as the ones he used to give me. "Thank you for telling me. It's going to be okay." I didn't tell him I was going to hunt down the man who'd stolen Claire's life. My dad had carried the aftermath of my sister's death for all these years. The burden of knowing what I was willing to do to avenge her would be more than his shoulders could bear.

I stood and gathered our coffee cups to refill, giving my dad a chance to rein in his emotions.

"Let me get that," Craig said, taking the cups from my hand and heading to the kitchen.

I shifted the conversation to my grandmother. "Did Grandma Dottie ever say anything about a man watching the house before Claire died?"

Dad looked up at me startled. "What?"

"Grandma Dottie left me a letter. It was in the glove compartment of my car, and I didn't find it until recently. In it, she said Mom caught some guy lurking around the house watching Claire and me. Did she or Mom ever mention it to you?"

Dad scowled. "No. Lila would have told me." He sounded defensive.

I was treading on delicate ground. The only thing my dad liked talking about less than Claire's death was my mother. Her leaving so soon after we'd lost Claire had been a one-two punch to us all.

I let it go. "It was probably nothing." I took the fresh cup of coffee Craig handed me gratefully.

"Can I see the letter?" Dad asked.

"I'm sorry. I didn't think to bring it." There was no way my dad could read my grandmother's letter. He had no idea either of us were necromancers, and the last time I mentioned seeing a ghost to him, it had landed me in three years of therapy. No way was I setting off that powder keg again. We may have made progress talking about Claire, but some things needed to remain unsaid. I changed the subject, fishing for a clue to revive a long-cold trail. "Did Grandma do or say anything odd before she left on her trip?"

He thought about it for a minute. "No. She acted normal—excited about her trip. Why?"

I shrugged. "It seems strange she'd leave a letter for me in the car but not tell me about it."

He sat up straighter in his chair. "You know, there was something odd. She sent a letter addressed to herself from Romania. At the time, I thought it was a souvenir or something."

"You didn't open it?"

"Of course not. It wasn't addressed to me."

I tried not to get my hopes up. "Do you still have it?"

My dad stared at Claire's photo on the buffet. He swallowed past the catch in his throat. "I put it with the condolence cards. They're in Claire's room. I couldn't open any of them."

I walked around the table and gave him a quick hug. "Do you mind if I look for it?"

"No. That's fine."

I looked at Craig and tilted my head toward the stairs leading to Claire's bedroom. "Do you want to come with me?"

He was watching my dad. "You go ahead. I'll stay and talk to your dad."

Dad's head jerked up in surprise, but he looked grateful to have something other than memories to focus on, even if it was a man he suspected of being street thug.

I forced myself to take the stairs one at a time instead of running up them. By the time I got to her bedroom, my heart was beating double-time in anticipation of another clue about my sister's death.

Claire's room looked exactly how it had the day she left it, from the pale-yellow bedspread to the photo collage on glittery paper she'd taped to her vanity mirror. The stack of cards wasn't hard to find laying on top of her dresser. I shuffled through them until I came to one addressed to my grandmother. I sat on Claire's bed, ignoring the dusty air I stirred up.

It was a standard business envelope, nothing fancy. Inside, I found a receipt for a safe deposit box with a Bucharest address and a key. No note. No explanation. I checked the outside of the envelope. It was postmarked the day before my grandmother died. I closed my eyes and took a few deep breaths, palming the key.

The air grew stifling as I considered the implications. Grandma Dottie had found something in Romania, and whatever it was had likely gotten her killed.

CHAPTER 8

After the turbulence and dysfunction of an evening with my family, Craig's presence was a refuge. Standing on the threshold between our hotel rooms, I leaned into his solid strength. He didn't hesitate, pulling me into his body and wrapping his arms around me. We stood like that for a long time until the last rays of daylight dimmed outside the window and my heartbeat was an echo of his. Craig didn't ask me a single question, and he didn't offer vague words of comfort. He just sheltered me in his arms as long as I needed. I felt something break wide open inside my chest, making room for him.

I raised to my toes so I could brush a tentative kiss against his lips, needing something good to balance out the bad. It was all the invitation he needed, his lips crashing into mine. Craig took control, allowing me to shut down the thoughts warring inside my head and just feel. He tangled one hand in my hair and dropped the other to the small of my back to press my body against his. I wanted him with a ferocity that should have scared me, but I was too far gone to turn back now.

I leaned back so I could tug his shirt from his waistband, unbuttoning it with trembling fingers. With a fluid motion, he pulled it over his head and tossed it to the floor. My mouth went dry at the sight of him, all hard muscle and satin skin. He removed my shirt and bra next before stepping back, those stormy gray eyes slowly roving over my body. I reached for the button of his jeans, but he stilled my hand.

"Not this time." His voice was rough. Before I could react, Craig picked me up and carried me to the bed. "This time, it's about me taking care of you."

He laid me on the bed like an offering, lifting my hands above my head and pressing them against the mattress. Looking at me from beneath hooded eyes, he trailed kisses from the inside of my wrist to my navel and back up again. When I reached for him, he tsked and pushed my arms firmly against the mattress again, waiting until I complied. He smiled when my breath quickened. Then, he lifted my hips and tugged my body to the edge of the bed. Craig watched me as he ran his hands up my thighs, dragging my skirt to my waist before removing my thong. His fingers brushed dangerously close to where I needed them.

He braced my legs over his broad shoulders and nipped the inside of my thigh. Craig tasted and teased me until I clutched the comforter, and my back bowed from the bed. He chased my orgasms as relentlessly as he did everything else, not stopping until I was shaking and hoarse from crying his name.

When he was finished, I couldn't have moved if I tried. I was grateful when he stripped off my skirt before tucking us both under the covers. He pulled my back to his chest and curled his body around mine. We laid like that for a long time until our breathing shallowed and our bodies heated again where they touched. I rolled over to face him. Although I was naked, he still wore his jeans. I ran my fingers along the waistband, but he stopped me before I could dip inside.

"We should talk." Craig climbed out of bed to grab his shirt from the floor and toss it to me.

I looked at him quizzically.

"If you're naked, talking is the last damn thing I want to do," he grumbled, then groaned when I stretched and reached for his shirt.

I took my time getting up, hoping to coax him back to bed. Whether he wanted to rehash what happened at dinner or talk about what I found in Claire's room, I wasn't ready to deal with any of it. Besides, we'd spent the better part of a year talking. We needed a lot of naked time to balance the scales.

The bed dipped under Craig as he sat on the edge next to me. He leaned in and brushed a strand of hair off my cheek. "There are things I need you to understand before we take things any further."

When it became apparent he was serious about the need to talk, I sat up and pulled his shirt over my head. "Okay." I tried and failed to keep my nervousness out of my voice as I ran through the litany of things he might need to tell me before we had sex.

What if he has a secret girlfriend—or worse a wife? No way. Not Craig. *What if gargoyles and humans are incompatible in the bedroom?* I eyed his tight-fitting jeans. Nope. All the right parts there. *What if all gargoyles take a stupid vow of celibacy? Oh my God, what if he's a virgin?* I dismissed the last as soon as I thought it. No virgin knew how to work a woman's body like that.

Craig stood. "I'll grab a glass of water and meet you in my room."

There was something about a barefoot man in a pair of broken-in blue jeans that fired all the right cylinders. I took a moment to admire the view.

What if he's about to tell me he has herpes?

Looking at his ass in those blue jeans, I wasn't sure even herpes would be a dealbreaker. I'd rather not risk it. *Please, don't let it be herpes.*

Before I could consider any more traumatic reasons for this conversation, I got out of bed and followed him into his hotel room.

Craig sat on the couch, looking much less confident than I'd ever seen him. I took a sip from the water glass and sat beside him. Seeing his solemn expression, I felt a flutter of nerves in my belly. I hoped whatever he was about to say wouldn't change things between us. He lifted my legs and spun me sideways, so he could rest them across his lap.

He took a minute to settle before he started talking. "I need you to understand some things about what it means to be a gargoyle and how that affects the relationships I have."

"Okay." I waited for him to continue, his words doing nothing to settle my nerves.

Craig traced the hem of the shirt I wore. Whether it was to soothe me or himself, I didn't know. "Has Meira told you much about gargoyles?"

I shook my head. "Nothing." Meira was my go-to for knowledge about supernaturals, but she'd been tight-lipped about Craig.

"As you've probably gathered, gargoyles are the protectors of the supernatural world."

I nodded, an encouragement to go on.

"We're territorial creatures. Except for family, it's highly unusual for two gargoyles to live in the same vicinity."

"That must make it hard to make baby gargoyles," I joked in an attempt to lighten his mood. Judging by his sharp look, the joke failed spectacularly.

"All gargoyles are male," he corrected.

I wondered if that meant gargoyles were made somehow rather than born.

Seeing my confusion, he explained. "We can have children but only once we've found our mates."

I choked on the drink of water I'd taken. *Wait. Was he actually a virgin?* "You can only have sex with your mate?"

Craig chuckled. "No. We can have sex just like humans, but we can't have children with anyone other than our mates.

I perked up a little at that. Unless he was about to tell me he had an STD, this could be a condom-free card.

Because we were talking about how babies were made, I was guessing he didn't mean mates in the British way. "By mate, I'm assuming you mean spouse?"

"Similar, but humans discard spouses like out-of-style clothing."

I appreciated the fact he used an analogy from my wheelhouse. Before I could tell him, he turned his head, meeting my eyes with an intensity I wasn't prepared for. "And gargoyles?" I asked instead.

"Gargoyles mate for life."

I couldn't tell how he wanted me to take that. Was he telling me if we ever got married, he wasn't the divorcing kind? Or was he saying once he found his mate, he'd forget I existed?

"Do gargoyles choose their mates?" I asked. "Or do you find the person fate meant for you?" I'd read my share of romance novels, but I'd always chalked that quirk up to wishful thinking. How wonderful to have some hottie destined for you—so blinded by fate, they'd adore even your morning breath and sing praises about your stinky gym socks.

Craig glanced at me. "A little of both, I guess. There are people who you feel an instant connection to, but they're rare. Once you find someone like that, you either chose to strengthen the bond or walk away." He stroked my bare thigh where the shirt had parted, meeting my eyes. "Gargoyles are not very good at walking away."

My breath hitched as much at his words as at the strong fingers brushing the sensitive skin of my inner thigh. "And when a gargoyle chooses a mate, it's for life?"

"It is."

I closed my eyes and let my head fall back against the couch, allowing the path his fingers were making distract me as they inched higher with excruciatingly slow movements. I forced a lightness in my voice. "It's good to know you're not the love 'em and leave 'em type." *Because I would definitely be needing a repeat.*

"I don't think you understand what I'm saying, Kali." Craig's hand paused. "You're it for me."

I jerked my head up and studied him. There wasn't a hint of teasing in his solemn face. He meant it, and he was waiting to see how I'd take it. I should run for the hills. This was a man I'd only officially been on a first date with. Then again, our world was largely incompatible with dating. Or doing anything in half measures. Whatever this was turning into, I wanted to be all in, but a lifetime commitment was more than I could wrap my head around.

"How long does a gargoyle live, anyway?" It was something I'd wondered but never gotten around to asking. With as many murder attempts as I'd been navigating recently, it didn't seem to matter much since old age was about as likely for me as winning the lottery.

"It depends. An unmated gargoyle can live hundreds of years."

"That's a long life," I said. "Are you about to tell me you're two hundred years old?"

"Close," he teased. "Thirty-two." Craig moved his hand to the opposite leg, repeating the featherlight attention he'd been giving my other leg.

"You said unmated gargoyles can live hundreds of years. What about mated gargoyles?" I wasn't sure why there would be a discrepancy based on relationship status.

"Mated gargoyles live as long as their mates."

I stilled his hand. "What do you mean?"

He stared at me unflinchingly. "As I said, gargoyles are natural-born protectors. There is no one a gargoyle protects more fiercely than his mate."

My stomach did a little flip. "So, the mate lives a long life because of that protection? Is that what you're saying?"

"No. I'm saying a gargoyle can't survive the loss of his mate."

I stared at him, the air suddenly grown stifling. "But I'm a human." Technically, I was a necromancer, but I was still clinging to human status. Not that it mattered. The life spans were the same regardless of what I called myself.

"You are."

"Why would anyone trade hundreds of years for the lifespan of a human?" I didn't add that my lifespan would undoubtably be much shorter than the average human given my growing fan club and propensity for trouble.

"Because a mate is worth the trade-off," Craig said simply.

I sat up, moving his hands to the couch beside him. "You're saying that I..." I trailed off, unable to finish the thought.

"I'm saying I choose you as my mate." There was no hesitation in his answer.

I stood up, feeling like I might hyperventilate. Craig stood up next to me and reached for my hands. "Breathe," he coaxed.

"But what if this doesn't work out?" *What happens if—when —I screw this up?* "You'd find another mate, right?"

He kept a neutral look on his face, but the tension in his shoulders was hard to miss. "No."

"But you'd die." I choked trying to get the words out. "Because of me." I closed my eyes. *I don't know how to do this.*

"No one is dying." His voice was calm. "The mate bond is only formed after both people choose each other."

I sucked air into my lungs, feeling part of the weight lift. "Okay. That's good." Once I calmed my erratic breathing, I asked him how exactly mate bonds worked.

Craig explained mate bonds were a lot like the human notion of soul mates, except these were literal soul bonds. If we chose each other, I would hold a piece of Craig's soul within my own, and vice versa. As a necromancer, I supposed it was possible I could sever those bonds, but that was completely unchartered territory. Looking at the determined set of Craig's jaw, I knew it wouldn't matter even if I could break it. He wasn't the kind of man who chose lightly or changed his mind once he did.

"Hey, look at me." He pulled his attention back to him. "I'm telling you because I need you to know this will never be casual for me. But I'm not asking for a commitment today," Craig reassured me. "I'm a patient man. I'll wait."

I let him pull my legs back onto his lap. But despite the reassuring smile I gave him, I was drowning in the fears that plagued me.

The time difference between Chicago and Bucharest meant my window for contacting a business there closed at nine a.m. I dialed the number on the receipt for my grandmother's safe deposit box on our way to the airport the next morning. Despite being transferred to three different people, every employee I talked to was adamant the only way I could obtain the contents of the safe deposit box would be to show up in person with an official copy of Grandma Dottie's will and the proper documentation to show my identity as her heir.

That presented two problems. One—a flight to Bucharest was obscenely expensive. And more importantly, two—my grandmother did not have a will. Without the will, my mother was next of kin, so even if I could get my hands on the probate documents, I still couldn't waltz in there and claim the contents.

The cab dropped us off at the airport, and Craig grabbed our carry-on bags. Once we were seated in the airport, I explained the problem.

Craig looked thoughtful. "What about your mom? Could she get it for you?"

I snorted. "No way. Even if I did have her phone number—which I don't—she would wash her hands of this."

While I appreciated the sympathetic look he gave me, I'd had years to accept the rift.

Our wait was surprisingly short, and soon enough we boarded the plane. Thankfully, Craig and I had seats together for the return flight. Since we'd been sidetracked last night, we spent the flight comparing the evidence from the two witch murders.

I opened my phone and located the photo of Fiona's sigil. "Can you pull up the photo from Anne?"

Craig scrolled to the photo, and we studied the two. I couldn't shake the feeling I'd seen both before. While it was possible they'd surfaced during my research into Zepar's sigil, I didn't think that was where I'd seen them. I closed my eyes and ran through the evidence again, looking for patterns.

As I started to drift off to sleep, something tugged at my memory, and I sat bolt upright. I pulled my purse from beneath the seat where I'd stashed it for the flight and pulled out the page we'd found in Fiona's fist. I flattened it on my lap and stared at the handwriting. "I know who this belonged to."

Craig looked surprised. "You recognize it?"

I leaned into Craig, keeping my voice low. "This is Samara's handwriting." Samara had been the teenage witch who had originally tried to raise Zepar in the 1950s. When the witches' council discovered she had summoned a demon, they sealed her in a cave, effectively ensuring her death.

"You're sure?" he asked.

I nodded. "Positive. I still have the diary I took from her room, and this writing matches it." Craig didn't ask me about how I'd acquired her diary, and I didn't volunteer the information. "I think this is a page from her grimoire."

Craig examined the page. "Do you think this is the same ritual Naomi used?"

"I don't know. It could be. I didn't get a good look at Samara's grimoire." I ran my fingers over the words and illustrations. At first, I thought the spell was in Latin, but Craig took one look and shot down that theory. Whatever language this was, neither of us could decipher it. Although there were symbols and drawings, there were no recognizable sigils. Since I'd accidentally raised Zepar without the benefit of an instruction manual, I didn't know whether sigils were typically recorded in the ritual or simply added to the circle. "How do you think this page ended up in Fiona's hand after the witches' council confiscated the grimoire from Naomi?" I asked.

Craig ran a hand across the back of his neck. "If it is from Samara's grimoire, then someone from the council either lost it or used it."

The thought of someone in such a powerful position targeting fire elementals made my stomach pitch. I hoped there was another explanation—one that involved a weaker witch prone to making the kind of mistake that would get him caught.

Craig and I went straight to my apartment from the airport to test my theory. When I pulled out Samara's diary to compare it to the page we found on Fiona, there was no question that the handwriting matched.

Craig sent Celeste a video call, and I grabbed us each a cup of coffee while we waited for her to answer. It took two tries, but Celeste finally picked up. We'd taken a six a.m. flight out of Chicago, so it was still early morning.

This was the first time I'd seen Celeste look less than polished. She was fresh-faced without a hint of makeup, which made her appear much younger than her thirty-odd years. She didn't beat around the bush. "I don't have a list of fire elementals for you. The witches' council refused to authorize the release of that information. They deemed it too dangerous."

Craig's mouth tightened in frustration, but he didn't push. "That's unfortunate, but it's not why I'm calling."

Celeste appeared relieved he wasn't going to argue the issue. "What can I do for you, Ward?"

Craig held up the page we'd found. "Does this look familiar?"

Celeste reeled back, her shock at the sight of the page genuine. "Where did you get that?"

"Answer the question, Celeste." Craig's tone was clipped.

"Yes. I recognize it. It looks like a page from Samara's grimoire. How are you in possession of it?" There was a note of accusation in her voice, and from the look on Craig's face, he did not appreciate the attitude.

"We found it clutched in the fist of the Chicago fire elemental who was murdered," he said.

Celeste swore under her breath.

"Exactly. Are you still in possession of the grimoire?" Craig asked.

Neither Craig nor I voiced our suspicions that someone on the witches' council could be one of the perpetrators. Right now, it was purely supposition, and accusations like that required more solid evidence before they were made.

Celeste stared at us for a minute before answering. "We are. It's held under lock and key and under wards I set myself. In fact, every witch on the council set wards to ensure none of us could access it alone. There's no way anyone has gotten to that book since it's been in our possession."

"Can you check to make sure?" I asked. Celeste might be confident the book was there and intact, but I wasn't as sure.

"Of course." Celeste motioned someone over and directed them to get the car ready.

Must be nice to have a personal driver. Meira hadn't been kidding when she'd said Celeste was a wealthy woman.

"Do you know if there were any pages missing out of the grimoire when the witches' council confiscated it?" I asked her.

"Maybe." Celeste frowned. "I didn't look at it closely. Samara's grimoire reeked of black magic. None of us wanted to spend any more time with it than absolutely necessary. But I'll ask the others and let you know if I find anything."

I held the paper back up where Celeste could see it. "Can you tell us if this is a demon summoning ritual like the one Naomi used?"

Celeste moved closer to the screen, and I obliged by holding the paper directly in front of the camera. "That's not a summoning ritual," Celeste said.

I moved the paper, my shoulders slumping with relief. "Oh good." The last thing I wanted was to chase another demon around Kansas City.

"I'm afraid it's far from good news." Celeste scribbled notes on a pad in front of her, then handed it to her assistant.

"What do you mean?" Whatever this was, it had to be better than a demon summoning ritual.

"It is a locater spell," Celeste said.

Craig glanced at the paper and back at Celeste. "Okay, so it helps a witch locate items. How is that bad?" Celeste looked like she was battling how much to tell us. Craig leaned close to the camera. "You had better put all the cards on the table, Celeste. Why is that a bad thing?"

"It's not just any locator spell." She sat up straighter and cleared her throat. "What you're holding is prohibited. It's black magic. The spell is not used to locate objects. It traces bloodlines."

"As in people? Like a magical family tree?" I asked.

Celeste sighed. "Basically, yes. With that spell, a witch could theoretically track down every descendant of a bloodline. You can understand how dangerous it could be in the wrong hands. Someone could wipe an entire bloodline from the face of the earth using that spell."

Craig swore. "All they'd need is this spell?"

"No," Celeste said. "They would also need a blood sample from a descendant."

"Which would be pretty easy to get from a crime scene where the attackers sliced open the veins of their victims," I finished. We'd been operating under the assumption the witch killers bled the victims for the ritual, but what if there was another reason?

Celeste paled.

"Let me guess," Craig said. "Fire elementals share the same bloodline."

Celeste grimaced. "Yes. They're pretty spread out now, but based on how concentrated magic is passed through generations, all the fire elementals could be traced back to a single ancestor if you went back far enough."

"Why is someone so desperate to change a fire elemental into a vampire?" I considered what we knew. "Maybe this isn't someone trying to change just one. Maybe someone wants to systematically hunt down and change all fire elementals."

Craig stared at Celeste. "Have there been any other fire elementals who have been attacked?"

Celeste paled. "One other went missing about a month ago. She was seventeen, and she was assumed to be a runaway."

"Why change fire elementals?" Craig ran his hand across his jaw, thinking. "Shit. There are three ways to kill a vampire, but only one of them is suited for warfare."

"Fire," Celeste said.

"Fire elementals would make the perfect lab rats. Turn them, and the vampires have a weapon they can use against the other witches. And if they die in the process, at least they eliminated the most dangerous weapon against them."

Craig paced the room, his shoulders bunching with anger. He paused to glare at Celeste through the camera. "If you won't give me the list of fire elementals, then it's on you to place every one of them in protective custody."

"I know." Celeste looked to someone off screen. "We'll be in contact about the remaining elementals within your territory to get them placed. No two should be in the same location for obvious reasons. And Ward, I'm sorry. We can't risk any one person outside of the witches' council knowing all their names, but we can quietly place them all within their own territories."

Craig grabbed the paper with the ritual on it and waved it in front of the screen. His gray eyes hardened. "It appears someone is making their own list."

"Why leave the ritual behind?" I broke in.

Both Craig and Celeste looked at me.

"Think about it. Fiona doesn't remember grabbing it, but her memory was intact from the moment she woke up. The only other explanation is that the witch killers put it there intentionally for us to find," I theorized. "The question is why?"

"I don't know," Craig admitted. "But it's not unusual for criminals like serial killers—for example—to leave taunting notes for the police. Maybe whoever did this is toying with us."

I studied the ritual. "If that's the case, then this must have been left for someone who would recognize the spell."

Craig stared at me. "Or the handwriting."

I'd had the same thought myself. There were only two people outside the witches' council who would recognize Samara's handwriting—Naomi and me. "How many people would know what this is?" I asked Celeste.

She considered the question. "Very few. Outside the witches' council, a handful, maybe."

So far, a lot of the leads seemed to be circling back to the witches' council. Before going down the path that was sure to land me in hot water if I was wrong, I had to check the other potentials off the list. "Would Naomi know what the spell does?" I asked.

Celeste looked thoughtful. "I imagine so since she was in possession of the grimoire, and it did belong to her aunt."

"And if they left it as a calling card for someone to recognize the handwriting, that also leads right back to Naomi," I added.

Craig glanced at me with a frown before he addressed Celeste. "We need to talk to Naomi."

Talking to the witch who tried to force a demon into my body wasn't high on my list of fun things to do, but I recognized the necessity.

Celeste shook her head. "That's impossible."

"Did you kill her?" I asked, feeling ambivalent about the answer.

"No."

"If she's alive, then questioning her is possible," Craig countered. "Where is she?"

Celeste leaned closer to her screen and dropped her voice to a whisper as if she didn't want anyone there to overhear her answer. "Naomi was sent to the Compound, so unless you know people a lot higher on the food chain than I do, there is no way you're getting anywhere near her."

Until she said that, it had never occurred to me that there was a higher up the food chain.

"I'll be in touch." Craig hung up the call without a goodbye, staring at the blank screen for several seconds.

"I'm assuming the Compound is some kind of supernatural prison?" I ventured.

"Something like that."

I stepped to the side, so I could see his face. "And they don't allow visitors I take it?"

"Normally, no."

"So that's it? We're out of luck?" It was getting increasingly difficult not to take these cases personally, particularly now that Naomi was implicated.

"Fortunately, I know someone higher up the food chain." Craig pocketed his phone and reached for his keys. "Let's go."

CHAPTER 10

The last time I'd bargained with the local alpha, I'd agreed to an undisclosed future favor that was still hanging over my head. I didn't like owing Max Volkov. Technically, I wasn't asking for a favor this time since the Tribunal had come to me for help, so I hoped we could call it a wash.

Craig tried to call Volkov on our way over, but there was no answer. Craig assured me Volkov wouldn't mind a spontaneous drop-in visit, given the circumstances. Based on my previous receptions, I wasn't convinced.

Craig rang the doorbell twice before we heard footsteps. When Volkov swung the door open, he was shirtless and barefoot. The pair of gray sweatpants slung low on his hips was the only thing between him and a peep show I wasn't prepared to see. His eyes flared in surprise. "You're back." He made no move to step aside and invite us in.

"Yeah." Craig pointed inside the house. "Can we come in?"

Volkov glanced behind him, his hand still clutching the front door, as if weighing his options.

"Where is the hot sauce?" a woman's voice called from the kitchen.

Volkov went even more rigid, something I hadn't thought possible. But then he wasn't the only one uncomfortable with this early morning visit. Before he could decide whether to invite us in or slam the door in our faces, I ducked under his arm and headed straight for the kitchen. It wasn't difficult to find. I followed the smell of bacon.

Volkov's kitchen was as upscale as the rest of his house, with polished concrete countertops, an expensive Viking stove that would make a chef salivate, and a massive refrigerator sized for a restaurant rather than a bachelor pad. At the moment, the door to the refrigerator was wide open, a woman's bare legs and t-shirt-clad back the only thing visible as she rummaged around presumably looking for hot sauce.

"Found it," she called, triumphantly waving the bottle in the air and closing the door. "Oh hey, Kali," Riley said. "You're just in time for breakfast."

I stared at her, at a temporary loss for words. Riley was standing in Max Volkov's kitchen dressed in what looked suspiciously like his t-shirt and a pair of boxer shorts. I didn't even want to think about whose boxer shorts she wore.

Riley handed me the bottle of hot sauce. "Hold this. I'll get you a plate."

Craig was getting Volkov up to speed as they joined us in the kitchen, but Craig stopped abruptly when he spotted Riley. While he had a much better poker face than I did, his eyes darted between the two of them before he looked at me.

"What?" Riley asked.

I finally found my voice. "You and…" I pointed to Volkov.

Riley waved me off. "It's not like that."

"So, the two of you didn't..." I couldn't bring myself to finish that thought.

Riley laughed. "Oh, we totally did, but it's not like we're dating." She winked at Volkov. "It's just a booty call."

Craig coughed into his fist. I glanced from him to Volkov, who was now staring at Riley, his face turning red. "It's a what?" Volkov asked.

Riley stared at Volkov. "Are you blushing?"

"I don't blush," Volkov bit out, right before he turned a darker shade of red.

Craig started laughing, not bothering with the fake cough this time.

Riley turned away from us and reached for the pan of scrambled eggs on the stove, moving it off the heat and fluffing them with a spatula. "You know," she said over her shoulder, "friends with benefits."

"We're not friends," he practically growled.

She shrugged. "Where are your plates?" When he didn't answer, she hopped up on his counter and started opening cabinet doors until she found them. "Ah ha." Riley pulled four plates down, jumped back to the floor, and started dividing the eggs. She piled some bacon and a single piece of toast on each plate before handing them out. Grudgingly, Volkov took the plate from her before telling us to sit wherever.

I moved to end of the island, but Riley stopped me. "Maybe not there." She laughed, tugging her shirt down lower on her legs. She pointed to the breakfast nook with a table and four chairs. I looked at the island and back at her. Riley threw her arm around me and leaned in, dropping her voice. "Turns out, he's not all lights-out missionary after all." She grinned at me and ignored him altogether.

I didn't know whether to laugh or cringe. I settled for

getting through breakfast without looking directly at either of them. I was still wrapping my mind around the idea of the two of them doing anything together other than annoying each other.

If Riley noticed the awkward silence, she didn't let on. "You want some hot sauce for those eggs, or are you going to eat them like that?" Riley waved the bottle in my direction. "Max didn't have any green chilies, or I would have made them right."

"I'm good."

"Suit yourself." Riley attacked the rest of her breakfast with her usual enthusiasm.

Craig waited until we finished eating to discuss the reason for our visit. He filled Volkov in on our Chicago visit, including the page from Samara's grimoire we'd found. "We need to interview Naomi. We need to know who had access to that grimoire and whether that spell was in there when the witches' council confiscated it."

Volkov's look turned calculating. "You suspect someone on the witches' council?"

Craig shrugged. "We need to rule them out."

Volkov took a drink of his coffee. "Did the witches tell you where Naomi was being held?"

Craig glanced away. "The Compound."

Volkov leaned back in his chair, running a hand over his stubbled jaw. "Shit."

"You know I wouldn't ask unless I thought it was our best shot," Craig said.

Riley snagged a half-eaten slice of bacon off my plate. "What's the Compound?"

"It's a high security facility to hold the most dangerous supernaturals," Craig answered.

"Oh, so like a prison," she said.

The two men exchanged a look. "Something like that." It was the second time Craig had answered the question vaguely, and it made me uneasy.

"Can you get us in?" I asked Volkov.

Volkov ignored my question as if I hadn't spoken and addressed Craig. "You're taking her? Do you think that's wise?"

I glared at him, not that he seemed to care.

"Naomi isn't going to talk to me." Craig held up a hand when Volkov looked like he had something to add. "Or you. Kali has a chance, at least, to get her talking."

Volkov grimaced. "I'll call Aleksei."

Craig clapped him on the back on the way to put his empty plate in the dishwasher. "Thank you."

Volkov took out his phone but made no move to call anyone. "When?"

Craig looked at me. "How soon can you go?"

"I have one order that needs to go out by the end of this week, but I'm almost finished. I can wrap it up tomorrow morning."

"I'll charter us a plane," Volkov said.

"You're going?" I tried not to sound disappointed but failed miserably.

"I'm the only way you're getting in." Volkov didn't look thrilled at the prospect of tagging along any more than I was at having him join us.

"Where is this prison, anyway?" Riley asked.

Craig watched me carefully as he answered. "Romania."

I sucked in a harsh breath and turned to Craig. "Why didn't you tell me?"

Craig looked apologetic. "I didn't want to get your hopes up if Max couldn't get us in."

Volkov studied me. "Why are you so interested in Romania?"

"It's personal."

He snorted. "Not if I'm escorting you, it's not."

"Do you have to go?" I tried—and failed—to keep the dread out of my voice. I watched the tic form in Volkov's jaw, unsure whether it was me questioning him or the thought of going that had him wound up tighter than usual. "Can't you just call and set it up?"

"No. Aleksei will never agree unless I accompany you."

"Who is this Aleksei, anyway?" I asked.

Volkov looked at Craig. Both men seemed uncomfortable with the question, but after a prolonged silence, Volkov answered. "My brother."

"Is he the warden or something?" Riley beat me to the question.

"Something like that," he muttered.

Riley tipped her chair back, balancing on two legs. "Can I come?"

Volkov reached over and pushed her chair back to the ground. "Absolutely not."

Riley pouted. "Why not?"

Volkov tilted his head and stared at her. We all knew why not.

"What?" she asked.

"Because you create chaos wherever you go, and we can't afford any distractions if we want to come back from the Compound in one piece," Volkov said.

That didn't sound promising, but I kept my reservations to

myself. Craig stood up, and I followed his lead, anxious to get out of here, so I could prep for the trip.

I leaned over Riley's head before we left. "Come by my place later." I looked at Volkov who was preoccupied. "I've got so many questions."

Volkov dismissed us. "I'll call you when it's set up." He didn't walk us out, too busy scowling at his phone.

Riley showed up at my apartment a couple hours later fully dressed. This time, thankfully, she was in her own clothes. She let herself in, and I glanced up from my laptop when she dropped onto the couch next to me. "Find anything?" she asked.

"Not really. Searching 'Compound' and 'Romania' pulls up a lot of sketchy real estate sites." I glanced at her. "What do you know about this Compound?"

She leaned her head back against the cushion and stared my ceiling. "Not a thing."

I followed her gaze, spotting the tiny black spider inching across my ceiling. Riley took her shoe off and climbed on the back of the couch to swat at it. She grabbed a tissue to wipe the spider remains off her shoe and handed it to me.

"Ew." I tossed the tissue in the trash and sat back down beside her. "Volkov didn't tell you?"

"Why would he tell me?"

"I don't know—naked confessions?" I grabbed the closest throw pillow and hit her in the chest with it. "What were you thinking anyway? Sleeping with Max Volkov?"

Riley grabbed the pillow out of my hands and tucked it behind her head, smirking. "Oh, we weren't sleeping."

Despite the very real fear that Riley had gotten in way over her head, I couldn't help the laugh. "How long has this been going on?"

She rolled her head toward me. "Since about eight o'clock last night."

I laughed. "And?"

"And nothing. It doesn't have to be a big deal."

"There isn't a chance in hell that man is capable of doing low-key casual."

Riley shrugged. "We'll see." She sat up and grabbed the map I'd printed a few minutes ago. "Why did you print a map of Bucharest?"

I shuffled the papers on the coffee table until I located the envelope addressed to my grandmother. I shook the key loose and held it up for her inspection. "Because this is a key to a safe deposit box located there." I pointed to the X I'd marked on the map she was holding.

Riley perked up. "Safe deposit box?"

I filled her in on my grandmother's strange self-addressed delivery and gave her the quick and dirty version of my family reunion.

She turned the key over in her hand. "What do you think is in it?"

"No idea, other than I'm pretty sure it's somehow connected to Claire." I took the key back and tucked it inside the envelope. "I called the place, but they wouldn't tell me what was in it, and they wouldn't ship it to me."

"You're going to go check it out when you're in Romania, right?" Riley guessed.

"I'd love to." I sighed. "But according to the company, they will only release the contents to me if I have my grandmother's death certificate and her will showing I am entitled to it. Unless you know someone capable of forging documents in the next twenty-four hours, I may never know." I ground my teeth in frustration. Being in the same city my grandmother died in but being unable to retrieve the one thing that might have given me answers was worse than not knowing anything at all.

Riley was sitting up, staring intently at the map. "I could get it."

I perked up. "You know someone who can forge a will?"

She waved a hand dismissively. "No. I mean I can get the contents of the box for you."

"No. It's too risky." I tried to snatch the map back, but she jerked it away. "The last thing I want is for you to get arrested and wind up in a Romanian prison."

"I won't get caught." She said it with absolute certainty, her blue eyes intense. "I never get caught. And I've stolen things behind security that makes this place seem like a kiddie sandbox."

"Such as?" I asked. Riley had been dancing around this conversation for months, offering hints about her life before she came to Kansas City without divulging the whole story. From what I'd gathered, the alpha who had taken her in as a kid had made her steal for him. What I didn't know was the scale and complexity of those thefts.

She gave me an assessing look. "If I tell you, do you promise to consider letting me get this for you?"

I knew I should say no, but as I clutched the key to the safe deposit box, I found myself nodding instead. "I'll keep an open mind."

Riley tucked her feet underneath her, angling her body toward mine on the couch. "Get comfortable then because I'm about to impress you with my life as a criminal prodigy."

I laughed. "Those two words don't normally go together. You know that, right?"

Her mouth quirked, but the traces of humor disappeared

as she told me about the years she'd stolen for her old alpha, Carl. What started out as simple pickpocketing and robberies escalated as she got older and more skilled. She added safe cracking and security evasion to her repertoire. As a goat shifter, Riley was hard to contain, which meant getting in and out of tight security was something she excelled at. Paired with her ability resist both alpha commands and vampire compulsions, and she was a natural. Riley spent four years under Carl's thumb, stealing everything from cheap electronics to magical artifacts that brought top dollar on the black market. She'd made Carl a rich man before she'd escaped at sixteen. By the time she left, she had become a world class thief with an entrenched distrust of authority figures.

I listened to her story with equal parts abhorrence and interest. As I looked at the rigid set of her shoulders and her guarded expression, I swallowed down the sympathetic words on the tip of my tongue. Riley wasn't looking for absolution. She wanted me to accept her—even the part of her that basked in the thrill of a good heist. And I couldn't find it in me to judge her, criminal tendencies or not. But that didn't mean I wanted to be the one to send her to jail.

I ran my index finger along the flap of my grandmother's letter, an action I'd repeated often enough that the envelope bore signs of wear. "Look, I really appreciate the offer, but the risk is too big."

She dropped her gaze to her lap. "You don't think I can do it."

I grabbed her hand until she looked up at me. "Listen. I know you could do it."

"Then why are you saying no?" When I didn't immediately

answer, Riley turned away. "You know you'd do it for me in a heartbeat. Friendships, they go two ways, Kali."

I sighed. "How would you do it?"

Riley walked me through her plan, and while it wasn't without risk, her confidence was contagious.

"We'd have to convince Volkov to let you come along," I said. "And he seemed adamant about you not going with us. I guess we could buy a ticket on a commercial flight."

"International flights are expensive," Riley countered. "Maybe you could check me as an emotional support goat."

I laughed. "I don't think that would work. Volkov is chartering a plane." I dropped my voice in a poor imitation of Volkov. "I don't do commercial airlines."

Riley made a face. "Of course, he doesn't." The glimmer in her eyes said her next idea was likely going to land us in trouble. "You know, I could sneak onboard. With a chartered plane, it wouldn't be hard."

"Wouldn't Volkov be able to smell you?" I asked. Shifters could detect smells at impressive distances, as I'd found out the hard way.

Riley leaned forward, her eyes glinting with mischief. "Not if we're smart about it."

"What do you have in mind?" I had flashbacks to the time I'd doused myself in scent blocker in an attempt to go undetected as I snuck around Volkov's backyard. It hadn't worked well with two hundred feet between us, so I doubted it would be effective in the tight confines of a plane. Even if the product did work as advertised, smelling a deer on a plane would be a surefire way to set off alarm bells. I told Riley as much.

"That's why we don't try to hide my scent from him." She lifted her shirt to her nose and sniffed before offering it to me.

Reluctantly, I sniffed her shirt. All I could smell was faint traces of fabric softener, but then I wasn't a shifter. I waited for her to explain.

"All you need to do is wear borrowed clothes—something Volkov will recognize as mine."

I grinned, catching on. "Your leather jacket."

"Exactly. Give him a reason why my scent is there and," she said, tapping my nose, "then overwhelm him with something else."

"Such as?"

Riley shrugged. "Just wear a bunch of perfume and carry something smelly."

"It could work." Even if it didn't, what was the worst that could happen? He'd boot Riley from the plane, and I'd be no worse off than if we didn't try.

CHAPTER 11

There was a stranger waiting for me outside my shop when I got there that afternoon. He appeared to be a few years older than me, with messy blond hair that looked like he frequently ran his fingers through it and a nervous energy that came from being self-conscious.

"Hi there," he said, thrusting out his hand. "I'm Parker, your new neighbor." He pointed to the storefront next door to mine.

"Oh hey!" I relaxed at his nerdy, nonthreatening appearance. "I'm Kali. Welcome to West Bottoms." I shoved my keys in my pocket, so I could shake his hand. I glanced at the store next to mine, but there wasn't a business sign up yet. "What kind of store are you opening?" From the faded Ramones t-shirt and skinny jeans he was wearing, I was guessing he either sold tabletop games or guitars.

Parker grinned. "Come on over, and I'll show you."

I glanced at my watch. Because our charter flight to Romania didn't leave until morning, I'd arranged to meet Meira in fifteen minutes to follow up on a lead. After Craig planted the seed that a necromancer could perform the demon summoning ritual as well as a witch could, I couldn't get the detail out of my head. I needed to talk to Meira to find out how many necromancers might be capable of such a thing.

I turned to Parker ready to beg for a raincheck, but one glance at the hopeful expression on his face, and the words died in my throat. The conversation with Meira could wait a little longer. I'd call and let her know I was running late.

"I need to grab something from inside and make a quick call. Then, I'll be right over."

Parker's smile brightened. "The door will be open."

After getting off the phone with Meira, I retrieved my throwing knives from under the counter where I kept them. With everything that was going on, having the knives gave me an admittedly false sense of security. I arranged the knives in their custom holster. The holster was my second attempt and had turned out much better than my first. My original design was functional but had to be worn on my thigh. As I quickly discovered, walking around KC with throwing knives strapped to my body not only garnered a lot of unwanted attention, it was also wildly uncomfortable.

I modeled my latest creation after a fabric rollup carrier for crayons I saw on Pinterest. The whole thing was made of a gorgeous camel-colored leather stiff enough to protect the knives but pliable enough to roll up easily to fit in the inside pocket of my purse. Each knife had its own compartment and when rolled up, the whole thing was secured with a thin strip of leather used for a tie. I'd even hand-stamped a floral pattern on the strip to jazz it up a bit. The end product came out so beautiful I used it for a prototype, making several more that sold out almost immediately online. Turns out, not everyone wants a boring black leather sheath for their knife collection.

I locked my shop and walked next door. Walls of stacked boxes greeted me. "Hello?" I called.

Parker popped out of the back. Between his slightly rumpled appearance and the nervous way he shifted his weight from foot to foot, I was guessing Parker was a bit on the shy side. I smiled to put him at ease.

He looked at the bag in my hands. "Do you want to set that down?"

Because I'd rather not have to explain why I toted around a full container of salt and a set of throwing knives, I held on to the bag. "No thanks. I only have a few minutes before I need to meet someone."

"Oh, okay." He looked at his shoes, clearly disappointed.

He reminded me of one of my childhood friend's awkward brother, and I immediately felt a tinge of protectiveness. A lot of people overlooked guys like Parker, brushing them off. I didn't want him to think that's what I was doing. "I'd love to come back when you're all set up though."

"Yeah?" He looked up again.

"Absolutely." I looked around at the half-assembled shelving and a multitude of boxes. He had his work cut out for him. "How do you like the building?" It wasn't the newest building, but the space next door had been perfect for me. I hoped it worked as well for Parker.

"Good so far," he said. "Other than a couple oddities."

"Oh?" That piqued my interest. "What kind of oddities?"

"Mostly the smell." He made a face. "It's like this musty decaying smell. I've searched everywhere, thinking there must be a dead mouse or something, but I didn't find anything. Do you smell it?"

Now that he mentioned it, I definitely could. "It's a dead animal smell alright, but not the kind you think. The last tenant ran a taxidermy shop in here. He left most of the animals behind when he took off in the middle of the night—probably skipping out on back rent, if I had to guess. Anyway, some of the animals were not fully preserved yet." I grimaced.

Parker took it in stride though. "Well, that certainly explains it. I suppose I better stock up on air freshener. Other than that and the weird glow-in-the-dark circle painted on the floor, the space is great."

I tried not to look guilty at his mention of the summoning circle. Riley had made it with a can of glow-in-dark hairspray she'd assured me would wipe right off. *Guess not.* Wanting to steer the conversation away from demon summoning circles, I looked around until I spied a few open boxes next to him.

Parker waited until I reached him to pull a couple items out of one of the boxes. "I know it's a little weird, but I'm opening a vintage music and movie store." He held out a VHS tape of Gremlins still in the shrink wrap.

"No way!" I took the movie and scanned the back before peering into the open boxes to inventory his selection. "This is incredible." I meant it. I was an old movie junkie and–until now—probably the only VHS owner in a hundred-mile radius.

"Really?" Parker chuckled. "You're the first person who hasn't told me I'm crazy to think there is a market outside eBay for this stuff." He gestured around the room.

I tucked the movie back in the box. "I can guarantee you'll have at least one rabid customer."

He beamed at me. "I should be all set up in a few days. Come back then, and I'll give you the friends and family discount."

"You don't have to do that." I knew firsthand how difficult it was to get a business off the ground.

"I want to."

"All right. I'll be back to stock up, and I'll spread the word. You'll have a line out the door before you know it."

"That would be amazing." Parker took a deep breath as if gathering his courage. "Maybe we could have a movie night sometime." He didn't look me in the eye as he waited for my response, the fear of rejection easy to read.

Normally, I could tell whether a guy was interested or being friendly, but with Parker's shyness, I wasn't sure. I chose the safe hang-out-in-a-group route to make it clear this wouldn't be a date. "I have a standing movie night with my friends Riley and Emma. You should totally join us."

"I'd love that." There wasn't a hint of disappointment on Parker's face.

I was relieved we were both headed for the friend zone. Who knew? Maybe he and Emma would hit it off. They'd be adorable together. After a few more minutes of chit chat and a standing invitation to our weekly movie night, I left for Meira's.

My mood darkened the closer I got to Meira's shop, with thoughts of the dead witches weighing on me. Meira was helping a customer when I came in, so I wandered around her store until she finished.

The first time I'd walked into Old World Occult & Curiosities, everything in here had felt foreign and ominous. Now, I took it for what it was—a store that catered to the hobbyists and the curious. The only things actual witches purchased from Meira were herbs and other spell ingredients. Most of the store consisted of crystals, candles, and oddities designed to appeal to those with an interest in the occult rather than daily practitioners.

After her customer left, Meira flipped her closed sign, and we moved to the back. As a Tribunal member, Meira was already aware of the purpose of our recent trip to Chicago, so I could skip right to the relevant part. I gave her a quick recap, ending with Craig's theory that necromancers were as capable as witches of performing summoning rituals and far more likely to be willing to work with a vampire. Meira stilled.

"Do you think it was a necromancer?" I asked.

Meira took off her reading glasses, letting them dangle from the chain around her neck, as she considered it. "Some necromancers would be capable of it, but I find it unlikely."

Typically, Meira didn't dismiss alternate possibilities so easily. Perhaps she didn't want to think people she knew might be capable of such a thing. I didn't blame her. Remembering how Anne and Fiona had been found, I didn't want to believe someone like me could do it, either. "Why is it unlikely?"

She frowned. "Statistical probability, for one. There are far more witches than necromancers, and when you narrow it down to those with enough power to perform a ritual like that, the discrepancy grows wider."

"I get that, but it's not enough to rule out the possibility." When she didn't respond, I pushed. "Exactly how many necromancers are capable of it?"

"In the world?"

I nodded.

"A dozen, maybe." Meira reached for the mortar and pestle on the table next to us, then dropped a handful of herbs inside and began grinding them. "I'll give you that it's a possibility," she conceded. "But it's more likely our original theory is correct, and a witch was responsible."

"Probably, but we need to rule out necromancers before dismissing them outright. Can you give me a list of those necromancers powerful enough to pull off the ritual?"

Meira dumped the spices she'd ground into dust into a small jar and set it aside. "Lists like that are dangerous." It was an echo of Celeste's concerns about fire elementals.

In the past, Meira had been quick to warn about the dangers inherent in keeping written records, something necromancers avoided. For the most part, our history was confined to oral stories passed from generation to generation.

"Perhaps you could tell me the names, and I could memorize them. We can split them into groups to make them easier to remember, and I can rule them out in batches." When she didn't object, I suggested we start with the four most powerful necromancers.

Meira gave me a wry look. "Two of them are standing in this room right now."

As much as Meira had given me in terms of knowledge and training, our relationship wasn't built on trust. I allowed myself to consider the possibility I had been avoiding. If a necromancer was working with a vampire, Meira was the necromancer most likely to be involved. Other than me, she was probably the most powerful necromancer alive. Thanks to Zepar's manipulations, I also knew she at least envied, if not outright coveted, the power I held. She also lived in Kansas City where the first murder occurred, and she had connections throughout the territory, including in Chicago.

But while Meira had both the means and the opportunity, I couldn't come up with a motive. If she wanted to create super vampires, why had she helped me send Zepar back to hell? Why train me to manipulate souls at all?

"Okay, give me the next four in line then."

She rattled off four names, and I committed them to memory. I'd pass them on to Craig and see what he could dig up. I hoped all four would prove innocent as much as Meira did.

That left two more items on my check-with-Meira list. I decided to save my personal quest for last. "We think whoever is trying to turn witches into vampires must be going after the fire elementals specifically."

Meira looked taken aback, which meant it was news to her. Craig must not have shared that detail with the full Tribunal yet. "Both witches were fire elementals?"

"They were—powerful ones. It's the only connection we've found so far to link the two women together, other than the fact they were both young witches who mostly kept to themselves."

"How are they finding them?" Meira wondered. "The witches' council guards the identities of their elementals as much as I would a list of necromancers. Fire elementals are rare and spread out across the country. Who would have that information besides the witches' council?"

I told Meira about the locating spell we'd found on Fiona and Celeste's theory that it had been used to trace fire elementals. "Unfortunately, Celeste refused to give us a list of the remaining fire elementals. She plans to warn them, at least, but I'm not sure how much good it will do. Neither of our dead witches saw the attack coming. They both woke up mid-ritual and were compelled to stay still as they bled out."

Meira looked thoughtful. "That explains the petitions for sanctuary we got this morning."

"What petitions?"

"Two fire elementals from rural covens petitioned the Tribunal for sanctuary here in Kansas City. One was from South Dakota and the other from Oklahoma. Their covens would be too small and too isolated to offer adequate protection."

"Who will be protecting them here?" I asked. Craig had his hands full with the investigation.

Meira sighed. "Since the South Dakota witch was already staying with those Stitch Witch women, we left her there."

"Olivia is a fire elemental?" That meant Janis's niece was in danger.

"She is. Do you know her?"

"Not well, but I've met her." Olivia had hardly seemed like a powerful witch when she'd been cowering inside a tire to avoid paintballs. If I could throw fireballs with my bare hands, I'd be flaunting my badass badge. "And the other?"

"A witch from Oklahoma was placed under Volkov's protection."

I made a face. "The Oklahoma witch certainly got the short end of the stick."

"At least with Volkov, the witch will be safe. I wouldn't put it past Helen and her friends to drag poor Olivia into more trouble than she's hiding from." Meira was about as polar opposite from Riley's witches as a person could get. While Meira exuded sophistication from her perfectly styled silver locks to her high-end neutral wardrobe, Riley's witches embraced the wild side.

Meira stood up and began putting away her herb jars. Before she could escape to the front of her shop, I stopped her.

"There's one more thing." When she turned back to me, I

pulled out the letter and the key I'd found in Claire's room. "Grandma Dottie rented a safe deposit box in Romania right before she died." I handed Meira the letter and waited until she finished reading it. "Do you have any idea what could be in that box?"

Meira frowned, turning the key over in her hand. "No idea." She looked at the date stamp on the envelope and paled. "Isn't that the day before Dottie died?"

"It is," I confirmed. "I don't think her death was an accident."

"Just because she rented a box and mailed a key to herself doesn't mean her death wasn't an accident," Meira said. She gave me an assessing look. "When are you going to see what's in the box?"

"No idea. They won't release the contents to me without a will and death certificate." I didn't mention the plan Riley and I had hatched to steal it.

"Well, don't jump to conclusions until you see what's in it." Meira dropped the key back in the envelope and handed it to me. "Besides, at the moment, all of our focus needs to be on finding and stopping this witch killer."

I didn't disagree, but I also wasn't about to stop digging into the clue my grandmother had left for me.

CHAPTER 12

There were several perks to flying on a chartered plane rather than a commercial flight. The one I appreciated the most was that it allowed Riley and I to get to the jet in record time. Like many chartered flights out of Kansas City, we were flying out of the downtown airport. It was a small airport with a few large hangars used for bigger planes like the frequently chartered Cessnas and even more hangars better suited to small private aircraft. With a small terminal and self-fueling stations, it saw plenty of business use.

When Craig offered to pick me up, I'd made an excuse, telling him I needed to make a morning stop, so I'd meet them at the airport. He'd grudgingly agreed. That allowed Riley and I time to get to the airport long before Craig and Volkov were set to arrive.

"How will we know which plane is the right one?" I asked Riley as we parked.

"I'll hang back like we're not together, and you can ask someone. Once you know, give me a hand signal like this."

Riley made some elaborate combination of hand gestures that would fit right in at a Royal's dugout.

"Um, how about I just wave?" I suggested.

"Boring." She veered off to the side, leaving me to cross the tarmac alone. Riley was dressed to blend in, wearing a black hooded sweatshirt, loose jeans, and her trademark combat boots. With her bright pink hair covered and her face shadowed by the hood, no one would be able to tell her age or gender at a glance. She slouched down next to a car parked in the adjacent lot to wait for my signal.

Fortunately, finding the right private jet proved easy since there was only one not parked in a hangar.

"Excuse me." I approached the uniformed man who was doing some kind of check and waited until he looked up. I gave him my sunniest smile. "I'm supposed to be on a flight with Max Volkov. Is this the right flight?"

"You're early." Although he smiled politely, I noted the edge of irritation in his voice.

"Sorry. Mr. Volkov makes me nervous. I didn't want to risk being late."

He relaxed. The man must have met Volkov and knew what an asshole he could be. "That's understandable. You've got the right place. I just finished the flight check." He glanced behind me to the building, no doubt hoping for a coffee and a few minutes of peace and quiet before being forced to spend the better part of a day in Volkov's presence.

"Don't mind me," I said. "I don't want to be a bother. You can do whatever you normally do. I'm happy to wait for the others onboard."

He wavered, looking uncertain. "I'm not supposed to let anyone on the jet until Mr. Volkov arrives."

"Oh, okay." The stairs were already in place, and the door

was open. I didn't actually need to go onboard though, so I was happy to play the little rule follower. I pointed to the chairs next to the building. "I'll take a seat over there."

The man let out a relieved breath. "Great. Can I bring you back a cup of coffee?"

"That would be wonderful." I followed a few steps behind him, so I could wave at Riley and point to the jet. I watched as she ran to it, climbed the stairs, and ducked inside. When I was sure she was safely onboard, I caught up with the man and began a steady stream of small talk to keep him distracted. By the time Craig and Volkov arrived, the pilot and I were chatting like old friends.

Volkov scowled as he approached, so I pasted on my biggest, fakest smile and waved at him. Craig scanned me with a puzzled expression as he took in my uncharacteristic outfit.

"Why are you wearing Riley's jacket?" Volkov asked, ignoring the pilot's greeting.

"Hello to you, too." I said cheerfully. I brushed my fingers across my shoulder. "I borrowed this. My jacket was at the dry cleaners." To make the jacket look less ridiculous on me, I'd coordinated my outfit—black-on-black with some metal stud earrings for good measure. Of course, I'd tied a red bandana into a makeshift headband to soften the whole look.

Seemingly satisfied with my answer, Volkov turned his back to me and started a conversation with the pilot and the copilot. While Volkov was distracted, I rushed to the stairs. With his long legs, it wouldn't take Craig long to catch me, so I sped up.

"What's the rush?" Craig asked.

I kept moving. "I've been standing here awhile, and I'm ready to sit down." I reached in my pocket and pulled out my keys, purposely dropping them off the side of the stairs as I climbed. "Shoot. Would you mind grabbing those?"

"Sure."

While he backtracked for the keys, I sprinted up the rest of the steps, so I would have a few seconds to unveil the second part of our smuggle-Riley-onboard plan. I had the plastic baggie out before I reached the top step. I opened it and pulled out the foil-wrapped sandwich I'd brought along. It was still warm, and as soon as it was out of the sealed plastic baggie, the smell of liver and onions permeated the confined space.

The chartered jet had luxury stamped all over it. With cream upholstery and a variety of seating configurations and conveniently placed tables, it was a huge step up from flying commercial. Unlike a commercial plane with its rows of seats and overhead storage, this jet was open, allowing for ample head space. However, it minimized the places Riley could have hidden.

"Riley," I hissed. "Where are you?"

I heard a tapping from inside the closet toward the back, telling me where Riley was camping out for the first leg of the flight. We figured once we were in the air, Volkov wouldn't waste time turning around. If we could get off the ground, we'd be golden.

I positioned myself in the seat near the closet door, so I could act as a human roadblock if anyone reached for it. I resisted the urge to plug my nose as I sat holding my stinky sandwich. Hopefully, the jacket and the sandwich would be enough to disguise Riley's scent.

I didn't have to wait long to find out. Craig stepped inside, with Volkov close on his heels. Both men stopped abruptly to stare at me.

Volkov made a face. "What in the hell is that smell?"

"Breakfast," I said cheerfully, waving the liver and onion sandwich around while trying not to gag. "You want some?"

"Absolutely not." Volkov moved to the opposite side of the aisle as far away from me as he could get. He had a small carry-on bag he shoved into an empty seat before turning back to scowl me. "Can you eat the damn thing already, so we don't have to smell it all the way to Bucharest?"

"Someone's not a morning person," I chirped.

Craig remained standing in the aisle, eyeing me skeptically. "You are going to eat that, right?"

I swallowed. "Yup."

He waited, watching me as I stalled. First, I dug through my purse for a napkin. I hadn't planned to actually eat it. Even if the smell hadn't enough to put me off, the idea of willingly eating liver was revolting. When Craig took a step closer and waited, I set the sandwich on the small table beside me. "Dang it. I forgot a drink."

Craig reached into the side of his duffle bag and pulled out a metal water bottle, handing it to me with a smile.

"Oh, I couldn't take yours. You might want it."

"I'm good." He thrust the bottle into my hands.

Having no other choice unless I wanted to open the door and confess while Riley clambered out, I grabbed the bottle. Then, I took what was probably the longest drink of water of my life. Out of stalling techniques, I brought the sandwich to my mouth and took a small bite. I planned to spit it in my napkin when they looked away. Unfortunately, both men watched intently, so I was forced to keep chewing. I swallowed the disgusting mess—all while keeping a pleasantly neutral expression on my face.

"How is your sandwich?" Craig asked, his eyes crinkling at the corners.

"Mmmm. So good."

"Good thing you brought such a big sandwich then," he said, crossing his arms and settling in for the show.

I nodded. "Mmmm hmm."

When it was obvious neither of them was going to look away, I took another bite, bigger this time. I wasn't sure which was worse, the smell or the taste, but I didn't want to drag this out any longer than necessary.

By the fourth bite, my strategy became chewing as little as possible before swallowing. Because I paused to wash each mouthful down with a big gulp of Craig's water, it was taking entirely too long. The next bite lodged in my throat, triggering my gag reflex. The more I thought about gagging, the harder it was not to do it. My eyes started watering, so I kept my lips pressed tightly together. And still I smiled and chewed.

Finally, I patted my stomach. "Well, this is one of those cases where my eyes were bigger than my stomach." I rewrapped the remaining half of the sandwich in tinfoil, leaving the corner open to avoid sealing up that God-awful smell. *I should have doused myself in deer piss and taken my chances.*

Craig reached for the carry-on I'd dropped in the aisle. Suddenly panicked he'd put it in the closet behind me, I grabbed the strap and started a tug-of-war. "I need that."

"Okay." After giving me an odd look, he let go. I snatched the bag to my lap, sending his open water bottle careening to the floor in my haste. I dove for it too late, and it splashed all over his shoes and into the aisle.

"Sorry," I mumbled.

"Are you always like this?" Volkov asked with a grimace.

"Like what?" I sat clutching my bag to my chest.

Volkov looked at Craig and shook his head. "This is going to be a long flight."

Craig tossed his bag in the seat across the aisle and bent to retrieve the now empty water bottle that had rolled underneath the seat. He shoved it back in the side pocket of his bag before pausing next to me. My heart sped up, and I avoided glancing back at the compartment where Riley hid. Finally, Craig sat down beside me.

He leaned in so he could whisper in my ear. "Stop trying to antagonize him."

"What?" I asked, genuinely confused.

"Volkov. I get that you're not happy about the Max-Riley situation, but come on."

I relaxed. "You're right. I'm being childish." As long as the two of them thought the jacket and the sandwich were attempts to annoy Volkov because I didn't like the thought of him with Riley, they wouldn't suspect our stowaway. I scooted the sandwich a little farther away from me on the table and buckled my seatbelt.

Takeoff was uneventful, as was the first hour or so of the flight. Then, all hell broke loose. Volkov was making his way to the back of the plane to use the bathroom when Riley decided she'd had enough of confined spaces. Whether it was on purpose or not, she waited until Volkov was even with her hidey-hole to open the compartment door and pop her head out. He did a double take before losing his shit.

Ignoring Riley for the moment, he backtracked so he could get right in my face. "Are you fucking kidding me?"

Craig put a hand on Volkov's chest and moved him back out of my personal space before looking to see what had him so irate. Riley poked her head around the closet door and gave him a little wave. Volkov stood in the aisle staring at her, his whole body tensing while he ran through a string of curses—some of them way more creative than I would have thought him capable of.

Riley waited until his tirade was over. "Hey, can you finish yelling at me after you move so I can get out of here? My legs are kind of cramped."

When he reached for Riley, I thought he was going to throttle her. I scrambled to my feet, but Volkov just pushed Riley back inside closet. He stared at her for a second, then closed the compartment door and locked it from the outside.

Instead of the outraged yelling I expected, Riley laughed, which pissed off Volkov even more. He returned to his seat —the bathroom forgotten—and grabbed an investment magazine. Had it not been upside down, I might have believed he was reading it. I was smart enough not to comment on it.

I chanced a look at Craig. "Really?" he asked.

It wasn't the kind of question someone expected an answer to, so I didn't bother. Riley banged on the door again, shouting vague threats both men ignored. I stood and attempted to slide past Craig.

Craig extended an arm, blocking my way. "Sit."

I pointed to the closet. "But Riley."

"Will be fine." He glanced at Volkov. "You need to let him cool down."

I felt like a crap friend leaving her locked in there, but I sat back down and stared out the window.

Riley knocked on the compartment door again. "Hey, Kali. Time me."

"What?"

"Time me," she repeated, louder this time. "I want to see how long it takes me to get out of here."

I looked at Volkov who continued staring at his upside-down magazine, the edges crumpling as he clenched his hands. I knew I probably shouldn't encourage Riley, but my curiosity to see how long it would take her to escape won out. Craig looked at the stopwatch app I opened on my phone and shook his head.

"Okay, go!" I made sure to say it loud enough Riley could hear me through the locked door.

She rustled around in the compartment for several seconds, and then it went quiet. I wondered if she was trying to pick the lock from the inside. *Is that even a thing?* Riley chose the more aggressive approach, as evidenced by the bleating coming from the closet. Before long, I could hear horns ramming the door, making me cringe. I didn't have to look to know she was denting the hell out of the storage compartment.

"Oh, for fuck's sake." Volkov tossed his magazine and stalked back to unlock the door.

Riley bolted out, careening into the seat on the opposite side of the plane before jumping up onto it and giving it a good bounce. Volkov reached into the storage space to grab Riley's clothes. He tossed her shirt over her head and quickly took advantage of her momentary distraction to scoop up her squirming body. It went far better than the last time he attempted to manhandle her in goat form. Within seconds, he had shoved her into the small bathroom and tossed her clothes in after her.

"Shift back and get dressed," he growled before shutting the door and going back to his seat.

Although he didn't make a sound, Craig's shoulders shook

with suppressed laughter. I studiously avoided eye contact with Volkov. A few minutes later, Riley came out of the bathroom fully dressed.

She paused in the aisle next to us. "Hey Kali, do you have any of that sandwich left?"

I handed her what remained of the foil-wrapped sandwich with a grimace. She snatched it and settled into a seat across from us where she polished off the rest of the liver and onions.

During most of the rest of the flight, Riley napped, while Craig and I planned our interview with Naomi. Craig had followed up on our leads so far but come up empty handed, so a lot was riding on this interview.

It took Volkov almost the entire flight to cool off enough to speak to any of us.

"Why did you come?" Volkov finally asked Riley.

She shrugged. "It's none of your business."

Volkov's eyes shifted to his wolf, but he kept himself in check. "I disagree. And if you want off this jet, you'll answer my question."

Riley glared at him, but she answered. "There's something I need to retrieve."

The jet touched down and rolled to a slow stop. Volkov was the first to unbuckle, standing up so he loomed over Riley. She remained sitting, making no move to join him in the aisle.

He stared down at her long enough, I squirmed uncomfortably. "This is not Kansas City," he started, a note of warning in his voice. "If you get caught stealing something, I have no pull with the authorities here."

I leaned closer to Craig. "How does he know she is going to steal something?"

He gave me his are-you-kidding-me look.

Riley curled her lip. "Have I ever asked you to use your pull with authorities?" She made air quotes as she said authorities. "No. I have not. Because one, I don't get caught. And two, you are not my alpha."

He smiled, but it was a little too sharp to be friendly. "What are you going to take?"

Riley pressed her lips together and glanced back at me.

Craig spoke before I could. "She's going to get into your grandmother's safe deposit box, isn't she?"

All eyes were on me. "Yes," I admitted. "They won't give me the contents without documentation I don't have, so Riley is going to retrieve it."

Even though Craig and I joined them in the aisle, it did little to defuse the fight brewing between them.

Riley stood and went toe-to-toe with Volkov. "It's an easy in-and-out job. I could do it in my sleep."

"You're going to rob a bank?" Volkov demanded.

"It's not a bank," she said dismissively. "It's a private safe deposit rental place."

Volkov turned to me. "Is it important?"

I swallowed. "It is to me."

He ran a hand through his dark hair. "Fine." He angled his head so he could look in Riley's eyes. "But if there are any signs of trouble, you get out and back to this jet to wait for us. You got me?"

Riley pulled back and eyed him suspiciously. "Wait. Why are you agreeing to this so easily?"

He smiled. "Because if you're off robbing some strip mall security place, you won't be at the Compound."

"She can't go while we're at the Compound because I'm going with her," I said.

Craig frowned down at me. "It's too dangerous."

He hadn't said a word when Riley announced her plans a minute ago, so it wasn't the break-in he was objecting to—it was me going. "No. It's not. Worst-case scenario, we're calling you for bail money."

Craig crossed his arms over his chest. "You can't go."

"Excuse me? I wasn't asking permission."

He turned around to grab both of our bags. "We can talk about this later."

One look at the stubborn set of Craig's jaw told me all I needed to know. No amount of talking would change his mind, so I wouldn't waste my time trying. When I didn't argue, he shot me a suspicious look. I ignored him.

"Why don't you want me at the Compound, anyway?" Riley asked Volkov. "Is it because you don't want me to meet your brother?"

"What? No," he said. "I don't want you doing something that will make you a permanent resident."

A chill ran through me at the dire warning. "What does that mean?" I asked.

"The Compound isn't a typical prison," Craig answered. "The kind of people housed there don't get visitors, and its exact location is a heavily guarded secret."

Volkov grabbed his carry-on and checked his watch. "Let's move. They're expecting us to land in four hours. We need to get out of the airport before they send the welcoming committee."

Puzzled, I turned to Craig. "What welcoming committee?"

He followed Volkov. "You don't want to know."

$\mathcal{A}$ dark gray sedan was waiting for us. I assumed the driver was one Volkov had arranged because he didn't hesitate as he strode to the car. The driver opened the trunk and waited until all our luggage was piled inside, then opened the door for Riley and me. With Craig in the back with us, it was a tight squeeze.

The driver seemed to know where he was going without being given directions. We stopped in front of a five-story luxury apartment building with an old-world feel and a uniformed doorman. Volkov didn't move to get our luggage, apparently used to having lackeys to carry around his things.

I suspected this was not an Airbnb. "Where are we?"

Volkov scanned the street. "My family keeps an apartment in Bucharest."

Riley raised an eyebrow but followed his gaze. "What are you looking for?"

"One at two o'clock," he said.

"Another at eight," Craig said.

They hurried us inside. Although the doorman greeted

Volkov, he couldn't seem to look anywhere but at Riley's bright pink hair. She lifted her chin and stared right back until he got the hint and looked away. "I'll have your luggage sent up, sir."

Volkov gave a curt nod. "Thank you." He bypassed the elevator for the stairs.

After hours on the plane, my legs protested the idea of climbing stairs. "Tell me you are on the second floor."

"Fifth." Volkov took the stairs two at a time, disappearing around the next bend.

"Is he claustrophobic or something?" I asked Craig, who was behind me, bringing up the rear.

"Elevators can be jammed."

"Okay."

He glanced behind him. "Let's save the questions for upstairs."

Several flights later, we followed Volkov into an apartment so large it had to take up most of the top floor of the building. Unlike the clean modern lines Volkov seemed to prefer in his own home, this place looked like every bad movie version of a Russian oligarch's residence. There was so much bling, all I could do was blink against the gaudiness of it all. I expected Riley to give Volkov a hard time about the silver spoon he seemed to have been born with, but she was subdued as she studied the surroundings.

Volkov and Craig went through the apartment like they'd done it a million times, checking rooms and peering out windows in perfect synchronization. Riley and I checked out the house while they finished their security check. When the doorman knocked with our luggage, Volkov waited for Craig to position himself against the wall next to the door before he opened it. This was over-the-top even for them.

After the doorman left, I asked the obvious question. "What is going on?"

"As I said Ms. James, the Compound is not a typical prison. The only way in is with an escort," Volkov said.

"And?"

"And it's not a friendly kind of escort."

I wasn't entirely sure what he meant, but it if it was putting Craig and Volkov on high alert, it couldn't be good. I glanced at Riley. "Are we safe here?"

"We are," Craig reassured me. He crossed to the window and peered at the street below. "Aleksei isn't expecting us until morning, but the Shadows down there will have notified him of our arrival by now."

I assumed by Shadows, he meant Aleksei's people who must have eyes on the building. *And I thought my family was dysfunctional.* If Volkov had wanted to arrive incognito, maybe an Airbnb would have been a better choice than the family apartment his brother would obviously know about.

Volkov moved to the opposite side of the room, phone to his ear. "We'll be in front of the building by 9:00 a.m." He hung up without elaborating, then turned to Riley. "As long as everyone stays inside, they won't come for us until morning."

The escort sounded more ominous than a prison shuttle, but both men were too preoccupied to share more information. That was fine. Riley and I had plans of our own.

Riley made a big production of yawning. "Where can I crash?"

Volkov grabbed her bag and headed to one of the guest bedrooms.

I followed Riley's lead with a yawn of my own. "Something tells me the two of you are going to be up for a while. I think I'll crash with Riley tonight."

Craig nodded. "Get some rest. Tomorrow will be a long day." He returned to the window where he could watch for movement on the street below.

Volkov deposited Riley's bag on the bed and turned with a lecture on his lips. Seeing me, he relaxed. "You're sleeping in here, too?"

I eyed the huge four-poster bed. "I am."

"Good. You brought her, so you can make sure she doesn't cause trouble." He closed the door with a firm click behind him.

As soon as Volkov's footsteps receded down the hall, Riley crossed the room and locked the door.

"Is that smart?" I asked. "If he tries the knob, he's going to know something's up."

Riley rolled her shoulders and neck, working out the stiffness. "No worries. I'll unlock it before we leave."

"How exactly are we getting out of here?" I was pretty sure her plan didn't involve slinking out the front door.

Riley crossed the room to peer outside. "Looks all clear."

I joined her as she was opening the window. There was no sign of anyone watching the side of the building like they were the front. They probably figured no one would be dumb enough to climb out a five-story window and leapfrog to the ground.

There were no screens on any of the windows, which made it easy for Riley to poke her head out. "Fancy," she exclaimed before pulling herself back inside. "There's a balcony on every level." She grinned at me. "Cake walk."

The so-called balcony was little more than window dressing—a small ledge surrounded by wrought iron. "I don't know if you can call that a balcony. It seems more decorative than anything."

Riley brushed off my concern. "All that matters is that it's sturdy. It'll be like climbing a tree."

I looked down at my cork-heeled wedges and ruby-red pedicure. "Do I look like I climb trees?"

"You could stay here, you know. I'll be in and out—half an hour, tops."

I narrowed my eyes. "That's not the deal. If you go, I go."

Riley grinned. "You'd better change those shoes then." She pulled an all-black ensemble out of her duffle, including a black fanny pack, and I stifled a gasp. Riley laughed. "Really? It's the fanny pack you have a problem with, not the criminal intent?"

"I can't help it if I have standards."

Riley dressed, rolling the ski mask she'd brought, so it looked like a normal hat. She moved to the bathroom mirror and tucked her hair beneath it. "Did you bring the contacts?"

I rummaged around in my bag. "Yeah, here." I tossed her the pair of brown contact lenses. They were cosmetic only, something I stocked in my shop to go with the costumes I sold, but they'd do a good job of disguising Riley's vivid blue eyes.

The outfit I'd packed was black like Riley's, but it had several distinctive features. Rather than a ski mask, I'd brought a black cloak I'd made for a cosplay costume. Unlike most cloaks, it was slim fitting through the torso with a loose black hood that dipped low over my eyes and a neckpiece designed to pull over my mouth like a balaclava. The cloak fastened with a funky little buckle at the shoulder but was open below to allow easy access to its pockets. I'd added rein-forced pockets inside the cloak to hold throwing knives on one side and slim flashlights on the other.

Since I hadn't wanted to risk smuggling my own knives

through the airport, I had to settle for two paring knives I'd swiped out of Volkov's kitchen when I got a glass of water. Because it was my first time on a chartered flight, I'd played it safe. Had I known what a free-for-all private flights provided, I would have loaded up on weapons.

A brown-eyed Riley came out of the bathroom, took one look at me, and broke into a huge grin. "You look ready to kick some ass, girl."

I rolled my eyes. "No ass kicking. In-and-out."

I tucked two Maglite flashlights—one for me and one for Riley—in the right-side pocket of my cloak. Sitting on the bed, I pulled on the boots I'd bought specially for this outfit. They were knee high and made with leather so supple they molded to my calves perfectly. The soles were broken in enough to be quiet but still had enough grip to prevent me from falling on my ass on the first slick surface. The final piece of my ensemble was a pair of thin black gloves I tucked in the outer pocket.

While I was dressing, Riley piled our clothes on the bed and arranged them under the blankets in the shape of our bodies. It wouldn't fool anyone if they looked closely, but a quick glance in the room shouldn't give us away.

Riley filled her oversized fanny pack with various tools she'd brought. When she was finished, she unlocked the door. "Ready?" she asked.

"Ready." The draw of getting my hands on whatever my grandmother had left in the safe deposit box overshadowed any nerves I was feeling.

Riley climbed through the opening and stood on the slim ledge facing me. "I'm going to drop to the balcony below. When you come out, wait for me to give you the all-clear. Then, I want you to climb over the railing and lower yourself from the bars. I'll grab you and pull you onto the balcony. Got it?" She waited for my nod. "Last chance to back out," she challenged.

"No way. Let's go."

Riley made it look effortless, swinging down to the balcony below in seconds. I wasn't afraid of heights, but the thought of dangling over a railing five stories above ground sent a shot of adrenaline crashing through me. Once I was on the balcony, I closed the window. Even though we were leaving through the window, we planned to come back through the front door, so there was no need to leave it cracked open. We were banking on the fact that whoever was staking out the front of the building would be on alert for people leaving, not sneaking back in.

I wiped my palms against my pants and put one leg over the railing. I stepped my second leg over, holding onto the bars in a death grip while trying my best not to look down.

"All right," Riley said. "If you hold on to the bars, you should be able to lower yourself down."

"Going somewhere?"

The sound made my heart hammer against my ribcage and my palms slick with perspiration. I didn't have to look up to know Craig was in his gargoyle form. The gravel in his voice was a giveaway.

"Damn it! You scared me."

"Good. You should be scared. Do you have any idea what a fall from this height does to the human body?"

"I wasn't going to let her fall," Riley called up to him.

Craig didn't reply, and he didn't give me the chance to step off the ledge. He plucked me off the railing, his arm like steel around my waist. The sound of his powerful wings keeping us aloft drowned out whatever Riley said next. "We'll meet you there," he snapped at Riley before shooting higher in the sky.

"I thought you'd take me back," I admitted.

"Would it stop you from trying again?"

We both knew the answer. Craig didn't ask for directions, and before long, we were standing on the roof of a building across the street from our target. Once my legs steadied, he let go. He surprised me by remaining in his gargoyle form.

"You'll have to go down the fire escape to get to the ground. I'll stay here and keep watch. If there's any trouble, get to the street, and I'll fly us all out of here."

"Thanks." In this form, Craig was all hard, terrifying stone, but I could sense the worry lurking beneath the surface. "I'll be careful."

He didn't respond.

I climbed down the fire escape and hid in the shadow of the building until Riley joined me. It was a long wait. "What took you so long?"

"I had to make a stop because I forgot to bring these." Riley opened her fanny pack and held up a pair of Channellock pliers. She titled her head back. "Craig up there?"

"Yeah. He's keeping watch."

"Good." Riley pulled her ski mask down. "Stay here until I get the lock off. When I give you the signal, you need to haul ass across the street and get inside the building." Riley darted across the street without waiting for an answer.

For a business that made money on security, the storefront was unimpressive—standard aluminum-framed glass like any other strip mall business. From watching Riley pick locks in the past, I knew she was good at getting into places she shouldn't. But tonight, I learned exactly how good she was. After a quick scan of the street, Riley gripped the round metal lock with the Channellocks, gave them a quick twist and pulled the lock—cylinder and all—out of the opening. She disappeared inside.

"Holy shit!" I muttered. When I got home, I was going to install a better lock on my shop. That had been way too easy.

When Riley waved me over, I sprinted across the street and into the door she held open for me. Inside, I looked up at the security camera mounted in the corner of the room.

"No worries. I used a jammer. There won't be any footage of us." Riley looked over her shoulder as she made her way deeper into the room. "You got the box number and the key?"

"Right here." I pulled my necklace from beneath my shirt. I'd put the key on a chain, figuring it would not only keep it safe but also within easy reach.

Riley moved behind the counter and rummaged around until she came up with a second key. "Let's go," she said.

I followed her down the hallway but stopped dead when I saw the vault. "Shit." No wonder it had been so easy to get inside the building. With a vault like that, it didn't matter.

Riley lifted her mask to the top of her head and peeled off one of her gloves. "Give me your phone."

I unlocked it and handed it over, not sure what good it would do us. Riley pulled up the timer app, put ten minutes on it, and handed it back to me. "You're on lookout. Hit start when you get to the front where you can see outside. Stay back far enough in the dark where you won't be visible from the street." She tapped the screen. "When this timer runs out, come back. I'll be in the vault."

I looked at the solid steel door skeptically. "You can get in there in ten minutes?"

"Seven or eight, most likely, but I'm giving myself a little buffer. It's been a while." Riley opened her fanny pack and pulled out a stethoscope, a folded piece of graphing paper, and a pencil. Then she put her glove back on and knelt by the vault door. "Now go."

Standing in the lobby of a business we'd broken into made those ten minutes the longest of my life. But when I got back, the door was open, and Riley was sitting cross-legged on the table in the center of the room, a smug grin on her face.

Three walls of the room were made of floor-to-ceiling safe deposit boxes in various sizes. Once I located my grandmother's box, my hands shook as I opened it and took out the contents. I stared at the single medium-sized manilla envelope that had been inside the box. Despite the overwhelming desire to rip it open, my gut churned at the thought of what I might find. The envelope was relatively thin, so whatever was in it couldn't be more than a few sheets of paper.

Riley put the box back and turned to me. "Not here," Riley insisted. "We need to go."

I tucked the envelope in my pocket for safekeeping. Riley put everything back the way we found it, including the lock on the front door. Hopefully, when staff arrived in the morning, they'd have no idea we'd been inside, and I'd be one step closer to finding Claire's killer.

We made our way to the roof of the neighboring building where Craig stood guard. Riley and Craig watched me expectantly as I took a deep breath and broke the seal, shaking out the contents of the envelope. A stack of photographs fell out. Riley leaned closer. Although the moon was full tonight, there wasn't enough light to see what was on the photographs. I dug my flashlight out and handed it to Riley, who held it steady as I went through the pictures.

The first was of a building I didn't recognize, but based on the architecture, it was taken here in Bucharest. I'd never seen a building that old in the US. It was a stunning multi-story mansion that managed to look both stately and wild. Windows were framed with ornate stonework whitewashed from the sun. The stairs leading up to the house had patches of moss growing between cracks in the stone, and the overgrown grounds and headless statues in front of the building hinted at decay and abandonment. The next two photos were different angles of the same building, one of which showed a street sign in the background.

It didn't surprise me my grandmother was drawn to such a place. Had these been the photos I found in the envelope she'd mailed to herself, I would have thought them nothing more than tourist mementos. But she hadn't. She'd developed the photos, sealed them in an envelope, and put them in a ten-year prepaid safe deposit box across the world from her home. This building was important somehow. I just didn't know how yet.

I flipped the photo over and checked the date stamp—a day before my grandma's death. Before I could flip to another, Craig held out his hand. I gave him the photo, and he studied it with a frown. "This was in your grandmother's safe deposit box?"

"It was." I handed him the photo with the full view of the building and the street sign. "Do you recognize this place?"

"It's Wallace Ratcliff's home."

"Who's Wallace Ratcliff?" Riley asked before I could.

Craig handed both photos back to me, and from his grimace, I was guessing Ratcliff wasn't an old friend. "Ratcliff is the master vampire."

I fumbled the photo as if it burned me. "Vampire?" Everything kept circling back to them. First, Twitch had stalked me, probably at Meira's request. Then, Durrand had campaigned for my death before attempting to kill me himself. Now, this Ratcliff had something to do with Claire's death.

"Not any vampire," Craig said. "The master."

I frowned. "What's a master vampire? Is he the head vampire in Bucharest or something?" *Does he wield the same kind of power Durrand had in the US?*

"Not a master vampire—the master," Craig corrected me. "As in, he rules all vampires."

Why would the master vampire care about a teenage girl living in the suburbs halfway around the world? I couldn't think of a connection that made sense. But if my grandmother had taken these photos and gone to all the trouble of renting a safe deposit box and mailing herself the key, there must be a connection.

I flipped to the next photo and stared down at it. It was of the same mansion, and I could barely make out the shadow of a man visible through the gauzy curtains of a main floor window. I couldn't discern his features though. I flipped to the last picture, my whole body tight with anticipation.

This one was a closeup of two men, both of them looking out the same window. Craig pointed at a man I didn't recognize. "That's Wallace Ratcliff." The master vampire was trim, with a softness to his features at odds with the intensity in his eyes. Although there was nothing physically intimidating about the man with his wavy hair and full cheeks, my gut said he was dangerous.

But it was the other man who stole my breath. The sights and sounds around me faded as I took him in until he was all I could see. I memorized the brute angles of his face, studied the familiar fanaticism lurking in his pale eyes.

"Kali." Craig's voice startled me. "What is it?"

"It's him."

"Who?" Riley leaned in for a better look at the man who commanded all my attention.

I pointed to him. "That is the man who killed Claire."

"Are you sure?" Craig asked.

"Positive," I said through clenched teeth. Some things you didn't forget. The face of the man who ran my sister down on a busy street in Chicago, smiling as he did it, was definitely one of them.

I looked up at Craig as the connection snapped into place. "Do you think Ratcliff ordered Claire's death?" My voice was barely a whisper, but once the question was out, I couldn't stop the endless barrage. "Was her killer a vampire?" There was nothing to indicate he was a vampire—either in the vision Zepar had shown me or in this photo. And yet, I knew it to be true the second the words left my lips. "Why my sister?" I jabbed the photo with my finger, my voice getting louder with each question. "And why was my grandma there? Did she suspect they killed Claire? Did she confront them?" I sucked in a breath. "Oh God, what if they killed her, too?"

I searched their faces looking for answers they couldn't give me, noting the sympathy on Riley's face and Craig's fear for what I might do. What I would do.

Craig reached for me, but I stepped away. "I need to go here." My voice was flat, even to my own ears.

"Listen to me." Craig gripped my shoulders and turned my body toward him. "These are just photos. We have no idea what they mean."

"Then, I'll go find out what they mean." I tried to step away, but Craig kept his grip on my shoulders.

"Confronting Ratcliff will get you killed."

The rage hit like a tsunami, threatening take me under. "I don't care."

"I fucking do." He growled and shook me. "Use your head and stop letting emotion rule you."

For the first time, I resented that stoic facade of his. I hated his calm in the face of my anger. I tried to jerk away, but he held on. "I need her killer to pay."

"And he will." Craig tilted his head down, and I saw the

resolve in his face. "I'll make sure of it, but first we need to be certain."

The urge to lean on him, to count on someone to be there in the trenches with me was so tempting. In the months after Claire's death, I had learned people saying the words I wanted to hear was easy, but them walking away was even easier. "Look, this isn't your fight."

"I'm making it my fight."

When my breathing was normal and the blood no longer pounded inside my head, he let me go. I held the photo up. "This is the man who took my sister from me. He was here, in the city I'm standing in right now. And this picture of him may be what got my grandmother killed. I don't care if I have to walk barefoot through a den of vipers. I'm going to this house, and I'm asking Wallace Ratcliff for the name of the man who killed my sister. Do not ask me to walk away from this."

Craig might force me to go back to Volkov's, but I needed him to know I'd find my way back, whatever the cost. I tucked the photos into the inside pocket of my cloak.

"Riley, are you okay getting back to the apartment on your own?" At her nod, Craig unfurled his wings and stepped closer to the edge of the roof. "Call Volkov when you're close, and he'll make sure you get past the Shadows safely."

Riley arched a brow. He may as well have dared her to get by them on her own. No way was she calling Volkov.

"Be safe," I told her.

"Be smart," she shot back before climbing down the fire escape.

Craig held out his hand, his face grim. "I'll take you because you cannot face this man alone."

We balanced at the edge of the roof while Craig spent the

next few minutes drilling vampire etiquette into me as if I should care about offending a seethe of murderous blood-suckers. Don't look them in the eye, so they couldn't compel me. Rein in sarcastic comebacks and avoid directly challenging them. Thank Ratcliff for his hospitality.

"I got it." The first I could do, but I wasn't making any promises about the second. And it would be a cold day in hell before I'd thank Ratcliff for his hospitality. Because I didn't want Craig to change his mind, I kept my thoughts to myself.

Craig bent down, so we were eye-to-eye. "You need to follow my lead." He grabbed me by the shoulders like he wanted to shake some sense into me. "Listen to me. Wallace Ratcliff is dangerous, and he will drain you for the sport of it. If you do anything reckless, I will remove you from Ratcliff's house, and this continent, if that's what it takes to keep you alive."

"I understand."

Craig pulled me against him and opened his wings. When he stepped off the roof, I was cocooned against his powerful body, but it would take more than strong arms around me to stop the need for vengeance beating a steady rhythm in my chest.

Because a seven-foot gargoyle walking down the streets of Bucharest was guaranteed to draw attention, Craig landed in the shadows of a nearby park and changed back into a human. We walked the rest of the way in tense silence. When Ratcliff's stone mansion came into view, Craig stopped me. "Stay close to me."

Although the mansion was in Bucharest, it may as well have been miles from civilization. Set on a large plot of land, the mansion itself was far from the road and shrouded in a dense fog like the one the witch had used to conceal the crime scene in Chicago. A tall stone wall surrounded the property on all sides, offering another barrier against prying eyes.

Craig didn't give me an opportunity to wander, leading me by my wrist as we entered the mansion's grounds. The cobblestone walkway had fallen into disrepair, weeds tufting between the cracks. I watched my step on the uneven ground. The closer we got, the less the moon seemed to light the path, and the more I stumbled.

We didn't make it to the front door before we were surrounded by vampires. I felt them before I saw them, my heartrate registering the threat long before my eyes. Craig kept his body loose, but the grip on my wrist told me he felt it, too. The vampires materialized, forming a circle that tightened around us until I felt a body brush against my side and a hand lift a strand of my hair. At my sharp inhale, Craig jerked me in front of him, pressing me against his chest. He maneuvered us both until his back was against a tree.

"That's close enough." Even though Craig was in human form, he sounded like the gargoyle he turned into. Craig's arms transitioned to stone, even as the rest of his body stayed flesh and blood. "I will take the head of the next vampire who touches either of us." His threat seemed to do the trick because the vampires stepped back enough to be out of reach.

An elegantly dressed man pushed his way through the others, stopping mere feet from us. "What is your business here, enforcer?" He spoke with an accent and held himself with an easy grace.

"We wish to speak to your master."

The man smiled, his teeth a flash of white against his dark skin. The smile transformed him from good-looking to gorgeous, and despite knowing what he was, I couldn't help but stare. "And you brought such a lovely gift."

Based on the way Craig's body was wrapped around mine, there was zero chance the vampire thought he'd brought me as a midnight snack. He was trying to get a rise out of Craig, an excuse to unleash the barely repressed violence all around us. Craig didn't take the bait. "Tell your master we request an audience."

The vampire's flinch every time Craig called Ratcliff his master was almost imperceptible, but it was there. He was a man with aspirations. "Do you know who I am?" He bared his fangs

"I don't need to know who you are." Craig patted the left pocket of my cloak where I'd tucked my stolen knives. He waited until I reached inside and grasped the handles. Then, he had the vampire by the throat, lifting him off the ground. I remained between his body and the pissed-off vampire who was trying unsuccessfully to pry Craig's hand from his neck. Craig used his other arm to prevent the vampire's legs from making contact with me. Although I held a knife in each hand, it was hard to look menacing while clutching a set of paring knives. Still, it was better than nothing. The other vampires stayed back for now, watching us with unblinking red eyes.

"You're wasting your time," the vampire choked out. "Ratcliff is not here."

Craig lowered him to the ground but kept his hand on his throat. "Where is he?"

"That is not your concern." Despite his precarious position, the vampire smiled at Craig. "You can be assured I will tell him you and your pretty friend were here."

Craig tightened his grip, and for a second, I thought he would rip the vampire's head from his shoulders. I had no doubt the threat to this vampire was the only thing holding the others back at the moment. I braced myself for their attack as Craig moved us away from the tree. I felt the change as it came over him, his body becoming impenetrable against me and his wings unfurling behind us. Craig wrapped his free arm around me and leapt for the sky, tossing the hissing vampire at the crowd as we left the ground. *So much for getting answers.*

CHAPTER 15

I woke to the sound of Volkov yelling. Although I covered my head with the pillow, the man had a voice that carried better than a sports announcer at Kaufmann Stadium. When I caught Riley's name, I got out of bed and headed to the living room to serve as referee. I didn't bother changing out of the yoga pants and camisole I'd slept in, afraid they'd kill each other before I could dress.

Volkov stood with his back to Riley, hands balled into fists at his side. "What part of stay inside this apartment did you not understand?"

Riley peeled a banana while he yelled at her. "I understood you fine." She waited until he turned around to make a face at him before taking a bite.

"It's seven o'clock in the morning. Why are you yelling?" I asked.

Volkov ignored me and went back to berating Riley. "I told you to stay put because this apartment is under surveillance. Why can't you do what you're told?"

Riley gave him an are-you-kidding-me look. "And I told

you I was going to get whatever was in that safe deposit box. Why can't you stop being such a control freak?" She finished her banana and stood up to throw the peel in the trash.

By the time she came back, Volkov had enough of a handle on his temper he was at least using his indoor voice. "How did you get past the doorman, anyway?"

Craig joined us, fully dressed and scowling. "They didn't."

We'd made it back late last night, and other than Volkov, none of us had gotten much sleep. I seemed to be the only one who looked it, though.

Volkov blocked Riley from exiting the room. "You climbed out a five-story window. Are you insane?" He didn't raise his voice this time. Somehow, he was scarier for it.

"Probably." Riley sidestepped around him and headed back to the guest bedroom. Not wanting to continue the conversation by myself, I stuck close to her heels.

By the time we left the apartment, everyone was uncharacteristically quiet, even Riley. I resisted the need to pull out the stack of photographs I'd stashed in my purse. Maybe I should have left them behind, but I didn't want to let them out of my sight. They weren't proof, but they were the closest thing I had to it.

In the light of day, the apartment lobby screamed old money. From the plush royal blue carpet to the crystal chandelier, it was built to impress. I thanked the doorman as I walked through the door he held for us, grateful to leave it all behind. It was already warm outside, which was a welcome change after the coolness of the building. We didn't get much of a chance to enjoy the beautiful morning though. Two steps from the front door, a black van squealed to a halt in front of us, and men in black tactical gear and masks jumped out of the back.

"Don't resist," Volkov warned in a low voice. "Riley, whatever you do, do not try to escape." When she bristled, he turned amber eyes on her. "They will kill you without hesitation. Do not test them."

We'd already gotten the pep talk before we left the apartment, so we all knew what to expect. They went for Volkov and Craig first, hitting each man with a stun baton. Despite Volkov's warning, I saw the panic rising in Riley's flushed cheeks as their bodies slumped. I grabbed her hand before she could bolt—or worse, attack. Before I could reassure her we'd be okay, rough hands forced us apart and yanked our arms behind our backs. One of the men shoved a hood over my head, plunging me into darkness. He gave me a hard shove in the direction of the van. I stumbled but caught myself before I face-planted.

"Watch it," I snapped.

"Not another word," the man said, his voice guttural. "Give me an excuse, and I will end you."

I swallowed and nodded my understanding.

"Smart girl."

"Enough with the theatrics," Craig said. "Get on with it."

We were shuffled into the back of the van and shoved forcefully into the seats. Someone grabbed my arms and bound them in front of me with a zip tie, then did the same with my feet.

He must have moved down the line because the same voice that had threatened me earlier now warned Riley. "Same goes for you, pink. Keep your mouth shut if you want to live."

"Big man, hiding behind a mask," she mocked.

Volkov swore.

"You want a taste of this, too?" our captor asked, the buzz

of electricity ensuring her compliance. "I can do this all day long, sweetheart."

Thankfully, Riley didn't push back again.

The only thing that kept me from spiraling into panic was the fact that neither Craig nor Volkov seemed surprised at our reception. This must be standard operating procedure then. I closed my eyes and leaned back against the headrest, concentrating on the steady breathing of whoever was in the seat next to me.

Either the Compound was a long, windy drive from the apartment, or our escorts liked driving in circles. With a bag over my head, it didn't take long for me to lose all sense of time and direction. The men who had accosted us were silent, which made the whole trip even more unnerving. After the earlier threat, I decided not to take chances and kept my mouth shut for the drive. The sounds of the road eventually lulled me into a false sense of calm.

The van slowed down, and I felt a zing of magic like we'd crossed some kind of ward. Regardless of whether it was set to keep the Compound secret or to keep the prisoners in, the residual shock told me it was powerful magic. When the van stopped and someone yanked me to my feet, the fear came roaring back. Once I was standing, someone cut through the binding on my feet, so I could walk. They left my hands tied in front of me.

I felt a rifle nudge the middle of my back, and my captor bent close enough to bark orders in my ear. "Get moving, princess."

I was a lot of things, but no one had ever accused me of being a princess before. I had always been more of a string-creepy-doll-heads-together kind of kid than a tiara-wearing one. Not that it mattered to the psycho holding a gun against my back.

I started walking. Without the ability to see, walking wasn't as easy as it sounded. I started thinking about all the things I could walk into or off, like a cliff. Between the disorientation, the threat at my back, and the hood blanking out the world, the panic started setting in for real. I could feel the hood close in on me, whatever air was beneath it seeming to go thin. The more I gasped for air, the more the hood sucked in, amplifying the sensation of suffocation.

Craig must have been close enough to hear my erratic breathing because he risked our captors' ire to try to calm me. "Easy," he said. "You're okay. Try to think about something else." He grunted as if someone hit him, but he kept talking anyway. "It's like breathing through a mask."

His voice grounded me, and I focused on anything except the hood—the smell of industrial disinfectant, the pressure of the binding cutting into my wrists, the sound of our footsteps echoing down a hall. Slowly, my breathing returned to normal.

One second, we were walking down an enclosed hall and the next we were in an outdoor space. From the sounds of flesh hitting flesh and metal on metal, we seemed to be in the midst of some type of training. At first, I assumed we were in the prison yard. I imagined heavy weights and tattooed prisoners, maybe even a boxing ring to channel all that pent-up aggression. Then, a deep voice barked orders, directing the combatants to strike harder. It didn't sound like the directives of a prison guard. I jumped when the first gunfire erupted to my left and stumbled backward imagining a prison break. The solid body behind me didn't budge though, and I righted myself. Another round of gunfire punctuated the air.

"A firing range," I whispered.

The man behind me gripped my upper arm. "Quiet, little mouse." *Closer than a princess, I supposed.*

"Do what they say, and don't engage with them, Kali." Craig's voice was close.

I nodded even though he couldn't see it. Then, I heard a thud like a baton or end of a rifle striking bone.

"Do that again, and I'll take the toy gun you're carrying and wrap it around your neck," Craig growled. Whoever the culprit was must have heeded his warning because I didn't hear another thump.

"Is there a point to this?" Volkov sounded bored. "Because if you're trying to intimidate us with your weapons demo, you're going to have to try harder."

Someone chuckled. "I'm surprised you recognize the sounds of combat, Maxim. I was afraid you'd grown soft looking after your little flock." The man's voice was smooth, cultured, and completely out of place among the din of fighting surrounding us.

"Practice and combat are two different things, brother," Volkov taunted. "Something you would recognize if you didn't waste your life behind these walls serving your handlers."

I waited for the sound of a blow to the head or the electric buzz of the stun baton blazing to life, but neither came.

"If we're done measuring our dicks, can we get on with it?" Riley asked. "Because I really need to pee."

The mystery man laughed. "Who do we have here?" The sound of fabric rustling told me they were removing Riley's hood. The man whistled, "Well, well, aren't you a surprise? You hardly seem like the kind of company my brother keeps."

"Leave her alone, Aleksei," Volkov said.

"Take them off," Aleksei ordered.

A second later, my hood was gone. I blinked against the harsh daylight. We stood on the edge of a training yard unlike any I'd ever seen. It was set up in a courtyard, with two stories of stone prison caging us on all sides. Armed guards patrolled the roofline behind coiled barbed wire barriers, but strangely, none of their guns were aimed our direction. Instead, they were all pointed to the outside world, as if to protect those inside the Compound.

In the yard itself, men and women wearing form-fitting black clothes honed a variety of combat skills. Some were locked in hand-to-hand combat, the kicks and strikes so fast, I could barely track the movements. Others wielded weapons ranging from battle axes to high-powered rifles. But the most terrifying thing was not the weapons or the fighting, it was the blank looks and cold efficiency with which every one of them seemed to operate. This might be a supernatural prison, but you wouldn't know it from these people. Everyone looked human—deadly, but human. I didn't know if it was because they were actually human or because they trained like they were.

"Where are we?" The question slipped out before I could stop it. The man beside me raised his baton, but Aleksei stopped him with an almost imperceptible shake of his head.

"Welcome to the Compound." Aleksei turned his scrutiny on me. "You must be the necromancer."

"I am." Since my silence no longer seemed a requirement, I pressed my luck. "These can't all be guards, right?" I looked around the yard where dozens of people were training. If these were all the prison guards, why were they all out here instead of inside maintaining order among the inmates? And why risk having an armory within the prison itself? Having a weapons cache inside the prison walls seemed like a recipe for mutiny to me.

"I suppose it would depend on how you define guards," Aleksei answered vaguely. Before I could voice another question, he turned to Craig who was standing next to me. "Ward." Aleksei sounded almost respectful.

"Is all this really necessary?" Craig gestured toward the men who still crowded us, batons at the ready.

"We can't be too careful these days," Aleksei said.

From the tactical gear of the group who had brought us here to the uniform-clad combatants in the yard, every one of them save Aleksei was dressed in black. Aleksei wore a light gray three-piece suit, and unlike his brother, he looked like he had been born for a boardroom. Something told me he was no less dangerous for it.

The family resemblance would be hard to miss though. Both men were dark-haired and powerfully built, but where Max Volkov looked like the kind of man you wouldn't want to cross in a dark alley, his brother looked like a wealthy playboy who paid a personal trainer top dollar. The few times I'd seen Max smile, there hadn't been anything friendly in the flash of his teeth. By comparison, Aleksei had an easy smile and the laugh lines to go with it. Both men were predators, but I was betting only one of them liked to play with his prey before going in for the kill.

Aleksei stepped behind us, pausing when he got to Riley. He bent his head as if he were about to tell her a secret. Instead, he inhaled, watching his brother stiffen next to them. "Hmmm, not a wolf, then. What kind of shifter are you?" He looked genuinely curious, even if he had asked the question to push his brother's buttons.

Riley turned her head, so he was staring down into her

bright blue eyes. "The kind who thinks bullshit power trips are a waste of time." She smiled, pulled her hands apart, and handed him the zip tie she'd somehow managed to get out of.

Aleksei took it, a gleam of approval in his eye. The guy closest to Riley took a menacing step toward her, but Aleksei headed him off. "Come." He led us past a set of steel doors into the building.

Four armed guards waited on the other side of those doors —three men and one woman. All of them were vampires. Aleksei canted his head to the right, and two of the guards moved that direction.

"If you'll follow your escorts, they'll show you to your accommodations for the duration of the interview." Aleksei made it sound like we were headed to a high-end hotel suite rather than a prison waiting room.

Everyone fell in line between the guards, but Aleksei dropped a heavy hand on my shoulder to stop me from joining them. "You're with us."

The female vamp and the remaining male flanked me, their stillness making my pulse speed up. The woman smiled faintly while tapping out the rhythm of my heartbeat on her pant leg. *And isn't that comforting?*

CHAPTER 16

$\mathcal{E}$very hall we walked down was indistinguishable from the next. An endless row of metal doors lined those halls. Periodically, we passed a larger room with reinforced windows allowing a view inside. One appeared to be a medical bay with hospital beds, monitors, and people coming and going in white lab coats and scrubs. Most of the beds were empty, but the few that were occupied all held patients who bore signs of violence—gunshot wounds, a severed limb, cuts, and burns. Although I glanced at Aleksei as we passed, I didn't ask questions.

Another room was subdivided into smaller glass cages, half of which were occupied. Most of them housed predatory shifters in various states of rage. I made eye contact with a prowling Bengal tiger who paced back and forth in the confined space. My steps sped up. A vicious wolf shifted from woman to beast and back again as we passed. A grizzly beat his massive paws against the glass while roaring his frustration. While I watched, a sprinkler nozzle descended from the ceiling of the cage, and a fine mist sprayed down on the angry bear. Within seconds, his body slumped to the floor.

Despite the obvious danger they posed, I bristled at their treatment. *This is why I hate visiting zoos.* "Why are they contained like that?" I asked Aleksei. The glass cages hardly provided adequate space for large predators.

Aleksei paused and surveyed the room, forcing me to observe along with him. "These shifters have gone feral. They're unable to control the shift from human to beast."

"So, you lock them up in tiny cages?" I watched the smallest shifter in the room—a mangy coyote with wild eyes—throw itself against the barrier again and again.

Aleksei looked down at me, the steel in his voice at odds with his easy smile. "I teach them control."

"It doesn't look like you're doing a very good job of it," I mumbled.

"Come." He led the way to the other side of the room, where a larger cage held a wolverine. Aleksei tapped on the window that separated us. Two guards wearing full body armor nodded and stepped inside the wolverine's cage. Each of them held a stun baton. As we watched, one guard struck the wolverine with his baton, the full charge striking the animal in the chest. Before the animal could recover, the other guard repeated the attack.

I pounded on the glass, yelling for them to stop, but they didn't so much as glance in my direction. Both men scrambled out of the cage, barely making it to safety as the wolverine flashed its deadly claws and bared its teeth.

Aleksei pointed. "Watch."

A voice came over the speakers that were piped throughout the room. "Change!"

Despite the wolverine's obvious rage, he shifted, leaving a

small scruffy haired man in his place. The man's lips were curled in a snarl, but he tempered his breathing and relaxed his muscles until he stood naked and unthreatening in the middle of his cage.

If Aleksei was looking for some kind of acknowledgment of the effectiveness of his methods, he wouldn't get it from me. "That's barbaric."

"That's necessary. When you host a dangerous predator, control is the only thing that separates man from monster. You either learn to command the beast, or you're consumed by it."

"Is this for their benefit or yours?" I asked.

Aleksei met my eyes. "Both. You can't fight an external enemy if you're battling your own nature."

He didn't wait for my response, continuing down the hall. Aleksei halted next to a nondescript metal door, waiting for one of our vampire escorts to open it. I hesitated on the threshold until the female vampire shoved me inside, her slight form disguising a surprising amount of strength. I studied the room. Except for the small metal table with a chair on each side of it, there was no furniture. The room was brightly lit but barren. There weren't any two-way mirrors in the room, but the blinking red light on the camera mounted to the wall made it transparent we were being monitored.

"Please." Aleksei indicated the chair with its back to the door.

From the position of the camera facing my chair, they seemed to be more interested in observing visitors than monitoring the inmates. Aleksei remained behind me, a blatant intimidation tactic. Even though I knew what he was doing, I couldn't help the slight tremble in my hands. Because they rested bound in my lap, I consoled myself that at least he couldn't see them. Just as my nerves were ready to snap, Aleksei moved around me, stopping on the other side of the table.

Aleksei didn't sit down. Instead, he braced his hands on the table and leaned over me for a beat, not an ounce of his earlier friendliness in his expression. I couldn't help but smile. I was guessing by his immediate frown lines, people in this room didn't normally smile at him.

I looked up. "You might as well sit down. I've spent enough time with your brother that I'm familiar with this particular tactic."

"Fair enough." He sat in the chair across from me and studied me for several seconds, taking in the bright red bandana tied into a headband and my matching lipstick. I'd left Riley's jacket on the plane, so I was far more hillbilly rock than tough girl. "You're not what I was expecting," he admitted.

"What were you expecting?"

"When Maxim said he was bringing a necromancer, I assumed you'd be older." His eyes sparkled with humor. "More crone than bombshell."

I snorted. "Bombshell? Really?" These men sure loved their pet names. More endearments had been thrown at me since being snatched off the street than in my last ten dates combined.

He smiled. "I like you."

"Awesome." I lifted my zip-tied wrists. "Then maybe you can remove this. It's chafing."

I didn't expect him to actually do it, but he reached in his pocket, pulled out a switchblade, and cut through the binding. "It's Kali, right?"

I nodded.

"Well Kali, you may have guessed that we're not your typical lockup facility. Visitors are rare, as you can imagine. I'm trusting you to follow the rules." He tucked the knife away, leaving the zip tie on the table as a reminder.

"What are the rules?"

"Do what I say, when I say, and don't ask questions."

"Definitely a family resemblance," I muttered.

Aleksei flicked a finger toward the guards behind me. I didn't turn around, but the door closing confirmed at least one of the guards had left.

"You'll have twenty minutes to question Naomi—not a minute more. Make good use of your time." He stood to leave. "When you are finished, I will escort you out."

I hadn't expected to question Naomi without Craig present, and I wondered whether that was Aleksei's doing or at Naomi's request. A few minutes later, Naomi slid into the chair across from me, my guards once again taking up sentry duty on each side of the closed door. *So much for even the illusion of privacy then.*

Naomi looked much like she had the first time I met her, minus the cloying cloud of cigarette smoke that had surrounded her back then. Getting locked up in a supernatural prison was probably a fast track to kicking the habit. She glanced at the guards before settling her attention on me, her dark eyes wary as she waited for me to speak first.

I didn't bother with niceties. We were long past friendly small talk. Once someone helped a demon try to take over your body, there was no going back to casual conversation.

"I need to know everything about the ritual you performed." When she said nothing, I started at the beginning. "When did you find Samara's grimoire?"

Naomi shrugged. "I may have to meet with you, but I don't have to tell you anything."

She wasn't wrong. I wished I had Craig or Volkov here to play bad cop. It certainly wasn't my strong suit. As we stared at each other and the minutes ticked by, I ran through my options. Physical intimidation was out. I also couldn't dangle the usual carrot of freedom. We both knew she wasn't leaving the Compound alive. I mentally kicked myself for not being smart enough to smuggle in cigarettes for a bribe. I'd watched enough prison movies to know the currency.

Before I could decide on the best way to approach Naomi, one of the guards spoke into the Bluetooth headset he was wearing. "Yes, sir."

I glanced up at the security camera trained on my face. If I had any doubt Aleksei was monitoring me, the guard's response erased it. Although I'd seen how fast they could move earlier, the guard took his time crossing the room. When he moved behind Naomi's chair, the slight tremble gave away her fear. The guard stared at me as he shot fifty thousand volts of electricity into her body. Seeing my flinch, he flashed his fangs. Despite everything Naomi had done to me, seeing an old woman shocked into submission made me sick. I couldn't help but look away when she screamed, her body as rigid as a board. She slumped into her chair, breathing ragged.

The guard bent close to her ear. "Answer the questions."

After a minute to regain my composure, I reached into my pocket and pulled out the paper we found on Fiona's body. I flattened it on the table between us, watching Naomi as the blood drained from her face. "Recognize this?"

She reached for it, but I snatched it back before she could touch it.

"Where did you get that?" Naomi demanded.

"Someone has been killing witches, trying to turn them into vampires the way you tried to turn me." I kept the anger out of my voice. As I watched her, I caught the barest glimmer of interest. It was something. "One of the dead witches had it in her hand."

Naomi scowled. "That's impossible."

"Is it?" When she didn't answer, I held the paper up where she could see it. "This is from your aunt Samara's grimoire, isn't it?"

Naomi leaned closer, studying the ritual written on the page. Her brows pinched together, and her eyes darted back to mine. "No."

"No?" I scoffed, turning my head to look at the page. "That is definitely Samara's handwriting."

"It's her handwriting, but that page wasn't in her grimoire." Naomi shifted uncomfortably. "I knew her grimoire like the back of my hand, and that page was not in it."

I didn't think she was lying. "Could she have had another grimoire stashed somewhere?"

"I don't think so." Naomi's lips thinned. "It must be one of the missing pages."

"Missing pages?"

Naomi reached a hand toward the page. "May I see it?"

Reluctantly, I handed it to her, ready to snatch it back at the first word of an unfamiliar language passing her lips. She studied it for a long time and then ran her finger across the edge.

"It must have been torn out of her grimoire before I found it," she said.

If the book hadn't been in Naomi's possession since Samara's death, who'd had it? And why would someone tear one page out of a powerful witch's grimoire and leave the rest? "When did you find the grimoire?"

"Several months ago." Naomi ran a finger across the surface of the paper, tracing the symbols absently.

"Where did you find it?"

Naomi glanced at the guards and then back at me. "It was on her dresser."

I leaned back in my chair. "Are you telling me that in all the years you lived in the house, you didn't step foot in her room until a few months ago?" It was entirely too convenient to be true. Naomi had lived in Samara's childhood home for decades after Samara's death. I'd been in Samara's bedroom. If her grimoire had been on the dresser, it would have been visible with even a cursory look into the room.

"No. That's not what I'm saying" Naomi stared at the paper still in her hands. "I searched her room dozens of times over the years looking for it. I didn't find it until that day."

I tried to make sense of her answer. "Was it warded so you couldn't see it? Did you break her wards?"

Even as a teenager, Samara had been a powerful witch, known for creating intricate and virtually unbreakable wards. As her niece though, Naomi would have been able to detect them, and because of their blood relationship, she would also have been the person most likely to be able to break them.

"Wards are not invisibility spells." Naomi's tone dripped with condescension. "The grimoire wasn't there until the day I found it."

"You think someone took it and then returned it to her room?" The idea sounded farfetched. Who would have taken it? And why go to the trouble of putting it back?

Naomi handed the paper back to me. "I don't know. Maybe. Or maybe someone took it before she was killed."

I thought back to Samara's diary. "Could someone on the witches' council have taken it from the cave?"

"Of course, they could have." Naomi harbored a burning resentment toward the council, and given that they had sealed her aunt in a cave to die, I couldn't blame her.

They could have confiscated it because it contained a dangerous demon summoning ritual. They probably would have wanted to keep a ritual like that out of circulation. But if that was the case, why would Celeste deny they had it? And why had a page from it surfaced at the scene of a murder? Unless someone on the council was connected to the two dead fire elementals, it didn't make sense. It was an angle worth exploring, but I didn't want to jump to quick conclusions and overlook something.

The only other person Samara mentioned in her diary was her boyfriend. "What about Freddie? Could he have taken it?"

Naomi looked surprised. "How do you know about Freddie?"

"I took Samara's diary the day I came looking for her grimoire," I confessed.

Naomi huffed and glared at me. I wasn't about to apologize. If I had the chance, I'd take it again.

Even though she was angry with me, Naomi answered the question. "Freddie could have taken the grimoire. He was the only person in the cave with Samara before he went to the witches' council for help when things got out of hand."

Out of hand didn't even begin to describe what Samara had attempted, trying to summon a demon as powerful as Zepar. "And that got her killed," I said.

Naomi couldn't keep the bitterness out of her voice. "Stupid man."

Whoever had taken the grimoire had given it back to

Naomi. The question was why? Whether someone from the witches' council had taken it or Freddie had kept it for himself, they were the ones with the access and the knowledge to have taken Samara's grimoire. They were also the ones who would know about Naomi's relationship with Samara. If someone wanted to raise a demon, who better to recruit than Samara's niece? According to Celeste, there was no official record of the council gaining possession of the grimoire, which suggested a witch acting independently.

"Do you know who from the council got to the cave first?"

"Ruth," Naomi spat.

Ruth had been the head of the local witches' council and the motivation for Samara to raise Zepar in the first place. Samara's diary outlined the plan she and Freddie hatched to summon Zepar. The goal was to use the demon to make Ruth fall in love with Freddie with the hope that Ruth would lift the archaic rules against human-witch relationships.

Samara's death had happened seventy years ago when Naomi had been but a child. If Ruth had taken the grimoire, she most likely had passed it down. "Did Ruth have any children?"

Naomi sneered. "She wasn't exactly the mothering kind."

"I know Ruth had sisters on the council. Did they have children?"

"No."

I'd have to verify that with Celeste. Naomi hadn't exactly proven herself trustworthy so far. But if she was right, either Ruth took the grimoire and a random person stumbled over it after her death, or Freddie took it.

"What was Freddie's last name?" I asked Naomi. Samara's diary hadn't mentioned it.

"It's been a long time." She concentrated until she had it. "Masterson. His name was Frederick Masterson."

"Did you stay in touch with Freddie?" Maybe she knew if he had children.

"No. I never saw him again. He didn't even show up for Samara's funeral, which was probably a good thing after what he did. Why?"

"I wondered if he had family in the area, someone who might have inherited the book and known what it was." I glanced at the clock. We didn't have a lot of time left, and Naomi clearly didn't have the answers to this line of questioning, so I moved on. "Regardless of how you got the book, why did you use it on me? What was in it for you?"

Naomi's face blanked, but not before I caught the flash of fear in her eyes. *Interesting.*

"It wasn't your idea."

Her body tensed. "No."

"Someone came to you?"

She didn't answer.

"I talked to the two witches who were killed recently." I studied Naomi's discomfort. "Both claimed a witch and a vampire were working together to turn them. Do you know who they might be?"

"Witches and vampires don't work together." Naomi spoke with the absolute certainty that came from a deep divide.

"According to the witches, there was one person present to perform the ritual and another to compel them into compliance."

Naomi studied me thoughtfully. "Why do you assume it was a witch who performed the ritual?"

"Because humans lack the magic to call demons."

"True," she conceded. "But necromancers are also capable of performing a summoning ritual."

Craig had mentioned the same thing.

Naomi noted my discomfort with a self-satisfied smirk. "You didn't consider that. I wonder why that is."

I had considered it, even if I didn't want to, but the names Meira gave me didn't turn up any red flags when Craig checked into them. "Is any necromancer able to perform the summoning ritual?" Only powerful witches had the magic to back such a spell. I wondered if the same was true for necromancers.

"No. There are weak necromancers like there are weak witches. And as you well know, there are powerful ones. But a demon summoning is easier for a necromancer than a witch."

That meant that the number of necromancers capable of performing the ritual was likely bigger than the list we'd investigated. "Why is it easier for a necromancer?"

Naomi tapped on the table. "Because you're already connected to the spirit realm."

I had suspected the answer, but I'd needed the confirmation. Filing the information away for later, I switched topics. "Was Zepar the only one you worked with? No vampire?"

Naomi narrowed her eyes. "I do not work with vampires." She glared at the guards when she said it.

"Yet, you have no problem working with demons to make vampires."

Her lips thinned, but she didn't answer.

"Do you know of any other witches in Kansas City who would want to turn fire elementals into vampires?"

Naomi jerked in surprise before catching herself and slipping back into a mask of disinterest. "How would I know?

The witches there had nothing to do with me." I could practically see the wheels turning in her head.

Time with Naomi was running out. I considered who might benefit from an army of super vampires, and one man rose to the top of my list. I reached into my purse and pulled out the stack of photographs, stopping on the one with the master vampire's face.

I glanced at the slow blinking red light of the camera, knowing what I was about to do was not my smartest idea. Still, I held up the photo facing the camera, so Naomi could see it. "Do you recognize this man?"

She squinted at his face, but there wasn't a glint of recognition. "Never seen him before."

Disappointed, I stuffed the photos back in my purse. "Look. Zepar left you in here without a backward glance. You were a tool to him like I was, and now someone is targeting lone witches as we speak, trying to turn them and killing them in the process. If there is anything you can tell me about the ritual or about what Zepar's plan was, it could help protect the next witch from ending up in here, dead, or worse, as a vampire."

Some might argue death was the worst option in that list, but based on Naomi's reaction, she was firmly in the death over vampire camp. "Zepar didn't tell me what he had planned, but based on little things he said, you were a key piece of it."

I pivoted back to the question she hadn't answered. "And he was the only one you worked with?" When she looked away, I pushed harder. "Because that would mean summoning him had been your idea. It would mean you personally choreographed this whole thing."

She dropped her head toward her chest, closing her eyes.

"There was another. He used a distortion spell, so I never saw his face or heard his real voice."

That fit with Anne and Fiona's experiences. "You're afraid of him."

"Of course, I am." She looked around the room, pausing on the guards. "The only reason I'm alive is because I'm in here."

The door opened behind me. "Time's up," Aleksei said.

I chanced a parting shot. "Why did you do it? What was in it for you?"

Naomi gave me a sly look. "A place at the table."

"What table?" I demanded.

Naomi ignored me. The guard crossed to Naomi and helped her to her feet before escorting her out of the room. Twenty minutes hadn't been nearly enough time. I was leaving with more questions than answers, but since there was nothing I could do about it, I watched her go.

Instead of binding my hands again like I expected, Aleksei reached down and picked up the zip tie, shoving it in his pocket. "Did you get what you needed?"

"I don't know what I got."

"Mmm. That's a shame." He sounded genuine. "Shall we?" Aleksei gestured toward the door.

Although I wasn't thrilled about the idea of walking with him at my back, I stood and left through the open door. In the hallway, he stepped up next to me.

"No blindfold?" I asked.

"Not yet," he said.

Minutes later, he led me into a comfortable break room with vending machines and an industrial-sized coffee pot. Riley, Craig, and Max Volkov sat at a long table. Craig scanned me as I walked into the room, no doubt checking for injuries.

"I'm fine," I assured him.

Neither Craig nor Volkov asked about my conversation with Naomi. I assumed it was because Aleksei made no move to leave us. He checked his watch. "Your transportation is running behind. They should return within the hour. Until then…"

"We're fine here," Volkov interrupted him, sounding even more surly than usual.

"No tour, then?" Aleksei mocked.

Volkov stiffened. "I've seen all I care to see of this place."

"You didn't always feel that way." Aleksei stood staring at his brother. Judging by his expression, whatever had happened between them didn't alter the fact Aleksei missed the connection the two of them once had. When Volkov said nothing, Aleksei's expression hardened. "Craig, may I have a word?"

Until the first-name basis, it hadn't registered that they knew each other, but the familiarity was unmistakable. Given Craig's relationship with Max Volkov, it shouldn't have surprised me. Max kept his expression blank as the other two men left the room for a private conversation, but the tic in his jaw said it bothered him.

"What did he mean about you not always feeling that way?" Riley asked.

Volkov looked away. "When I was younger, I trained here."

It was a half-answer, which sparked even more questions. "Trained for what?" Riley asked.

Volkov's eyes flashed to his wolf, and he clenched his hands into fists. "Whatever they wanted."

Riley and I exchanged looks, but we knew better than to push further. When Craig came back in the room a few minutes later, he didn't share what Aleksei had wanted, and Volkov didn't ask.

The escort out of the facility was as friendly as our ride here. After a new round of zip ties and hoods, we were all shoved back in the van. At least our contingent of super soldiers were less abrasive on the way back. Again, the van drove in what I suspected were pointless circles. Since we had found out Max had trained at the Compound in his younger years, the whole cloak-and-dagger routine made even less sense. Obviously, this was all show for the benefit of the newbies. Knowing that went a long way toward dispelling my fear.

This time when the van stopped, our hoods and bindings were removed before we exited the vehicle. I assumed they didn't want to deal with the fallout of dropping kidnapping victims off at an international airport. As soon as we were all out, they slammed the doors shut and drove off.

Riley looked around the airport. "Why did they drop us off here? All our stuff is at the apartment."

"I had Theo deliver our bags to the plane already," Volkov said.

"Who's Theo?" Riley asked.

Volkov opened the door to the terminal and waved us inside. "The doorman."

Before I made it inside, a man stepped into my path, cutting me off from the group. Through the window, I could see several more men surrounding the other three. The men were all dressed in expensive business suits, and from most vantage points, they would look like a group headed to a professional conference or a business retreat. From where I stood, though, I had a clear view of the weapon pressed against Riley's temple. Even though Craig was virtually bullet proof, Riley was not, and holding her at gunpoint meant no one would risk doing something heroic.

The man blocking my way smiled, making it a point to show me his fangs. I waited for a compulsion that never came. "Master Ratcliff extends an invitation for an audience."

I tamped down the urge to roll my eyes.

The vampire extended his arm to indicate the car idling at the curb. "Shall we?" He smiled before turning back to the car and opening the passenger side door.

CHAPTER 17

J'd stared at my grandmother's photo long enough to recognize the man sitting in the back seat. Judging from the long legs stretched out in front of him, Wallace Ratcliff was taller than I'd expected. He still had that soft look about him that he wore in the photograph, but I'd been around enough vampires to know not to trust it.

His minion checked his watch. "Master Ratcliff's time is precious."

I glanced back at the airport terminal, but the wall of vampires blocked my view. My heartrate accelerated as I climbed in the car, the door slamming shut behind me. The interior was all soft leather and expensive upgrades. No matter how luxurious the ride, the present company guaranteed I wasn't going to enjoy it.

Ratcliff got right down to business. "Do you know who I am?" The undercurrent of menace was difficult to miss.

"I do." I watched him warily, expecting a strike at any moment.

He extended a pale hand—the same hand that may well

have killed my grandmother. I tried not to think of that as I reluctantly reached out to shake the master vampire's hand. Instead of shaking it, he lifted my hand, brushing his cool, full lips against my skin. I didn't bother hiding my revulsion.

He held on even when I tried to pull away. Finally, he released my hand. "Wallace Ratcliff III."

If I were a hundred-plus-year-old vampire named Wallace, I'd make it a point to change my name to something much cooler, like Darius or Angelus. Any name with an *-us* at the end qualified as an appropriate vamp name in my book. But Wallace? No one was going to quake in fear at the mention of Wally the Vampire. I was smart enough to keep my musings to myself.

With his tousled golden hair and full cheeks, Ratcliff looked angelic—at least until you caught sight of his eyes. It wasn't even the blood-red glint to them that unnerved me, although that was enough to send chills skating through my body. His eyes were flat, as if a human soul had never resided in his body. From Meira's lessons, I knew the original soul must still be in him. A vampire was made when a ritual called forth a demon and forced it into a dying host, the demon using the human soul as an anchor. Once inside, the demon overwhelmed and suppressed the soul. This vampire had buried the soul so deep, there wasn't even a hint of humanity left.

"I understand you have been asking about me," he said.

I nodded. "I'm glad your vampire gave you the message." With Craig's etiquette lessons in mind, I aimed for polite despite the way Ratcliff made my skin crawl. "I appreciate you taking the time to answer my questions."

Ratcliff leaned back against his seat, studying me as if I were a sideshow curiosity. I kept my gaze fixed on the lower half of his face, not wanting to risk a compulsion. Ratcliff had a soft jawline, his pale skin smooth and clean shaven. I wondered how many people fell prey to that baby face, not seeing the predator until his fangs were buried in their veins.

His lips curved. "You surprised me wandering into my domain like a lamb to the slaughter."

I stiffened.

"If not for your bodyguard, we may have chatted sooner."

I wondered if he had been inside the house, watching us through the first-floor window just as he had watched my grandmother all those years ago.

"I decided it better to bide my time so we could have a one-on-one chat." Seeing my dawning understanding that—somehow—he had been watching and waiting for the opportunity to take me, his smile widened. "I have eyes and ears everywhere, you know." He leaned closer. "Even at the Compound."

I thought back to the camera in the room where I interviewed Naomi and wondered if Aleksei was the one who told him. Even though I didn't trust Aleksei, I didn't want to think he worked for this man. More likely, one of the vamps who had been in the room where I questioned Naomi tipped Ratcliff off.

I ignored his last proclamation, unwilling to stroke his ego. "And here we are." I reached inside my purse for the photos, but Ratcliff stopped me with a sharp shake of his head. "Not here."

When I'd gotten in the car, I'd hoped to have our chat while driving around the block. Obviously, that had been wishful thinking. The longer we drove, the more my heart raced and my breathing shallowed. Before the panic could overtake me, soft wings stirred against my breast. My skin warmed where my tattoo was etched, which I found oddly comforting. The magic swelled within me, the tattoo calling to it. Whatever residual magic existed in the tattoo bound the crow and me together, and it lent me strength. My senses were sharper than normal, bringing me sights and sounds from distances beyond those of a human. I silently gave thanks for sketchy tattoo artists and magical ink, even if I didn't understand how it worked.

I had no doubt Craig would find a way to neutralize the threat to Riley and come for me. But it would take him awhile to find me and even longer to get past the horde of vampires someone like Ratcliff surrounded himself with. For now, I was on my own.

According to Meira, I would one day be able to control vampires. While I could sometimes break a vampire compulsion and occasionally locate the human soul within a vampire, so far, that was as close as I got. As I sat across from Ratcliff, I wondered if my new tattoo might give me the power boost I needed. Because there was no time like the present to take it for a test run, I snapped my focus to the spiritual plane and searched for the soul that Ratcliff ruthlessly repressed. Spotting the barest glimpse of a human soul coiled inside him, I reached for it, ready to hold on to it like a puppet string. Before I could make contact, a barrier slammed into place, locking me out.

"Are you really so arrogant you think you can control a master vampire?" His laugh was throaty and good natured. His eyes told a different story.

The car slowed to a stop, and I looked out my window. My grandmother's photos hadn't done the master vampire's home justice. In person, it was more beautiful for the worn edges, the crumbling stone steps, and the note of decay it wore like a warning. The car stopped mere feet from the back entrance. Here, there were no prying eyes. While I'd been nervous crammed in the backseat with Ratcliff, the idea of stepping foot in his home amplified my fear.

The driver opened my door and extended a hand to help me out like a gentleman. I found it difficult to reconcile the veneer of politeness vampires seemed to embrace with the violence and darkness residing within them. I ignored his hand and climbed out on my own.

Ratcliff got out behind me, his eyes blown red and the compulsion rolling off his tongue before I could brace for it. "Come," he demanded.

I fought against his hold. Unfortunately, by the time I broke free, we were already inside.

Wallace Ratcliff led me to his front parlor like a Victorian spinster. "Welcome to my home." He stood far too close to me for my comfort.

I quickly assessed the threats in the room. Two vampires behind me and one very dangerous master vampire next to me. Using my budding necromancer skills was out. While I was confident I could yank the souls out of the two vampires at my back, I'd already tried and failed to control Ratcliff. And three against one wouldn't be good odds even for a skilled supernatural fighter. While I was physically stronger than I had been a year ago, I wouldn't be winning cage matches against vampires any time soon. There would be no fighting my way out of this one. I hated being weak in a world dominated by the strong.

Ratcliff watched with amusement as I catalogued potential escape routes. "Why is it you came looking for me, Ms. James?"

I reached into my purse for the photographs and held up

the one of his house. "My grandmother took this photo almost ten years ago. Do you remember her?"

He didn't glance at the photo. "Who is your grandmother?"

"Dottie Barron," I said.

"I have no recollection of anyone by that name."

I dug in my wallet until I found the old photo I carried of my grandmother, Claire, and me. As I held it up for Ratcliff's inspection, I watched him carefully for signs of recognition, but he was impassive. I pointed to my grandmother. "Do you remember seeing this woman?"

"She hardly looks like the kind of woman I associate with." It wasn't a denial as much as a dodge. He returned his gaze to me, but after his earlier compulsion, I made sure to look anywhere but his eyes.

I flipped through the stack of photos, stopping on the closeup of Claire's killer. "Who is this man?"

Even if Ratcliff was telling the truth about not knowing my grandmother, his gaze lingered too long on the man's face for him to be a stranger. "Did you really come here to show me your photo collection?"

"I need to know his name."

"I'll answer your question if you answer mine," he challenged.

"Deal. What's your question?"

"You're quite the unusual necromancer, Ms. James. I have it on good authority you have a remarkable skill set."

I weighed which response was less likely to get me killed and went with the truth. "So I am told."

"Rumor has it you briefly hosted a powerful demon before somehow managing to expel him from your body. Is that true?" Ratcliff's voice was rife with skepticism.

"It's true." I lifted the photo of the man's face again, putting it in Ratcliff's line of sight. "Now I've answered the question, so it's your turn. Who is this man?"

"He's no one of consequence," Ratcliff said.

"He is to me."

"And why would a guest in my home ten years ago be of interest to a woman like you?" he asked.

"He killed my sister."

Ratcliff tsked. "Such messy business."

I bit the inside of my cheek, the tinge of pain a distraction from the urge to attack him. "I'd like his name."

"I'm afraid I can't help you, there." He brushed it off as if it were an inconsequential thing.

Another vampire walked into the room, interrupting us before I could press further. "I'm tired of waiting." She didn't specify what exactly she was waiting for, but she ran her tongue across the tip of her fang when she caught me looking.

She was as tall as the master vampire and reed thin, but unlike her master, there was nothing angelic about her. If not for her flushed cheeks, rabid smile, and eyes that hinted insanity, she might have passed for pretty. However, I found it impossible to see beyond the crazed predator circling me.

The vampire stepped behind me and tilted her head, so she was inches from my throat. Although the urge to step away was strong, I didn't move. Everything with a vampire was a head game. I held my ground.

"Kenzie, would you escort our guest to the dining room?"

There were a lot of ways I would have liked to spend the next hour—almost all of them resulting in Ratcliff losing his head—but a dinner party wasn't among them. "I'm not hungry."

His smile was predatory. "Oh, but I am."

My heart raced, as he'd probably intended. Kenzie stared

at the pulse in my neck as if hypnotized. Before I could react, she leaned down and swiped her tongue up the side of my throat. I jumped and put some distance between us, wiping my neck with the collar of my shirt. "Gross. What is wrong with you?"

She clapped her hands in my face. "Run along, then. You don't want to be late." She glided to the other side of the room, opening a set of pocket doors to reveal a formal dining room.

When I didn't immediately follow, it earned me a jab to the kidney from one of the vampires behind me.

"We can continue our conversation over dinner," Ratcliff said.

I didn't believe he had any intention of giving me the name I came here for, but outnumbered as I was, I didn't have much choice. Because the last thing I wanted to do was turn my back on a master vampire, I edged toward Kenzie without letting him out of my sight. Ratcliff seemed to find me endlessly amusing.

I didn't get a good view of the formal dining room until I was poised at the entrance. A long wooden table stretched the expanse of the large room. At least a dozen chairs around it were occupied. I was guessing they were all vamps. In the time I'd been in the house, I hadn't heard a sound to indicate this room was anything but empty. Even as I stepped inside, the room was unnaturally silent. The vampires' stillness was so complete, it was as if they were carved of wood rather than born flesh and blood. As one, a dozen pair of red-ringed eyes turned to look at me. Kenzie skipped to an empty seat. When she sat, her face blanked, and her body mirrored the stillness of the others.

I took an involuntary step back, but Ratcliff stood behind

me blocking my exit. He cupped a hand beneath my elbow and propelled me toward the only remaining seat. When we reached the head of the table, he forced me into the chair.

The table was set for a feast, laden with fine China, polished silver, and crystal goblets. In the center of each place setting, a crimson napkin was folded to resemble a lotus flower. However, there was no trace of food or wine anywhere, and no scent of cooking hung in the air. Near the head of the table was a single bone-handled knife, the kind more likely to be used to slice through a human vein than to cut up a steak.

The master vampire placed a heavy hand on my shoulder. With his free hand, he reached around me for the nearest goblet and raised it in the air. "Soon, we will break our fast together. But first, if you will all humor me, I have some questions for our guest."

No one moved. It was like sitting at a table of creepy-ass dolls, their blank faces inspiring more terror than bared fangs ever could. To avoid the unnerving stares of the vampires seated around me, I kept my gaze fixed on a divot in the wall. Slightly larger than a fist, I wondered if the divot had come from a head slamming against the wall.

Ratcliff leaned into my chair, his voice close to my ear when he spoke. "How is it possible, Ms. James, that you expelled a demon?"

I shrugged, gauging the distance to the bone-handled knife. "I don't know," I answered truthfully.

"And Zepar, no less," he marveled. "May I see his mark?"

"Why?" I asked suspiciously.

"Call it curiosity, if you will."

Feeling the stirring of wings on my skin, I brushed my shirt aside. "His mark is beneath this tattoo."

Ratcliff stepped in front of me, examining the crows far longer than I would have preferred. When he looked up, his eyes were wary—not the reaction I'd expected at all.

"What are you going to do with me?"

"That's a good question." He tapped a finger against the crystal goblet he still held. "I'd planned to cut your throat, tap your vein, and then toast to eliminating the threat to our continued survival with a glass of your blood."

I'd hardly categorize the possibility I could one day compel vampires as a threat, but Ratcliff was serious. The crow began to stir, the connection between my magic and that of my tattoo flared to life. Whatever this magic was, my fear slid away, and in its place settled a cold determination to become the threat he feared.

I went for the knife, but Ratcliff anticipated my move. He forced my hand flat and embedded the knife between my fingers, my hand pinned like a butterfly to his table. I hissed in pain.

He kept his hand on top of the knife. "Now, I think I will keep you for a while, lest you prove useful."

The tattoo pumped me full of adrenaline until the knife in my hand felt no worse than a paper cut. I smiled at him, meeting his gaze. He tried to compel me, but nothing happened. He took a step back, letting go of the knife. I smiled wider, grasped the handle of the knife and yanked it from my hand.

Before I had time to bury it in his eye, the sound of glass breaking drew my attention. It was the only warning before figures in head-to-toe black surrounded the table, a familiar face the last to join us. Aleksei leaned against the door frame, still dressed in his tailored suit.

At the sight of Aleksei, my magic receded, the crows

settling back into flat ink against my skin. The pain now radiating from the stab wound had me clutching my hand and gasping.

Ratcliff stepped closer to Aleksei. "You dare too much." Ratcliff's fangs dropped from his gums as he hissed the warning.

Kenzie tipped her chair back, forcing the man behind her to step back to avoid the crash. She latched onto his thigh in an instant, grinning around the blood pouring from the wound. The man swung the baton, connecting with the back of her head, but she held fast.

When he raised it for another blow, Ratcliff snapped, "Enough." The man stilled his hand for a second, and Kenzie grudgingly removed her fangs from the leg she had been gnawing on.

Throughout all of it, Aleksei appeared unconcerned. "We've come for the girl."

"On what authority?" Ratcliff demanded.

I scanned behind him, expecting Craig to be there, but there was no sign of him.

"She is under the protection of the Enclave and is not to be touched."

The angelic mask Ratcliff wore slipped, the demon visible in his rage. "Since when?" he ground out, eyeing me like a rare steak.

"Since Zepar tried to possess her." Aleksei sounded bored.

No one was more shocked by that pronouncement than me. *How could I have been under some kind of protection order for over a month and not known it?*

Before Ratcliff could question him further, Aleksei brushed a piece of lint off his sleeve. "That's all you need to know, Ratcliff. Anything else is above my pay grade."

Ratcliff slammed his goblet on the table, shattering the crystal, then stormed out of the room.

Aleksei looked at me and snapped his fingers. "Come."

I reared my head back. "Are you serious?" Even if he had just saved my ass, I didn't appreciate being called to heel like a pet dog.

Aleksei turned for the door. "We should leave before he decides against graciously accepting my authority on the matter."

Unwilling to leave any of my blood at Ratcliff's table, I wiped the bloody knife on my pant leg and tossed it on the table. On shaky legs, I followed Aleksei Volkov out of the vampire's domain before Ratcliff had a change of heart and decided to put me back on the menu.

CHAPTER 18

Jackassery must be genetic because Aleksei refused to answer even the most basic questions on the drive to the airport. It was a long drive though, and I continued firing questions at him, hoping to wear him down. I never did.

When we arrived, he deposited me curbside with a business card tucked into my purse and a cryptic message that Craig would be back to collect me, like I was a forgotten piece of luggage. It was petty, but I flipped off his car as it merged into traffic.

Before I had a chance to text Riley and Craig to let them know I was here, I spotted Craig walking toward me. Worry lined his face, and as soon as he reached me, he scanned me from head to toe, checking for injuries. He paused at the white gauze Aleksei had wrapped around my injured hand.

Aleksei had assured me there wouldn't be any permanent damage, even if it did hurt like a sonofabitch. "I'm fine."

"That makes one of us," Craig said.

Most men I knew made a big production out of their anger —all bluster and aggressive body language. Craig wore his anger like armor. And from the rigid way he held himself as he unwrapped my hand, he was madder than I'd ever seen him.

"Stab wound." There was no trace of sympathy in his pronouncement.

I tried to make light of it. "Nothing a couple painkillers won't solve."

"We need to go."

I turned toward the airport terminal, but Craig's hand on my arm stopped me. "We'll be flying without the plane."

It wouldn't be the first time he'd taken me up in the sky, but flying from Romania to KC? I followed him as he hailed a taxi. "Where are Riley and Volkov?"

"We thought it best to get the plane out of Bucharest." Craig opened the door for me. "And you and I need to have a conversation about what just happened."

I climbed into the back of the taxi. "You're flying us the whole way home?" *How is that even possible?*

Craig slid in beside me and gave the driver directions before answering. "Not quite. I'll get us to the private airfield where Max had the plane land."

The taxi dropped us outside of the city, which meant the trip cost a ridiculous sum. By the time the taillights disappeared, it was almost dusk.

Craig turned to me. "We'll wait for the cover of night to leave." He wouldn't look at me as he headed for some flat ground near a grove of trees. "Sit."

I sank to the ground without argument, resting my back against one of the trees. He lowered himself to the ground across from me, bracing against another tree. I started to tell him what happened, but he cut me off with a look. I waited, not sure what to say anyway.

Craig studied my face, his eyes dipping back down to my hand. "Why did you get in that car?"

I let my head drop back against the bark of the tree. "It was my shot to get the name of Claire's killer."

Craig shook his head. "You had a photo of the man, Kali. Did it occur to you that there might be another way to get his identity that didn't involve you jumping into a car with Ratcliff?" He let out a frustrated breath. "I would have taken care of it when we got back to the States. I could have run his photo through facial recognition software."

"Maybe," I conceded. "But the photo is grainy, and the man is more than likely a vampire. It's a fifty-fifty shot at best that you would find a match. I was one hundred percent sure Ratcliff knew the man's identity."

"And did you get his name?"

Even with my eyes closed, I could feel the weight of his stare. "No," I admitted.

"So, you risked your life for nothing." He sounded weary.

I recognized the undercurrent of fear he felt, and I searched for something to say but came up empty. I could insist there was had been no choice, that the master vampire would have forced me into the car if I had declined. But I didn't know because I hadn't declined. Craig and I sat in silence for a long time, the sun painting a brilliant sky as we waited for darkness to come.

I looked at him. "I'm sorry I scared you. But I can't stand by and wait for you to take care of things. Not when it means ignoring a lead to the man who killed Claire." My need for vengeance may have lain dormant for a while, but the encounter with Zepar had made it roar back to life within me.

If I was honest, it had been my guiding light so long, I didn't know how to function without it.

"I won't ask you to stop looking for justice, but you can't keep doing this—throwing yourself into danger with no thought of how you'll get out of it." Craig watched me with an intensity that shook me. "Whatever this survivor's guilt is that you're carrying, you need to let it go before it drags you down into the grave with her."

I didn't even try to stop the tears suddenly blurring my vision. The grief hit so deeply, I couldn't speak around it. All I could do was open the floodgates and let it take me.

But Craig wasn't done with me yet. "Because that hole Claire left when she died," he said, tapping his chest with a fist, "is the same hole you'll leave in me when you get yourself killed, and in Riley and Emma, in your family, and in anyone else who gives a damn about you. Claire's not the only one who matters, so stop acting as if she is."

He was right. My recklessness no longer endangered just me. Even though Craig wasn't finished being angry, he crossed the ground and held me while I cried. Whatever walls I had left came down in his arms. I didn't know if I deserved him, but I was going to do my best to hold tight to him anyway.

I couldn't find the words to reassure him, so I nodded. Then, I tore a chunk of gauze off my hand and dried my eyes.

"Good," he said. "Now tell me what happened."

I filled Craig in on everything that had happened after I was taken, including Aleksei's declaration I was now under the protection of the Enclave.

"I have no idea what that means," I admitted.

From Craig's expression, he did.

I sat up straighter. "What is the Enclave? A secret organization?" That would at least explain why Aleksei had been so tight-lipped.

"Not exactly," Craig said. "The Enclave is the ultimate authority for the supernatural world. Most supernaturals know of its existence, but because so few have direct interactions with the group, most of what is known amounts to rumor and conjecture." He glanced at me. "Plus, the members' identities are closely guarded secrets."

That didn't sound so different than a secret organization to me. "If so few people come into contact with the Enclave, then how do they govern?"

"You may have noticed we are a hierarchal bunch."

I snorted. That was the understatement of the year.

"As you know, local matters are handled by the leadership of each group—shifters, witches, vampires, and necromancers."

I nodded and counted myself fortunate to be in the latter category. Meira might not be my favorite person, but I couldn't imagine living within the rigid confines of either the shifter or vampire communities.

"Each of those groups also has national and worldwide leadership," Craig elaborated. "What can't be solved within the community's governing structure is handled by the Tribunal of that territory. Above all of those is the Enclave, which rules all supernaturals."

"Do Tribunals refer problems they can't solve to the Enclave?" I jumped in, wanting to get this all straight. Like it or not, my life was now subject to rules I barely understood.

"It's not quite that linear." Craig thought about it for a bit before putting it into terms I'd understand. "The Tribunals manage the practical governance tasks and enforce the Enclave's edicts. Think of the Tribunals like the court system and the Enclave as a group of the world's most powerful leaders."

I had a hunch the Enclave's members shared more in common with dictators than democracies. "How many members are on the Enclave?"

Craig shrugged. "No one really knows. The predominant theory is that each faction has a representative. How they're chosen and who they are is anyone's guess."

It sounded like a lot of power in very few hands to me. "And Aleksei and the Compound—where do they fit into all of this?"

From the tensing of his body, it was a subject Craig didn't care to discuss. I was surprised when he answered. "They're our version of the CIA."

I whistled. "So, it's not a supernatural prison?" That would explain the plentiful weapons and intense training.

"It's a prison of sorts, but only the strongest supernatural criminals are sent there for rehabilitation." Craig looked away.

"I'm guessing rehabilitation doesn't involve art therapy and GEDs."

Craig chuckled. "No. It most definitely does not. The Compound takes supernaturals with exceptional abilities and turns them into spies and assassins. We call them Shadows because no one sees them coming."

"Wouldn't that make them hard to control? I mean if you take the strongest criminals and train them to be even more deadly and stealthy, what stops them from going rogue?"

"Magical collars."

"Was everyone there collared?" I asked.

"Most. Aleksei is an exception. He's there voluntarily. Because he was not sentenced to serve the Compound, he's not bound with a collar."

I watched the last color leach from the sky. "Aleksei said I have been under the protection of the Enclave since Zepar tried to turn me. Did you know about that?" I stared in Craig's direction. With only a sliver of moonlight tonight, I could no longer read his expression.

"I had no idea. You're sure Aleksei said the Enclave?" Craig sounded worried.

And that, in turn, made me nervous. The last thing I needed was to land on the radar of a group who governed like gods. I tilted my head back against the tree and studied the stars lighting the night. "Positive. What exactly does it mean to be under their protection, anyway?"

"The governing bodies will be made aware of your protected status."

My head snapped up. "That's it?" *What kind of protection is a stiff warning?*

Craig sighed. "No. Anyone who attempts to harm you will be dispatched by the Shadows assigned to monitor you. Few people defy the Enclave and live to tell about it."

I swallowed, not liking the idea of having deadly assassins as babysitters. "You're telling me these Shadows have been watching me for a month, and none of us knew it?"

"That's exactly what I'm telling you. They're called Shadows for a reason, Kali. You'll have no idea who they are, but I guarantee they'll be somewhere nearby. Even if you managed to spot one, another would be sent to take that Shadow's place."

Despite the mild temperature, I shivered, imagining people watching me without my knowledge. *I better not wake up with the creepers standing over me in my sleep.*

Craig stood and extended a hand, pulling me to my feet. "Time to go." He took a step back and shifted into his other form, a massive, seven-foot-tall gargoyle with the strength to decapitate with his bare hands and skin thick enough to be bulletproof. Despite an appearance so terrifying that even supernaturals gave him a wide berth, I went to him without hesitation. Underneath that fierce exterior beat the same steady heartbeat as the man I was falling in love with.

Craig bent down so I could wrap my arms around his neck and lifted me with an arm locked around my waist. Before he could leave the ground, I asked the question that had been in the back of my mind since this conversation began. "Volkov said he trained at the Compound. Was he trained as a Shadow?"

Craig prepared to launch us into the air, his wings unfolding behind him. We cleared the tree line before he answered. "We both were."

As soon as I boarded the plane bound for Kansas City, I was out, sleeping the entire flight home. I woke to Craig shaking my shoulder when it was time to get off the plane. Despite my half-hearted protests, he insisted on driving me home. "I'll bring you back for your car tomorrow, but you're in no shape to drive."

Riley joined us. "Unless you want me to drive it to your apartment."

I laughed. "You're funny, but that would be a big nope. I just got it back from the shop, and I'd rather not have to send it back."

"Can't blame a girl for trying." Even though her words were teasing, the hug she gave me was tight enough to let me know I'd scared her. Riley may not have read me the riot act like Craig and Volkov had, but her worry hit me even harder. After a quick goodbye, she wandered over to where Volkov was unloading the rest of the luggage. Either Craig had gotten her up to speed while I slept off my adrenaline crash, or Riley was waiting until tomorrow to ambush me for all the gory details.

After the extended nap I'd taken onboard, I was wide awake by the time we made it to my apartment. As usual, Craig insisted on walking me up and doing a quick sweep. Remembering the promise of Shadows watching my back, I closed all the blinds. Then, I draped a bath towel over the top of my bedroom curtains for good measure.

Craig was waiting for me when I came back into the living room. I moved in for a hug, and he tucked me against his chest, holding me tightly enough I knew he was still shaken up about my abduction.

"I'm okay," I reassured him.

"I know." But he squeezed me a little tighter. "Tomorrow, I'll run the photograph and see if I can get a name."

"Thanks." I didn't get my hopes up that he'd hit a match.

Craig leaned back to look at me. "In the meantime, you'll stay out of trouble?"

I knew what he was asking. He didn't want me chasing down Claire's killer without him. I planned to sketch out Freddie's family tree to keep me busy. "How much trouble can I get into doing genealogy research like an eighty-year-old?"

Craig gave me a dubious look. "If anyone can make genealogy dangerous, it's you."

I may have laughed, but I didn't deny it.

CHAPTER 19

When I got to the Stitch Witch, a fabric store in Brookside owned and operated by Riley's witches, Alyce was in the middle of a quilting demonstration. Based on their appearances, Helen, Janis, Bea, and Alyce couldn't be more different. Helen was the pint-sized power-house, Janis the henna-dyed hippy, Bea the sexpot, and Alyce the quintessential grandma. What they shared was a shit-ton of magical ability and a penchant for trouble. Because of Alyce's old-fashioned aprons and cherub cheeks, people mistook her for a sweet old lady, which was why her quilting demos were so popular.

Alyce had a stack of quilt blocks in front of her and a prefinished quilt folded neatly on the table behind her. By the time I took a seat in the back, she was almost to the big quilt reveal. Having been to a couple of these before, I knew she demoed technique first, helped her eager apprentice quilters complete a block or two following her pattern, and then ended her demo with the big unveil.

Alyce worked her way around the room, peering over

shoulders and praising everyone's efforts. She paused next to a dour-faced woman who was meticulously hand stitching her block. "Beautiful work, Ethel."

Ethel inflated her chest at the praise, looking down her nose at the less impressive attempt of the woman next to her.

"May I?" Alyce asked. At Ethel's pleased nod, Alyce held up her square to show the group.

My favorite part of Alyce's quilting demos was trying to guess what her finished quilt would look like based on a single quilt block. Ethel's block included a brightly colored paisley background with a salmon-colored piece taking up most of the right side of the square. Ethel had embroidered delicate lines on the block, giving it depth and dimension.

Alyce handed the square back to Ethel with an approving pat on the back. "Okay, ladies. Now for today's prize." Alyce held up a prize pack that included an assortment of fabric and a generous store gift card. "Whoever guesses the design wins this goodie bag including the iridescent butterfly fabric that was on special order for months."

Everyone oohed and ahhhed over the fabric she held up.

"Who wants to guess first?"

Ethel raised a prim hand. "I think it's a fox quilt." She held up her square and pointed to her embroidery. "These are the whiskers."

Alyce called on three more people with a twinkle in her eye. Animal guesses were popular today. One woman guessed an owl and another a baby seal. Someone guessed a flower quilt. When their competitiveness kicked in, the women started talking over each other. Alyce held up a hand, then picked up her folded quilt and waited for the room to quiet down.

Bea dropped into a chair next to me. "This is the best damn part. Watch their faces."

Alyce shook the quilt out with a flourish. The craftsmanship was truly impressive. Alyce created the most detailed quilts I'd ever seen, and this one was no exception. It didn't take long for the room to erupt in chaos, with half the women angling for a better look and half screeching in outrage.

Ethel had more color in her cheeks than the quilt block she was holding. She pointed a bony finger at Alyce's quilt and stuttered. "That's a, well it's a…" She couldn't finish her sentence.

Bea cackled beside me, clutching her side as she laughed. "It's a ball sac!"

Alyce beamed, shaking her five-foot penis quilt in triumph.

"Oh my God, the paisley," I choked out, laughing even more at the looks several of the little old ladies were throwing our way.

Despite the outrage, several women purchased full kits to replicate their own penis quilts, complete with instructions on stitching realistic scrotums. Once the crowd had mostly cleared out, I cornered Alyce for the favor that brought me here.

"Word on the street is that you're a genealogy wizard. I need some help tracking down a family tree, but all I have to go on is a name and a city. Can you help me?"

Alyce's eyes lit up. "I love a good genealogy challenge. Of course, I'll help you." Alyce motioned to Olivia who was working at the Stitch Witch while job hunting. "Olivia, can you watch the front? I'm going to go show Kali the new software program I got. It makes family searches so easy."

"Yeah, sure." Olivia finished refolding the stack of fabric

she'd been working on and moved to the counter to help the quilters lining up to purchase their kits. Olivia avoided looking at the photo of the finished quilt Alyce had generously included with each purchase.

I followed Alyce to the back and perched on a chair next to a cluttered desk that held a dinosaur of a computer.

"How is Olivia holding up?" I asked. Knowing a killer was out there hunting down fire elementals must be terrifying, particularly for someone who had grown up in small town America.

Alyce turned on the computer, which took forever to boot up. "She's handling it much better than any of us expected. Even though that girl seems timid, Janis told me when she was younger, she got in with a rough crowd. I'm betting she saw some bad apples back then because she's not letting her fear get out of control. She went to an all-girls boarding school for her last year of high school and came back the sweet girl she is now."

"An all-girls boarding school?" I cringed. That sounded awful.

Alyce gave me a conspiratorial look. "I know. Can you imagine? That's probably why she can't look at my quilt without blushing." Now that the computer finally was on, Alyce pulled up her genealogy program. "Okay, what's the name and city?"

"Frederick Masterson. I know he lived in Kansas City in the 1950s, but that's about all I have to go on."

Alyce scrunched her brow. "Why does that name sound familiar?"

"He was Samara's lover." I didn't have to explain who Samara was because Alyce had been right there with me when

I'd tried to fix the mess Samara started by attempting to summon Zepar so many years ago.

Alyce's eyes sharpened. "Is this related to the witch attacks?"

"Maybe." I explained my current theory that one of his descendants might have got ahold of Samara's grimoire and was using it to target witches. I didn't mention the black magic spell we found on Fiona, knowing Celeste wanted to keep knowledge of it locked down.

After an hour of searching, I left armed with genealogy notes that were largely disappointing. I'd hoped to find marriage and birth records that could lead me to modern-day relatives. What we found was Freddie's lineage dating back several generations. He was born in a small Missouri town in 1934 to Frederick A. Masterson and Cybil K. Frances. Because he was from a poor family rather than a rich one, Frederick P. Masterson had a junior after his name rather than a Roman numeral. He had one sibling, a twin, who died when she was twelve years old. There were no records of a marriage or children that we could find for Freddie.

We found a couple passing mentions of Freddie in old newspaper articles from his hometown—sports accomplishments and such—but his adulthood was a big dead end. It was entirely possible he'd moved away, started a family, and lived a quiet life. But it would take a considerable amount of time to track that history down, and time wasn't something we had an abundance of.

After leaving the Stitch Witch, I couldn't shake the feeling of eyes on me wherever I went. Ever since learning about the Enclave and its network of spies and assassins, I imagined every new face I saw was that of a Shadow. First, it was the stranger who hung around the bus stop for over an hour staring at the front of the store while I was inside. While walking to my car, I checked over my shoulder so often, I got a kink in my neck. When I stopped at the corner drugstore, there was a weird cashier who asked if I wanted some company at girls' night when I purchased a big bottle of fingernail polish remover and some nail decals. After making a noncommittal comment, I quickly stuffed the items in my purse and rushed out the door without waiting for my change.

I was fumbling with my keys to unlock my costume shop when someone tapped me on the shoulder. After jumping, I reluctantly turned around, fully expecting one of Aleksei's Shadows to be looming behind me. Instead, I came face-to-face with Meira.

"You scared me!" I accused.

Meira's lips turned down in disapproval. "You should really be more aware of your surroundings with the witch killer on the loose."

I held the door for her and led her to the back. Meira glanced around with distaste. "How do you find anything in this mess?"

I shrugged, not feeling the need to justify how I kept my workroom. With half-sewn costumes, stacks of fabric, and bins of embellishments, it may have looked to be in disarray, but I preferred to think of it as an unconventional organizational system.

Meira's gaze caught on the mannequin I used for a knife-throwing dummy. If she noticed that it shared her fashion sense, she didn't comment on it. "You said you had the photographs to show me?" She reached for the reading glasses she wore on a chain around her neck and perched them on her nose.

"I do." I grabbed the stack of photographs I'd been carting around since Bucharest and laid them out on my work bench.

Meira's expression darkened as she looked through them. "Tell me you did not sneak around in the bushes like a peeping Tom to take these photos."

"I did not. Grandma Dottie did."

Meira's eyes widened. "These are what she left in that safe deposit box?" she guessed.

I nodded.

"Why would she do that?"

"All I know is these photos are connected somehow to Claire's death." Craig still had the photo of Claire's killer, so I couldn't ask Meira about the man I was hunting. Instead, I pulled the closeup of Wallace Ratcliff, the master vampire, and pointed to him. "I'm pretty sure he ordered her death."

"Kali," Meira said softly. "Have you considered that Claire's death might actually be the result of a drunk driver?"

I gritted my teeth. "It was not." I didn't have the patience nor the desire to try to convince her. That wasn't the reason I was showing her the photos anyway. I pointed again at Ratcliff. "I take it from your reaction you know who this is."

She didn't have to glance down at the photo to answer. "I do."

"After my run-in with Ratcliff, I think he's behind the witch killings." I headed off her lecture. "He sent his goons to the airport to collect me."

Meira stared at me. "Why do you think Wallace Ratcliff is the witch killer? Both witches were killed in our territory, halfway across the world."

"I didn't say he killed them. I said he was behind it." Supernatural or human, men in power rarely got their own hands dirty. They recruited cannon fodder for those jobs. Before she could object, I pushed. "Who benefits more from a bunch of super vampires than Ratcliff? Think about it. By turning powerful witches, he'd have an edge over the other supernatural groups. And by turning fire elementals, he'd neutralize the biggest threat against his vampires."

"Fire." Meira looked thoughtful. "You have a point. But why now?"

"I've been thinking about that. He knew about Zepar's attempt to turn me. I think maybe that's where he got the idea."

"The timing makes sense," she conceded.

"If we're right, that solves half of the equation. We still need to identify the witch who is working with him."

Meira took her glasses off. "Any theories?"

I shared my suspicions that either someone on the witches' council at the time of Samara's death held on to her grimoire, or Freddie took off with it. Meira confirmed that Ruth's bloodline ended with her death.

"That leaves Freddie, then." I pulled my genealogy notes out and added them to the photos spread out on my work bench. "From a cursory search, I can't find any indication Freddie had children—no marriage license or birth certificate listing him as the father. I couldn't even locate his death certificate." I rubbed the knotted muscles in my shoulders. "Everything is a dead end."

Meira picked up the paper and stared at it thoughtfully. She ran her finger down the list of names, stopping on Freddie's grandmother. "Abigail Frances." Meira looked up at me. "Abigail Frances was a necromancer."

I rocked back on my heels. "If Freddie Masterson had a daughter," I started.

"You think she could be a necromancer." Meira finished the thought.

"I think we solved the rest of that equation." I snatched a pen out of the cup holder and circled the name. "I need to tell Craig."

Although we still didn't have a name for the daughter, at least we had a viable lead now. With the full resources of the supernatural community behind the search, we could find her quickly. "If we find her, she can lead us straight to Ratcliff."

Meira stepped closer to me and dropped her voice. "You need to listen to me. These are not the kind of accusations you make lightly. Do not repeat this theory to anyone other than Craig." She started to leave but turned back. "And then let him handle this, Kali. If Ratcliff is involved, you are not equipped to go up against the master vampire. You don't need to draw his attention."

I decided against mentioning the assassins supposedly guarding my back. If Meira was warning me away from getting on Ratcliff's radar, I had a pretty good guess what she'd have to say about the Enclave's sudden interest in me.

CHAPTER 20

When I called Craig, he told me he was headed to Volkov's because there had been another attack. He'd said there was another attack rather than another body, so I assumed the victim was still alive.

Craig swung by to pick me up on his way to Volkov's.

"Who was attacked?" I asked as I settled into his truck.

"Xavier," Craig said.

"Who's Xavier?"

"He is the witch from Oklahoma who asked for sanctuary." The witch Volkov was responsible for protecting.

"He was attacked in Volkov's home?" I asked. *Ouch.*

"Someone abducted him from Volkov's home," Craig corrected.

"He's missing?"

Craig frowned. "Not anymore. He was found in the woods behind Volkov's house an hour after he was taken. That's all I know."

We had ten minutes of driving in front of us, and I wasn't in the mood for silence. "So, witches aren't all women?" While my interactions with witches had been limited, every witch I had met had been a woman.

"Witches are predominately women, but there are a fair number of male witches, as well." Craig shook his head. "You've got to stop getting your knowledge of supernaturals from 80s movies."

He explained that at one time, both men and women practiced magic at roughly even rates. During the various witch trials, many male witches gave up magic to avoid persecution. Women were a more popular persecution target throughout history. For women, it meant the more powerful the witch, the less likely she'd be caught because powerful witches could tap into spells, wards, and sometimes even the elements to protect themselves. Weaker familial lines were often wiped out entirely, making it a survival of the fittest scenario. Although there were still some powerful male witches, they were the exception rather than the norm these days. The power structure of most modern covens was decidedly matriarchal.

The witch history lesson kept us occupied for the rest of the drive. When we arrived at Volkov's house, Craig punched in the gate code and parked by the front door.

I could see Volkov through the library window, and even from this distance, I could tell he was livid. Craig opened the door without knocking, and we went inside.

We followed the sound of Volkov's voice to the library. Although the room was a book lover's dream with floor-to-ceiling bookcases and soft ambient lighting, I'd spent enough time in this room searching for summoning rituals and sigils that it didn't give me warm fuzzies to be back here.

Craig caught Volkov's eye. "I'm going to do a quick

perimeter check." He bent down to me. "Hold tight, and please don't antagonize him."

The man was a powder keg. I wasn't going anywhere near him.

The library was a large room, but with so many people crowded in, it felt claustrophobic. Even without Craig in here, Volkov took up plenty of space on his own. There were also two men and a woman I didn't recognize in the room.

From the state of the library, the attack must have happened here. Volkov's normally tidy desktop was in disarray, as if someone slid across its surface. One of the library chairs was busted, and another tipped on its side. A cup of coffee was knocked over, dripping down the edge of the library table onto the floor.

Volkov had a man and a woman cornered, interrogating them. I was happy for once to not be the object of his ire.

"How the fuck could someone get to him?" Volkov pointed at the second man who lounged on the couch.

If the guy on the couch hadn't been sporting the beginning of a black eye, I would have wondered what he was doing here. Even I could tell he wasn't a shifter. From the rodeo buckle on his Levi's to the scuffed cowboy boots on his feet, it wasn't hard to peg him as the witch from Oklahoma. He stood out in this crowd.

By comparison, the man and woman currently getting their asses chewed were dressed for the secret service. At the moment, both of them looked at the floor, avoiding eye contact with Volkov.

The woman braved an answer. "That's on me, sir. Ian was out patrolling the perimeter, and I left Xavier alone in the kitchen to go to the bathroom. I wasn't gone more than a few minutes. By the time I heard the commotion, he was already gone." She kept her eyes down.

Some of Volkov's anger dampened. "Alright. I need the two of you to try to track the sonofabitch who broke into my house."

Relieved, they were out the front door in record time. I wondered if either of them was a bloodhound shifter, which would come in handy for tracking. The man certainly had the soulful brown eyes of one. Now didn't seem like the best time to play guess-the-shifter though, so I didn't ask.

Volkov moved on to the witch as Craig came back into the room. "Nothing?" he asked Craig.

"Signs of possible forced entry in the living room, but otherwise, it's clean." Where Volkov ran hot, Craig was all cold efficiency as he examined the scene. It was probably why they worked so well together.

After taking a quick inventory of the room, Craig stopped in front of the witch, who looked far less shaken up than I'd expect someone who was recently attacked to be. Craig studied the shiner the man wore on his left eye. "Anywhere else you're hurt, Xavier?"

"Just the eye." Xavier's voice had a touch of down-home Southern in it. He uncrossed the leg he had slung over his thigh and sat up straighter, making room on the couch. When he moved, he exposed a splotch of blood on the t-shirt tucked into his blue jeans.

Craig didn't miss it. "And that?" He pointed to the blood.

"I got caught up in some brambles when I tried to escape," Xavier said without looking at the injury. "It looks worse than it is."

Craig nodded. "All right. Tell us what happened."

"I was at the bookshelf over there." He pointed to the wall opposite the door. "And I felt someone behind me."

"Your back was to the door?" Volkov interrupted. At Xavier's affirmative nod, he said, "You couldn't have been in here long because you were only left alone for a few minutes." Volkov narrowed his eyes. "In the kitchen." When Xavier didn't react, Volkov pressed. "What were you doing in here?"

Unlike the shifters, Xavier had no trouble meeting Volkov's eyes. "You've got quite a collection. Figured I might as well take advantage while I was here and do some light reading."

Because Volkov was a collector of rare volumes of dangerous magic, his library was off limits to most people. Something I was sure Xavier had been warned about. He appeared to be one of the few people on the planet not wary of incurring Volkov's wrath.

Craig took over the questioning. "You said you felt someone come in behind you. Did you see who it was?"

"Whoever it was hid behind a distortion spell. I couldn't make out the person's features."

"Was it a man or woman?" Craig asked.

"I assume a man based on the fact that I'm not a small guy to attack, but I can't be sure."

The lull in questioning gave me an opportunity to insert my own. "How does a distortion spell work exactly? Is it something you have to continually use magic to maintain, or is it like a ward—something a powerful witch can make for someone else?" If it required constant magic, it would rule out Freddie's offspring as my primary suspect. Necromancers might be able to summon a demon and mint shiny new vampires if we put our minds to it, but as far as I knew, we could not cast spells.

Xavier's attention swung to me for the first time since I'd entered the room. "Who are you?" he asked bluntly.

"Sorry. I'm Kali."

Xavier gave me the once-over. "And you're a witch?"

"Necromancer," I corrected.

"So, you're the one." Xavier went from assessing to looking at me like something unsavory stuck to his shoe.

"Excuse me? The one what?"

Xavier stared at me awhile longer before answering. "The one who summoned the demon."

Geesh. Word apparently got around fast in the supernatural community. "I'm the one."

At last, Xavier answered my question. "Distortion spells are tricky spells to cast and require a great deal of skill. But like wards, once they are cast, they remain active until the magic fizzles out."

"And a witch could make one for someone else?" I asked.

"Sure."

That meant a necromancer could have done it with a purchased spell. "How long would a spell like that last?"

"Depends on the witch who cast it. Most witches capable of making a distortion spell would only have enough juice for it to last an hour—two at most. If the witch is particularly powerful though, the spell could be made to last days."

Great.

Craig redirected the conversation. "What happened after you spotted the guy?"

"He attacked as soon as I turned around," Xavier said. "He had a stun gun in his hand."

Bringing a stun gun probably meant the attacker wasn't confident in his or her ability to physically overpower the victim. It was the same reason I carried a stun gun, and Craig and Volkov did not.

Craig searched for marks on Xavier. "Where did the attacker hit you with it?"

"Here." Xavier pulled his t-shirt to the side, showing two small marks on his neck.

"And then?"

Xavier looked away. "I don't remember."

"Did you fight?" Craig asked.

As a witch, I expected Xavier to have at least tried to fight his attacker off with magic.

"I punched him in the face, but he zapped me again." Even though Xavier referred to the attacker as a man, every detail he shared made me more convinced this was the work of Freddie's daughter—whoever she might be.

I frowned. Defaulting to a physical attack seemed odd for a fire elemental. Xavier wasn't a small man, but he wasn't a bruiser, either. Judging from Volkov's reaction, I wasn't the only one surprised.

Could he be the Shadow? I wondered. At this point, I suspected every stranger who crossed my path, but Xavier had turned up at an opportune time. I stepped closer, but Xavier didn't spare me a glance. That, of course, made me even more suspicious.

Craig stared at Xavier's unblemished knuckles. "You punched the attacker?"

Xavier nodded.

"Then what?" Craig prodded.

"He came at me again, and shoved me into the table over there," Xavier said. "After that, he stunned me again, and I woke up in the forest."

"Then, he just let you go?" Volkov asked.

There was a hint of a smile on Xavier's face. "Something must have scared him off. When I woke up, he was running away."

"You didn't think to detain him?" Volkov didn't hide his frustration.

"Nah. I'm a witch, not an enforcer." Xavier stared at Craig when he said it.

I tamped down my suspicions about Xavier not being what he seemed because it wasn't relevant to what had happened here. Xavier was the only witch who'd made it out of the confrontation with this attacker alive, which meant he might have noticed something that would help nail the witch killer.

"Was your attacker alone?" I asked.

"As far as I could see. Why?"

"In the other attacks, there was both a witch and a vampire," I answered before Craig gave me the stop-sharing-information look. *Fine.* I'd be less forthcoming.

Xavier blinked in surprise, probably at the thought of a witch and vampire willingly partnering up. "There was no vampire," Xavier assured me. Even after running through what happened in excruciating detail, Xavier didn't give us anything useful about his attacker.

Volkov's shifters came back empty-handed, claiming the trail went cold mere feet from the front door. Xavier theorized it to be the work of a spell. I perked up at his mention of a scent masking spell. I'd have to hit up Helen and the witches for one of those, which would be so much more pleasant than eating liver and onions or spritzing myself with deer urine.

Despite the shifter's report, Volkov wouldn't be satisfied until he checked the grounds for himself. While Volkov had Xavier take him to the place in the woods where he woke up,

Craig and I remained in the library. I updated Craig about what I'd found searching for Freddie's offspring. He said he'd get his contacts to dig into it. Hopefully, they could track down a name of Freddie's daughter if she existed.

When Volkov came back, his face was grim. He posted Ian outside the room with instructions to keep everyone else out, then closed the door.

"What did you find?" Craig asked.

"Nothing much. The ground had been disturbed where Xavier woke up, like someone had cleared away the debris to form a circle," Volkov said. "But that's not what we need to discuss. Aleksei just called." He leveled his stare at me. "Naomi is dead."

I sat on the couch in shock. Naomi hadn't exactly been a spring chicken, but judging from Volkov's demeanor, she hadn't died of natural causes. "What happened?"

Volkov glanced at Craig as if asking how he should field my question.

"How did she die?" I demanded, not appreciating the attempt at shielding me.

"Strangulation." He looked at Craig again, but at least he'd answered. "The attacker used piano wire."

"A professional, then."

Volkov nodded, his face grim.

"I'm assuming they didn't catch the attacker?" Craig asked.

"No."

"How is that even possible?" I asked. "The Compound has more security than Fort Knox. How on earth could someone get in, kill Naomi, and then escape undetected?"

"I don't know." Volkov sounded as frustrated as I felt.

I dropped my head into my hands when I realized why both men were watching so studiously for my reaction.

"That's why the witch killer left the page with the spell. The killer knew Naomi had been in possession of Samara's grimoire, so the witch killer left the page knowing we'd connect it to Naomi." I forced myself to lift my head and look at them, my voice rough with guilt. "We led the killer right to her. If we hadn't gone to see her, the wards on the Compound would have prevented the killer from ever finding her." There was no love lost between Naomi and me after what she'd done, but I still hated that I'd played a part in her death.

Craig dropped a comforting hand on my shoulder, but I brushed him off. I didn't want comfort at the moment. I wanted to catch the witch killer before someone else ended up dead.

CHAPTER 21

$\mathcal{I}$t didn't take long for the Tribunal to call one of their emergency meetings. I wondered if they even had a normal meeting schedule. They certainly didn't keep minutes or take public comments, so I couldn't really see them bound by anything so mundane as regular meeting times. I received the official invitation the same way it always came—Craig showing up on my doorstep.

"Is this about Naomi's murder?" I asked as I buckled my seatbelt.

Craig started his pickup. "Partially. Volkov wants everyone to be up to speed on the investigation."

"And the other reason?"

When Craig didn't answer right away, I let my head hit the headrest, knowing I wasn't going to like whatever it was.

"Durrand's replacement has been chosen."

Lucky me. Another vampire. I would get a front-row seat to the introductions. Lucian Durrand's seat on the Tribunal had been vacant since Craig had killed him for attacking me. *What are the chances the next vampire on the Tribunal is an upgrade?*

"Please tell me this one is dark and broody and sparkles in the sunlight."

Craig looked at me in confusion.

"Never mind," I mumbled. Craig didn't get a lot of the pop culture references I handed out like candy. I'd have to work on that. Maybe I needed to invite him to movie night sometime. Seeing how much of the truck cab he filled up with his size, I'd probably have to get a bigger couch if he and my new neighbor showed up on the same night.

"What do you know about Durrand's replacement?" I asked.

Craig merged onto the interstate, leaving the industrial West Bottoms behind for the decidedly more bougie neighborhood where Volkov lived. "Next to nothing. All I know is his name and that he's showing up today to meet the rest of the Tribunal." Craig didn't volunteer the name, but from his sudden tension, he was concerned about something.

"What is his name?"

"Garadin Aldea."

He was a stranger then because his was a name I'd remember. "What an unusual name."

Craig's hands tightened on the steering wheel. "It's Romanian."

I jerked my head to stare at him. "Why would a Romanian be appointed to a Tribunal in the middle of the US?" The longer Craig took to answer, the more nervous I got.

"I don't know, but we suspect Wallace Ratcliff personally selected Aldea."

"Shit." Given my last run-in with the master vampire, that couldn't be good.

"Ratcliff probably wants eyes on you." Even though Craig

tried to reassure me, the grip he kept on the steering wheel spoke volumes.

"Maybe. Or he wants someone loyal to him on the Tribunal to run interference in the investigation into the witch killings."

From the set of his jaw, Craig had already thought of that possibility. He parked in front of Volkov's house, and I tried to push aside my growing unease as I walked up the long drive.

We arrived a few minutes early, with Meira and Celeste close on our heels. I hadn't seen Celeste in person since she'd warded my place after my run-in with Zepar. Today, she had on a gorgeous tangerine dress worn toga-style with an antique broach at her shoulder. After complimenting her fashion sense—something I rarely did with this neutral-obsessed crowd—we filed somberly inside, each of us lost in our own thoughts.

"In here." Volkov directed us to the library like we didn't all know that's where we'd end up.

"Are we still waiting on the vampire?" Celeste asked with mild curiosity.

Volkov's lips thinned. "He arrived half an hour ago." With Max Volkov, the only thing he hated more than being kept waiting was someone showing up early and forcing him to entertain. He was far from a gracious host, but werewolves weren't known for their welcoming natures.

The vampire in question stood at the front window, hands clasped behind his back as he gazed outside and ignored us as we filed into the room. The man was dressed impeccably in a dove gray suit and was shorter and far stockier than Durrand had been. He didn't turn around immediately to greet us. Both Meira and Celeste frowned at the slight.

Volkov cleared his throat. "Now that we're all here—"

"Introductions are in order," the vampire cut in. Still, he didn't turn around. I'd costumed enough actors to know a drama queen when I met one. With Volkov's short temper and Meira's sense of decorum, the combination should be interesting at least. I was imagining the fireworks when Garadin Aldea finally turned around.

I swayed, and Meira reached out to steady me, concern etched on her face. "Kali, what's wrong?"

Everyone's eyes turned to me, but all I could see was Aldea's smug face. I stepped closer, stopping with only a few feet separating us. When my knees trembled, I braced myself on Volkov's desk to keep them from buckling.

"Are you okay, child? You look like you've seen a ghost." While he sounded sincere, the mocking tilt of Aldea's lips said otherwise.

I kept my gaze locked on his face as I went for the letter opener on Volkov's desk. Before anyone had an inkling what I was doing, I buried it hilt deep in the side of the vampire's neck. I reveled in his momentary shock and welcomed the rage that overtook him next. I could hear the others shouting, demanding I stop. It was all background noise to me. I gripped the letter opener in my fist, working to widen the wound by sawing it back and forth even as his hand closed around my throat, the other going for my makeshift weapon. Aldea's blood coated my fingers, making the handle slick, but I held tight.

Before I could yank it out and bury it in his neck again, Aldea threw me across the room. I landed on the corner of Volkov's desk, the wind momentarily knocked out of me. I reached for the magic in my tattoo and drew its power into my body. When I staggered to my feet, the pain dulled to an ache, and I lunged for Aldea again.

He held his arms out wide and laughed, the blood still trickling down his throat. "Come on then, little girl."

I swung a right hook at Aldea's face to draw his attention and grabbed a fistful of the family jewels with my left, giving them a brutal twist before strong arms pulled me off him. I didn't care whose arms they were, only that they were holding me back. I fought with my whole body, all flailing limbs and blunt teeth.

Craig stepped in front of me, temporarily blocking my view of Aldea. "Kali, stop." He nodded sharply at Volkov, who was struggling to contain my thrashing body.

I was long past any of the moves I'd learned in Krav Maga. I was fighting on instinct alone, the wild desperation of being within striking distance of my sister's killer lending strength to my attack. For a second, I broke loose, but Volkov grabbed me around the waist and yanked me back. I threw my head back, not caring if I broke his nose as long as it got me free.

Before I could do more damage, Craig grabbed both of my arms. He pinned them to my sides, then he nodded for Volkov to release me. Craig spun me around faster than I could react, wrapping me in a bear hug. "Get him the fuck out of here," he ordered.

As Volkov ushered Aldea out of the library, I took great pleasure in the blood staining the pristine white of his dress shirt and the letter opener he had to pry from his neck. I bared my teeth at him, the power surging through my crow tattoo firing my veins.

Aldea stared at me as Volkov pushed him out of the room, leaving me with a parting shot. "Master Ratcliff sends his regards."

"Kali, you have to stop," Craig said, still holding me immobile like he feared I'd go back for round two as soon as he let go. He wasn't wrong. Out of everyone in this room, he was the only one I'd shown my grandmother's photo. He was the only one who recognized Aldea's face, and yet, he held me back.

When Volkov returned moments later, he was alone.

"Where is he?" I demanded.

"Gone." Volkov shook his head, frowning. "You can't stab people in the middle of a Tribunal meeting." For once, Volkov was the voice of calm while someone else raged.

Even with Aldea gone, it took a minute before the blood-lust cleared enough for me to speak coherently. "He's not people," I snapped. "It's him."

"Who?" Meira asked.

My throat closed, and I couldn't force the words out as I replayed the last time I'd seen Aldea's face and every time after when he'd come back to haunt my dreams. "Aldea is the man who killed my sister."

Meira gasped and took a step back, her gaze searching the door for any sign of him. "How could you know that?"

I bit my lip and struggled to get my ragged breathing under control. "Because Zepar showed me his face."

The room went quiet.

"Kali," Celeste soothed. "Zepar was a demon. He could have shown you anyone's face."

"No." I leaned as close as I could get to her with Craig still pinning my arms against my body. "That man killed Claire. She showed me his face long before Zepar did."

Volkov tilted his head toward the door. "Take her home, throw her in a cold shower or something until she cools off." He leaned down until he was even with my face, so I was forced to look at him. "A vision from a demon is not evidence. If," Volkov emphasized the word, "he killed her, then it will be handled by this Tribunal. Do not go after him again, or there will be consequences."

If I managed to kill Aldea, I wouldn't care about his consequences. Volkov straightened and moved away from me.

"And this incident?" Meira asked.

Volkov shrugged. "A wound like that is barely more than a paper cut to a vampire. As far as I'm concerned, no harm, no foul."

"Agreed," Celeste and Meira said in concert.

I was quiet on the drive home, busy planning all the ways I could take Aldea's head.

When we got to my apartment, I took Volkov's advice and took a cold shower, but it did little to cool the rage heating my blood. After ten minutes of shivering, I gave up and got out. Once I was dressed, I went to the living room where Craig was camped out. Whether he was acting as babysitter or bodyguard, he was adamant about not leaving me on my own. Aldea owed him a thank-you card for that.

Craig was on the phone when I got back. "You're positive?" he asked whoever he was talking to. "Do you have a location?"

I kept one ear on the conversation as I climbed on a chair to reach my liquor cabinet above the refrigerator, grabbing the new bottle of tequila. Resisting the urge to drink straight from the bottle, I pulled a couple of small glasses out of the cabinet and assembled our shots. After adding salt and lime, I carried them out to Craig. He hung up the phone as I came in the room and accepted one of the shots without comment, throwing it back at the same time I did mine.

I sat beside him, looking at his phone on the coffee table. "Who was that?"

"Volkov." Craig held out his shot glass. "Do you have more tequila?"

I poured him another shot and waited for the bomb he was about to drop. He didn't disappoint.

"Volkov did some checking. It seems Aldea has been in Kansas City longer than we knew."

The blood drained from my face at the thought of him being here so long. *Have I crossed paths with him? Did he watch me now like he'd watched Claire and me as teenagers?* "How long?" I asked.

"He signed a lease three months ago for a luxury condo. According to his neighbors, he moved in a couple months ago." Craig watched closely for my reaction.

I gripped the arm of the couch to steady myself. "You know where he lives?"

He stiffened. "I do, but it's not information I'll be sharing with you, for obvious reasons."

I ground my teeth in frustration. "Then why are you telling me this?" I asked, knowing the second he left, I'd be making a list of every luxury rental in the city limits. I might even call Jack Gates to help me track the guy down. Jack might be dead, but he was the best investigative reporter I knew.

I may have waited a decade to bring this man to justice, but now he was tauntingly close. The need to end him beat like a drum inside my head.

Craig turned me to face him, waiting until some of the fight left my body. "Set aside your sister's death for a second." When I reared back to object, he tugged me closer. "For the sake of this conversation," he clarified.

I nodded.

"Consider the timing. Aldea has been in Kansas City for a couple months—the same time frame as the witch murders.

And he wasn't appointed to the Tribunal until a few days ago, so why would he be here all this time?"

I stilled. "You think he's the vampire working with the witch."

"I do."

"It makes sense," I agreed. "No one has more to gain from a new army of super vampires than the master vampire himself. And Aldea is obviously Wallace Ratcliff's lackey, as the appointment to the Tribunal demonstrates. It makes sense he'd put Aldea in charge of turning new vamps." I let out a heavy breath. I'd rather end Aldea now than do whatever Craig was about to propose. "What's your plan?"

"I know you want Aldea to pay for what he took from you." Craig avoided saying Claire's name, probably afraid it would set me off again. "But this is our best shot at justice. If we can nail him for the witch murders, he'll get a death sentence, and we protect the rest of the fire elementals in the process."

I thought of the two who had sought sanctuary here in KC and the countless other fire elementals who had to constantly live in fear that they would be next. They deserved to be able to rest, knowing the killer was no longer a threat to them.

Craig saw my hesitation. "As long as he ends up dead, does it really matter if it's on Claire's behalf or Fiona's?"

He was right. Anne and Fiona deserved justice as much as Claire did. Even if I could take out Aldea on my own—and I was more than willing to die trying—killing him now would leave the identity of the witch killer a mere theory.

"You're right," I finally conceded. "What do we need to do?"

raig and I camped out on the couch in my apartment with the bottle of tequila and a legal pad to come up with a workable trap to draw out the witch killer. The plan wouldn't be without risks, but with the bodies piling up and bloodlust riding me, they were necessary risks.

"Who serves as bait?" I asked.

"It would have to be one of the fire elementals," Craig said.

I wondered if either of them would sign on for something so dangerous. They'd come to Kansas City for safety. Volunteering to be bait for a witch serial killer was the opposite of safe.

"Do you think either of them would do it?" Forcing them into a dangerous situation like that without their full consent was out of the question.

Craig looked thoughtful. "Xavier might."

"Yeah, but Xavier wouldn't make good bait. He's already fought off an attempt to take him. Olivia is the obvious choice." Olivia might be a powerful fire elemental, but she had easy target stamped all over her. From her slight stature to her timid personality, she'd be like catnip for our witch killers.

"I know." Craig rubbed his jaw, not liking the option even if she was the logical choice.

"I'll ask her," I offered.

"Thanks." He looked relieved. "If she agrees, we'll set the trap. We'll need a location where she can appear to be alone but somewhere with enough cover we can have a team in position. Then, we'll leak information about where she'll be."

I considered it. Whatever scenario we came up with had to be convincing, or Aldea would never bite. "She could be at my shop, helping with inventory or something. Olivia has been working at the Stitch Witch until she finds a job, so it wouldn't be much of a stretch for me to hire her."

"Too risky," Craig argued. "If you're with her, they'll either kill you to get to her, or grab her and take her to a second location we don't control."

"What if I had her cover the shop for me while I went to an appointment?"

Craig thought about it. "It's not perfect, but it could work. It's a familiar environment to anyone who'd be on our team. We could place our people in the shop and in the empty building across the street."

"How are we going to get in the building across the street?" I couldn't imagine Craig breaking and entering, but he'd surprised me before.

He must have suspected what I was thinking because he shook his head, smiling. "I know the landlord."

"Oh."

"What about your new neighbor?" Craig asked. "We can't risk a human stumbling into the middle of this."

"He doesn't live above his shop like I do, and I've only seen him there during the day. If we do it in the evening, we should be clear." With the exception of haunted house season, this part of Kansas City was largely a ghost town after five.

"Good," Craig said.

I refilled our glasses and lifted mine for a toast. "It sounds like we've got ourselves a plan."

Craig didn't reach for his. "There is one thing I need to do first," he said grimly.

"What's that?" I set my glass back down on the coffee table, not liking the sound of that.

Craig took a steadying breath before he hit me with his curveball. "Ratcliff is currently in D.C. on vampire business." He didn't volunteer how he knew Ratcliff's travel itinerary. "Volkov is following up with Aleksei to see how the Enclave connects to all of this, but it can't be a coincidence they put you under their protection. And they extended that protection by sending Aleksei into Ratcliff's seethe to retrieve you."

The same thing had occurred to me. "You think they know what Ratcliff's up to?"

"I'm not sure, but before we move forward with this plan, I need to find out how deep their interests run, and I need to establish a connection between Ratcliff and Aldea."

"Okay," I reasoned. "So, we go to D.C."

Craig pulled away, pacing to the window. He peered out of the curtains, and I recognized it for the stalling tactic it was. His deep sigh confirmed my suspicions. "I need to go alone." He turned back to face me, heading off the objections he must have known were coming. "Listen to me. You're lucky to have gotten out of Bucharest alive, Kali. Going back to Ratcliff's domain is too dangerous. Not to mention, you are on everyone's radar. The Enclave has Shadows watching you. Aldea has his eye on you. If you get on a plane for D.C., we might as well send Ratcliff a party invite." Craig reached for my hand and tugged me closer.

I held myself stiffly, but I didn't pull away.

"Let me lock this down, so we can nail Aldea."

His reasons were logical, but I felt the old fear bubbling up. "We could take a chartered plane. I could stow aboard like Riley did, so no one would know I was on it."

Craig didn't say anything.

"Meira could cover for me," I pleaded.

"I'm asking you to trust me." Craig leaned in, his serious gray eyes like still waters on a winter day.

Trust wasn't something that came easily for me. Maybe once it had, but then everyone I'd trusted left me behind. First, Claire, through no choice of her own. After her death, the people in my life fell like dominoes—my friends who couldn't cope with a girl changed by the loss of her sister, my mother who simply walked away, even my father and brother, who stayed but as shells of themselves. And lastly, my grandmother who chased ghosts to her grave.

Each loss had frayed my ability to rely on anyone except myself. Even Riley, who crashed through my walls, I mostly trusted at my side where I could see her, where I could at least pretend to have some control. What Craig was asking tapped bone deep into my insecurities. He was asking me to trust that when he left me to handle this, he would come back.

I stared at him, swallowing past the fear welling in my throat. "Craig, I..." I faltered, closing my eyes.

Craig bent toward me until his forehead was touching mine.

"I'm afraid you won't come back," I whispered, the admission itself terrifying.

"Look at me." He leaned away from me, his hands going to

my shoulders. He waited until I opened my eyes. "I will always come back." It wasn't a soft promise.

I wanted to believe him. Even though the silence stretched between us, Craig didn't flinch. And he didn't pull away. He sat with me, gaze steady, the weight of his hands an anchor where they rested on my shoulders.

"Okay." My voice was as raw as I felt. "When will you leave?"

"As soon as Volkov gets the flight arranged."

I expected him to gather his phone and leave right away, but he grabbed my hand instead. "Come on. You need to get some rest."

Craig laid down beside me, tucking me against his body. Wrapped in his arms, I fell asleep to the steady sound of his breathing.

Later, I woke in a panic, cold sweat drenching the silk sheet covering my body, I knew without turning my head, Craig was gone. While I'd signed up for this, the old anxiety settled into my chest. Knowing I wouldn't be able to go back to sleep, I sat on the edge of my bed in the dark debating what to do.

In the end, I went all in with the trust fall, dialing the number by heart.

"Kali?" Riley's voice was muddled with sleep. "What's wrong?"

"Can you come over?" My voice cracked. "I don't want to be alone."

She didn't ask any questions. "I'll be right there."

To keep my mind off the multitude of things that could go wrong the next day, I distracted myself with an eight-hour sewing marathon. On the positive side, I finished four in-progress custom orders and shipped the costumes out a week early. I also started Emma's gown for this year's Kansas City Renaissance Festival. I was making her a gorgeous corset-style overdress made with burgundy velvet I'd found at a pop-up vintage fabric stall in West Bottoms. It would take hours of sewing, but the end product would be worth every second of my labor.

By five, I was ready for a hot bath and a bad movie. Parker caught me as I closed the shop.

"Hi Kali." He leaned the stack of empty cardboard boxes he was carrying against the side of the building.

"Still moving in, I see." I grabbed a flattened box as it flopped over and returned it to his stack.

"I am." He looked into the window of his store and shook his head. "It's a mess. At this rate, I'll be lucky if I'm open by Christmas." He sounded so dejected.

"Do you need help unpacking?" I offered.

His whole face lit up. "Really?"

"Really." It would be a win-win. His unpacking efforts would be supercharged with a helper, and I wouldn't sit around my apartment plotting Aldea's death. We could even order a supreme pizza and a liter of pop. I'd be so high on carbs and sugar, I wouldn't even worry about Craig.

"That would be amazing." Parker started gathering the boxes into a pile, but because of the wind that kept catching the flaps, it was a losing battle.

"Here, let me help you." I took half the stack, leaving him with the rest.

As we headed to the alleyway by my apartment where the

trash and recycling dumpsters were, the wind picked up, blowing my cardigan off my shoulder. I had a tank top underneath, so I wasn't concerned about flashing the neighborhood, but Parker's attention snagged on my tattoo.

"Wow!" He moved to get a better look. "That's a beautiful tattoo."

He was standing close enough that it made me take a step back. Seeing my discomfort, he cringed and ran a hand through his hair. "I'm sorry. I'm not the best with social cues," he apologized.

"It's okay." I felt bad for overreacting. I tugged my shirt to the side to give him the full view of my crow tattoo. "I just got it recently, and I have to admit I love it."

"I can see why."

Feeling the now familiar stirring of wings, I hastily covered it up before Parker noticed the movement and started asking questions. "Do you have any tattoos?" Parker didn't seem like the kind of guy who would consider ink.

A boyish grin lit up his face. "Believe it or not, I do." He pulled up the sleeve of his t-shirt to reveal an equally beautiful tattoo on his bicep. It was tailor made for a music lover, with a trumpet surrounded by flaming musical notes. He held my gaze. "We're not so different, you and I."

I tossed the boxes in the recycling bin and changed the subject, eager to get our feet firmly back in the friend zone. We were back to talking about bad horror flicks when we rounded the corner to head back inside. Parker stopped short, his eyes narrowing.

I turned to see Craig standing next to the door of my shop. He had a duffle bag slung over his shoulder and exhaustion written in the lines of his body. He didn't spare Parker a glance.

My stupid heart tripped all over itself. "You're back," I said, stating the obvious.

Parker shifted awkwardly beside me, looking between the two of us. "Who's this?" he asked.

"I'm sorry." I turned back to him. "Parker, this is Craig Ward."

Craig held out his hand, gripping Parker's hand lightly as he shook it. Except for a polite glance at Parker, he kept his gaze on me. "It's nice to meet you, Parker. I'm Kali's boyfriend."

If I kept smiling like a middle schooler, I was going to hate myself in the morning.

"I'm so sorry, Parker, but can I help you set up shop another time? Craig got back from his trip earlier than I was expecting him."

Parker looked away, his face flushing a little. "No problem. It was nice of you to offer. I'll take any help I can get."

"I'll stop by tomorrow, and we can make plans."

"That would be great." Parker mumbled a goodbye before sidling past Craig and disappearing into his shop.

When we got upstairs, Craig dropped his bag inside the door of my apartment and leaned in for a soft kiss.

"Are you hungry?" I asked when we broke apart.

"Starving." He stared at me, and I wasn't sure if he was talking about food or something more.

"Come tell me about the trip, and I'll make us sandwiches." I was far from Suzy Homemaker, but even I could pull together a tasty sandwich on short notice. We sat at the kitchen table to eat.

I waited until he finished his sandwich before pushing for details. "So," I prompted. "What did you find out?"

Craig stood to put his dish in the sink. "I talked to Ratcliff, and it's clear he knows Aldea." He sat down across from me, his face troubled. "But Ratcliff swore that he didn't put Aldea on the Tribunal. He claims Aldea was requested by name."

"Requested? By whom?" I scowled, trying to make sense of the game Ratcliff was playing.

"He claims that a representative from the Tribunal contacted him and requested that Aldea fill the open position."

I laced my fingers on the back of my neck and looked up at the ceiling, trying to make sense of it. "Do you think he was lying?"

Craig shook his head. "I think he was telling the truth." At my inquisitive look, he explained. "It's an oddly specific lie to tell, first of all. But more importantly, if Ratcliff put him on the Tribunal, he's the kind of man to rub salt in the wound, not deny it."

Craig had a point there. Ratcliff seemed to love nothing more than to lording his upper hand over those he felt beneath him. "Who would request Aldea?"

Craig stared at me blankly. "I have no idea."

It was late, so there was no chance we'd get answers tonight. I put our plates in the dishwasher and tidied up the kitchen. When I turned back to Craig, he was watching me with heavy lidded eyes.

"You look exhausted."

He smiled. "A little, but sleep can wait."

"Are you sure?" After a trip like that, he had to be dead on his feet.

"Positive," he said. "I've been waiting all day to do this."

"Do what?" I asked.

Craig backed me against the refrigerator, caging me in his arms. He stared into my eyes long enough my breathing shallowed in anticipation. When he kissed me, he left no doubt how awake he was. Although it was far from our first kiss, there was a possessiveness in this one that was new. I parted my lips, inviting him to take more. By the time he pulled back, I was trembling with need, ready to have crazy back-against-the-fridge sex. I didn't even care the living room blinds were open.

Craig had other ideas. He stepped back, giving me enough space to choose. This wouldn't be just sex, not with us.

I reached out and ran my fingers across the stubble on his cheek, swallowing past the lump in my throat. He was worth the risk. "This will never be casual for me either," I whispered, holding his gaze. "I'm all in." I grabbed his hand and led him to the bedroom.

Craig undressed me slowly, peeling away the layers as if unwrapping something precious, his lips blazing a path down my body. When I stood naked before him, he looked at me with reverent eyes. "Beautiful." There was gravel in his voice and a fierceness in his touch.

I tugged his shirt out of his pants and waited until he ditched the rest of his clothes. And then we were a tangle of limbs and tongues, trying to climb inside one another and blot out the ugliness of the world around us.

The good news from Romania was that the Enclave would not interfere with the investigation into the witch murders. According to Aleksei, Craig had the green light to do whatever needed to be done. Despite their stamp of approval, we still had no clue how much the Enclave knew or how invested they were in the outcome. Aleksei claimed not to know anything about why I was under their protection.

While Craig worked to pull a team together, I drove to the Stitch Witch to enlist Olivia's help. Although Volkov was a necessary part of the plan, we all agreed to keep Riley out of it.

"Hey, Olivia. Do you have a minute? I need to talk to you about something."

Olivia stopped winding the bolt of crushed velvet in her lap and looked up at me. "About what?"

I watched as a customer positioned herself close enough to eavesdrop. The problem with catering to the sewing crowd was they were notorious gossip hounds. "It's better if we talk in private."

Olivia narrowed her eyes suspiciously but set the bolt of fabric aside. "Okay. We can talk in the back."

Janis watched us with interest.

"You might as well come, too, Janis," I called over my shoulder.

When all three of us were settled in the back, I explained the situation as thoroughly as I could without divulging details I didn't have authorization to share. To my surprise, Olivia agreed to help us without much discussion.

Janis wrung her skirt in her hands but sighed. "I don't like this, but it's your choice, Olivia."

Olivia gave her a reassuring squeeze. "I'll be fine." When she turned to me, I didn't like the hint of excitement in her eyes. "What's the plan?" she asked.

I ran through the basics, including the where and when. I detailed the fail-safes we would have in place to make sure the witch killer never got a hand on her. By the time I was done, Helen had closed the store, and all four of the older witches were rallying around Olivia.

Helen gave Olivia a protection amulet that she tucked inside her shirt. The amulet would ward Olivia against most physical attacks, including a knife. Even if the witch killer figured out the ward, the time it would take to dismantle it would give us enough time to get to her.

Alyce's contribution to the cause was a mason jar full of moonshine and a pair of earplugs to block out vampire compulsions. No one was sure whether the earplugs would work, but we all figured it was worth a shot. I confiscated the moonshine after Olivia choked on her first swallow. Olivia seemed more like a sip-a-wine-cooler drinker, and Alyce prided herself on making moonshine that could, according to her, "burn the hair off a man's ass."

Our plan was to have Olivia watch my shop from four to six. To ensure word got around, I called Volkov to get his permission first. Even though we were playacting, it grated on me to ask permission. Volkov put me on speaker phone in the middle of a debrief for the attack on Xavier, ensuring he had a roomful of shifters and Xavier present for my ask.

Although the wards on my shop weren't a secret, any witches worth their salt would know wards designed to protect me wouldn't be a barrier to snatching Olivia. Helen and Bea also made it a point to ask Olivia about her shop-sitting duties throughout the day as customers came and went. If anyone could spread the word like wildfire, it was Stitch Witch regulars.

After leaving the Stitch Witch, I checked in with Craig who had arranged for a team of shifters he trusted to be on site. Craig had tried to convince me to stay away, but there was zero chance I was leaving this fight to other people. The plan was for me to join his team in the empty building once I left Olivia in my shop. Then, all we had to do was wait.

With the pieces in place, I had several hours to burn before we laid the trap. Fortunately, I had a rain check to cash in, which would occupy me for the better part of the afternoon.

I found Parker crouched amid piles of vinyl records and movies in his shop.

"Hey, Parker."

Startled, Parker spun around to face me so quickly he sent several towering stacks of VHS tapes crashing to the ground. He clutched his chest as if to ward off an imminent heart attack. "You scared me."

"I'm sorry. I called out when I came in, but no one answered."

He smiled sheepishly. "Not your fault. Sometimes I get so preoccupied, I completely zone out."

I handed Parker the gift bag I'd brought along.

"What's this?" he asked.

"A little business warming gift."

Parker pulled the tissue paper off the top and grinned when he saw what I brought him. Inside the bag was the biggest, strongest-smelling candle I could find.

"I figured it would help with the smell in here," I said.

He took the candle out of the plastic wrap, and even unlit, the smell of pumpkin pecan waffles scented the air. Parker put the candle on the counter and used the matches that came with it to light all four wicks. "Wow! That should do the trick."

"By the time we're done here, we'll both be craving waffles badly enough to make an emergency waffle run." I was only half joking.

"I could get behind that plan," Parker said.

"All right." I bent down to help reassemble the stacks of tapes scattered across the floor. Picking up a romantic comedy and campy horror flick lying next to each other, I held them both up, looking to Parker for direction. "Umm. What's your system, here?"

Parker raked his fingers through his already messy hair while he surveyed the chaos. "I was hoping you could help with that," he admitted. "I'm better at collecting than organizing."

"Lucky for you, I'm an organizing fool." The only person better suited for the task was Emma, but since she was still out of town, he was stuck with me.

"I might not have waffles, but I've got drinks in the back. Do you prefer soda or beer?"

I looked at the rows of empty shelves and the mountains of boxes stacked between them. "Definitely beer."

As Parker disappeared into the back, I checked my phone and saw a missed message from Craig. I pulled up the voicemail. "Xavier is missing. Volkov has shifters scouring the property, but so far, there's no sign of him. I've sent two guards for Olivia. They'll stay out of sight, but I want eyes on her until tonight."

I texted a quick response but closed my phone when Parker returned with two open beer bottles. There was nothing I could do, so I tried to tamp down my nerves.

"I hope you don't mind an IPA." Parker held out one of the bottles apologetically. He pulled it back before I could reach for it. "I should have grabbed light beer."

"IPA is perfect." I pulled the bottle from his hand and took a long swig to prove my point. Although I liked my beer more sweet than bitter, I didn't want Parker to stress over it any more than he already was. It wasn't the worst beer I'd ever drank. "I haven't had a light beer since high school."

Parker relaxed and settled in next to me. We spent the next fifteen minutes in work mode, sorting movies and music into piles, then moving them to the shelves I'd labelled by genre.

We fell into a companionable silence, which left my mind free to stress about all the ways our plan could go wrong tonight. If anything happened to Olivia because I'd convinced her to be our bait, I couldn't forgive myself.

Although I wasn't a big IPA fan, my nerves were stretched tight enough I drank half of it despite the bitter taste. Between the higher alcohol content of the craft beer and the lunch I'd skipped today, I already felt a little buzzed. We still had about three hours before show time. I assured myself by then, any semblance of a buzz would be long gone.

Because Parker's shop wasn't officially opened yet, he hadn't bothered to lock the door after I came in. When the bell chimed above the door, I turned to see who it was, the movement making me dizzy. I closed my eyes for a second to make the room stop spinning. I opened them again, but the room was blurry. My eyes focused enough to make out the man coming through the door, and the onslaught of disorienting symptoms suddenly made sense.

The first thing I noticed about Xavier was his black eye was miraculously gone, probably because it had never been there in the first place. No wonder he knew so much about distortion spells. The second thing I noticed was that he wasn't alone. He held Olivia in front of him like a shield. She was gagged and wrapped from shoulder to hip in duct tape. Even so, her green eyes shimmered with rage. Xavier gave her a little shove toward Parker, and she lost her footing, landing with a crash near me.

I tried to clear my head, but the dizziness intensified. "Hang on, Olivia. It's going to be alright." Because it was hours before our planned trap, no one would be in position watching the place yet. I doubted Craig's guards had made it to Olivia before Xavier took her. They'd be looking everywhere but here when they discovered she was missing. With only a nerdy human and me wavering on the brink of unconsciousness to save her, things weren't looking good.

I turned my head with great effort until I had Parker's face in my sights. Saving Olivia was going to be a daunting enough task given my current state. I needed to get Parker out of here, so I didn't have him to worry about as well.

"You need to go," I begged him, but Parker watched Xavier and ignored me. For a human with no knowledge of the supernatural, it must have been a shock to have a witch to barge into your brand-new business chanting in a long-dead language. I had to get Parker out the line of fire, so I tried again. "Parker. Listen to me. I need you to go get help," I told him, my voice breathy. Speaking was becoming increasingly difficult, so I put everything I had in my last attempt. "Run!"

My yell was enough to get his attention. Parker moved until he was kneeling beside me. "Shhh. Everything is going to be fine." As I hit the floor, I saw the hem of his jeans as he stood up and walked away.

Despite my dizziness, I could hear fine, and I didn't recognize the words coming out of Xavier's mouth. I didn't need to know what he was saying because there was no question he meant me harm. The wards that protected me in my own shop didn't extend to Parker's place, leaving me vulnerable to attack. I reached for my purse, but my movements were clumsy. When I grabbed it from the nearby shelf, it tipped over, spilling the contents on the floor. A lipstick, a lint roller, and my brand-new bottle of fingernail polish remover fell out. The one item I could use—my custom holster with throwing knives rolled up in it—remained snug in the inside pocket. I pulled the purse closer, but Xavier walked over and kicked it away from me.

With every second that ticked by, my vision grew blurrier, my thoughts muddier. Whatever spell Xavier was using made me feel like I was sinking to the bottom of a lake. I could still see his face above the surface, hear his voice, but everything was distorted. I tried to move, but my limbs refused to work, hanging like so much dead weight at my sides.

I went under.

CHAPTER 24

Consciousness came back in increments, first a twinge in my fingers, then a flicker of light. My senses sharpened even as my vision cleared enough for me to make out the rest of the room. My gaze landed first on the tipped over beer bottle and second on Parker. *The bastard put something in my drink.*

He sat in a chair watching over me. When he saw I was awake, he smiled. It was only when he leaned forward in his chair that I noticed the page he was holding—a page torn from the very grimoire that started all of this.

"How did you get that?" My voice was hoarse. There was nothing left of my shy, awkward neighbor. Parker held himself with the confidence of someone used to calling the shots, and his eyes were cunning as flipped the page so I could see it. Suddenly, the last puzzle pieces clicked into place.

"Parker. Frederick Parker Masterson. You're Samara's lover." I hadn't found a trace of a daughter because there wasn't one. The only one way he could be sitting here today, decades past when he should have died, was if Zepar hadn't been the only demon he'd talked Samara into summoning. "You're hosting a demon."

He clapped, and his eyes darkened to pits of black. I pushed myself to a seated position and waited for the dizziness to recede. A quick inventory of the room showed Olivia bound in a new summoning circle, fire-retardant oven mitts taped to her hands. Her mouth was still gagged, but instead of whimpering in fear, she glared at Masterson with a fury that promised retribution. Xavier stood over her, and when his eyes met mine, they were ringed in vampire red.

"You turned him," I whispered. How long had Xavier had been a vampire, and why he had been the only one successfully turned? "Is that why he's been helping you hunt the other elementals?"

Masterson bristled at the suggestion. "He's a tool—no more, no less. I don't need anyone's help to turn witches." He glanced at his watch as if he were waiting for something.

"There's no vampire compelling the witches." We'd gotten so wrapped up in our assumptions, we stopped looking beyond them. Just like witches weren't the only ones who could summon a demon, vampires weren't the only ones able to compel a witch. Whoever the demon was inside Masterson, he was more than capable of compulsion.

Masterson smiled again. "You're slow on the uptake but getting warmer."

"What do you want with me? I'm not going to let you put a demon in me." My voice sounded more certain than I felt.

I tried to get to my feet, but I was still too weak to stand. When my body failed me, I turned to magic. My crow could function even when the rest of me could not, so I focused all my attention on reaching for the black tendril of my crow tattoo. It wasn't until my magic was wrapped tightly around it that I realized my mistake. The oily touch of a demon was familiar, and this one had burrowed deep into the crow, and, by extension, into me.

Masterson watched as realization dawned. Then, he threw back his head and laughed. "You already did."

I stared at the sleeve of his shirt that covered his own tattoo, done in familiar black ink, and recognized it for what it was. "The tattoo is a demon mark."

"Clever, no?" Masterson tugged his sleeve up to caress his mark.

"I'm going to kill Dingo when I get my hands on him."

Masterson smiled indulgently. "I beat you to it."

"Why?"

"He knew too much. I don't leave liabilities alive."

I had no doubt Masterson killed Naomi for the same reason. The guilt over leading him to her reared its head, but I pushed it down again and focused on trying to get out of here alive with Olivia.

I looked at the circle where Olivia was bound. "How are you planning on finishing the ritual?"

"That's the beauty. I don't need to," Parker said. "You summoned the demon all on your own this time. All I had to do was make sure you carried his mark."

What if it was too late to stop what was in motion? While this demon was weaker than Zepar had been, I'd called on its power a dozen times already. Feeling tentatively for the soul bond, I pulled back as soon as I felt the pulse of its power. I was still in control—for now, at least. "I won't call on it again," I swore.

"We'll see." Masterson watched me with interest. "I have a surprise for you." He glanced at his watch as the door crashed open, and Garadin Aldea rushed into the room.

The mystery of who had called him to Kansas City was solved. Masterson had been playing chess with us all along. We just hadn't known it.

Rage pumped through me at the sight of Aldea. Xavier intercepted Aldea, keeping him occupied long enough for Masterson to give me a parting shot.

"Your choice." He tapped the crow on my chest. "Die like your sister at the vampire's hands, or use this to fight back." Parker canted his head toward Olivia. "Bring her."

Xavier hit Aldea with a wall of magic, temporarily holding him at bay, then bent down and grabbed Olivia, slinging her over his shoulder. By the time the magical shield broke, Xavier was out the front door and disappearing down the street.

Rather than going after them, Aldea turned on me. He stepped close enough, I could see the red rimming his eyes. As we stared at each other, this moment felt inevitable. Looking into the face of my sister's killer, I reached for the darkness, praying I was strong enough to keep it from overtaking me.

I dug deep, finding the demon where it coiled inside my crow. The bond was already in place. It was too late to undo this, so I was going to use the weapon curled on my chest. Although I'd never been able to see my own soul before, I saw it now—a scarlet thread that rose from my body like a flame. I pushed every last bit of my energy to my crow. Despite the cloying demon weighing it down, the magic unfurled its wings and dove for my soul.

When the two collided, the crow finished bonding my soul to the demon's, winding them together until the inky black was encased in scarlet. Then, the heavy body of the bird settled back into my skin. The demon pulsed power as Aldea came for me. I drew on it like a battery.

Aldea reeled back when he caught sight of my eyes—the demon must be bleeding into them. "Abomination," he snarled. "Like your sister."

He was wrong. Claire had been just a girl, but I was something else now. Aldea's eyes were lit with the same fanaticism as they had been when he'd driven his car into the body of my fifteen-year-old sister. This was a man willing to die if it meant taking me with him.

A calm settled over me as I searched the room for a weapon that would end this. I took a step back, inching toward my purse and the throwing knives hidden there. I tried to keep Aldea's attention off what I was doing. "Why did you kill her?" My voice came out hoarser than usual, and I wondered if that was the demon.

"To stop her from becoming a weapon," Aldea said contemptuously.

"She was a child." The break in my voice had everything to do with the loss of my twin sister.

"I should have killed you both when you were children." Aldea spit on the floor as he said it.

I took another step toward my purse, so it was within reach. "Why didn't you?"

"It was obvious she was the strong one. I thought the ability would die with her. You were just a silly, frivolous girl content to play dress up. You were hardly a threat." He sneered. "I should have killed you, anyway."

Aldea settled his weight on the balls of his feet, and in doing so, telegraphed his next move. I sidestepped as he came for me, the demon lending me speed. I dove for my purse. Aldea recovered too quickly for me to go for my knives that were still bundled up in a neat little roll, so I grabbed the only weapon within reach, unscrewing the cap of the fingernail polish remover as I came to my feet.

Aldea looked at it with scorn. "Still wasting your time on stupid, pretty little things," he mocked me.

I smiled. Then, I tossed the acetone at him. He threw his hands to protect his face, blocking most of it from getting in his eyes. Aldea laughed again, but I hadn't been aiming for his eyes. I stepped to his side and hit him with a textbook round-house powered by demon strength that sent him careening into the counter. He fell exactly where I wanted him, landing on the flames of the pumpkin pecan waffle candle. I watched him catch fire.

Aldea made no attempt to put out the fire licking up his body. He looked at me through the flames and bared his fangs. "War is coming."

I watched him burn until all that was left were embers and ash. Although a demon was still inside of me, it was the human who reveled in Aldea's death.

The crash of the door slamming open drew my attention. Of all the people who could have come through the door, Olivia was the last person I expected. I opened my mouth to tell her everything would be okay, but I choked the words down when I registered what she held in her hand.

"Is that what I think it is?" My voice was calmer than was reasonable for the day I was having. I wondered if I had my new resident demon to thank for that.

Olivia spun the head she was holding by the hair, Xavier's face frozen in shock. "Ding dong, the vampire witch is dead." She was still dressed like normal Olivia, except for the machete sheathed on her back. When her face broke into a wide grin, she looked like a pixie—a happy, bloodthirsty pixie.

I stared at her for a full minute before I could form words. "And his body?"

Olivia waved dismissively. "I made arrangements. It'll be disposed of properly." She pointed to the pile of ash. "And that is?"

"Garadin Aldea." I couldn't manage to put any remorse in my answer, but at least I wasn't sing-songing about it like she had about Xavier.

"And the witch killer?" She looked around for Masterson.

"Gone."

I tried to reconcile the wide-eyed witch from South Dakota to the machete-toting badass in front of me. Hell, I'd felt sorry for Olivia when she'd curled up in the fetal position in an old tire to avoid Paintball War. I looked at her now–all swagger. "You deserve an Oscar for that paintball performance."

Olivia grinned. "What can I say? I'm a witch of many talents."

"So, you're the Shadow, huh?"

Olivia didn't answer. Instead, she tossed Xavier's head in the nearby trash can and held out her palm. A ball of fire formed, and she lobbed it in the trashcan after him.

I plugged my nose, anticipating the smell, but I couldn't tear my eyes away. "Do you think he did it willingly?" I asked her. Because he was the only witch Masterson had success-fully turned into a vampire, I suspected Xavier had welcomed the demon with open arms.

"Maybe." Olivia pointed to the trash can. "I don't concern myself with motivation, only with the outcome."

Olivia tousled through her wind-blown hair. "He was a low-level fire elemental, but he had enough power to block my flames with his own." She tapped her machete and gestured to the still-smoking head. "That's why I had to resort to violence."

"You do know lighting someone on fire qualifies as violent, right?"

Olivia looked pointedly at the pile of ash on the floor. "Speaking of lighting people on fire," she said. "We should probably find a broom."

CHAPTER 25

Cleanup turned out to be an all-hands on deck affair. Craig got to me first, with Volkov and a crew of shifters close on his heels. I recounted what happened, skimming over the part where I paid someone to tattoo a demon mark on my body. When they pushed for more details, I put them off until the emergency Tribunal meeting Volkov called for tomorrow morning—sans Aldea, of course. I needed time to come to terms with what I had become and decide what I wanted to do about it.

Craig cornered me coming out of the bathroom in the back of Parker's shop, where I attempted to wipe the worst of the ash off my skin. He stood with his hands fisted at his sides. I couldn't tell whether it was because he wanted to touch me or because he could sense the demon writhing beneath my skin.

"Are you okay?" he asked.

"I don't know." I admitted. I filled in the gaps, telling Craig about how I got the tattoo and unwittingly bonded with the demon attached to it. "But I've kicked one demon out, so I've got some practice with this whole eviction process." I tried to sound confident, but my lip trembled. Right now, it was everything I could do to keep a stranglehold on the demon pushing up through my skin.

Craig pulled me in for a hug, his breath fanning across my hair. He looked like he always did—a bulwark of calm. Based on his racing heart, he was taking this as hard as I was. He might be good at fighting all manner of supernaturals, but standing by while I battled an enemy he couldn't see or touch rendered him powerless. Craig wasn't a man used to being powerless.

Although he tried to persuade me to go home and leave the aftermath to them, the last thing I wanted was to be alone with a demon. Instead, I got to work. The first thing I did was grab my cell phone and take photos of the blood-red circle spray-painted on the floor and the sigils ringing it. Then, I gathered the contents of my purse and set it by the door. Between all of us, we had the place set to rights within an hour. I even insisted we go through Parker's boxes looking for anything that might help us locate him, but other than movies and old music, there was little to find.

Despite my assurances I would be okay, Craig refused to leave me alone. Once we were in my apartment without the distractions of other people or tasks to keep us busy, we both fell silent. After several minutes, I couldn't take the tension anymore.

"I'm going to take a shower." I stared down at my singed clothes and headed to the kitchen to get a trash bag. The clothes could go on my balcony for tonight. Tomorrow, I'd toss them in the dumpster.

I glanced at Craig, who took up all the space in my small apartment kitchen. He looked lost. I opened the cabinet that held my basics—sugar, flour, oil, salt. "My kitchen isn't as well stocked as yours, but if you'd like to bake, it's all yours," I offered.

In the midst of dealing with Zepar, Craig had told me he baked when he was stressed. Right now, he was definitely stressed. I didn't have it in me to comfort him, so this was the best I could do.

"That's a good idea." He looked down at me for a second, like he had something else to say, but then he walked to the sink to wash his hands.

In the bathroom, I stripped down and searched my body. Other than my tattoo, which shifted and moved as I watched it in the mirror, I looked the same. I ran a finger across my crow and felt for the demon beneath it. I'd covered one demon mark with another. This one just came in pretty ink unlike the calling card Zepar had carved into me.

Masterson had carved similar marks into Anne and Fiona. I frowned at the reflection of my tattoo. Patterns generally served a purpose, so why had Masterson broken the pattern with me? *Was it because I booted Zepar out?* This tattoo was more insidious, lulling me into accepting it in increments. *What did it mean that Masterson and I both wore ours in the form of tattoos?* Maybe he broke the pattern because I served a different purpose. Anne and Fiona were meant to be soldiers, but maybe I was meant to be something else.

I stepped in the shower and turned the hot water as high as I could stand. Then, I scrubbed my skin raw with a loofah. No matter how hard I scrubbed, the demon still itched beneath my skin.

The rich smell of coffee and chocolate lured me back to the kitchen. Even with my limited baking supplies, Craig managed to make cappuccino muffins that were perfectly browned and smelled divine. Normally, I would devour them, savoring every delicious bite. But tonight, although I voiced all the usual compliments, I couldn't taste a thing.

When I finally fell asleep, I dreamt I was surrounded by hell fire, the heat of it so intense, I woke drenched in sweat. Craig reached for me, but I slid from the covers and went to the bathroom. I stared into the mirror for a long time, watching my eyes turn from brown to demon black and back again. I turned on the shower, but no amount of water washed away the darkness clinging to me.

The drive to Volkov's in the morning was as strained as the night before had been. We'd left the apartment early, so we could stop at the neighborhood diner for steak and eggs. Fortunately, the diner had its fair share of shifters as customers, so the waitress didn't bat an eye when I asked for a rare—as in bloody and still mooing—steak.

After several minutes of quiet stressing, I turned to Craig. "Am I a vampire?" I kept my voice low so the humans around us couldn't overhear.

"No." He sounded confident. "The demon might drive you to crave blood, but you won't need it."

"That's disgusting." Even as I said it, the pang of hunger that hit when the waitress set a bloody steak in front of me confirmed my days of medium-well were behind me.

The breakfast took long enough that Craig and I were the last to arrive at Volkov's. The mood in the library was so somber, it felt like walking into a funeral wake. In some ways, I supposed we were.

This time, when I told the story of the tattoo and the

demon attached to it, I didn't leave any details out. By the time I finished, they were all looking anywhere but at me. Even Volkov stared at the floor.

"How do I get this thing out of me?" I asked.

Meira and Celeste exchanged a look.

My stomach pitched. "What?"

"Kali, that's not possible." Celeste's gentled her tone as if talking to a misguided child.

I gritted my teeth. "There must be a way."

Meira met my eyes. "There isn't."

I grabbed an armful of Volkov's books and slammed them on the table. "We just have to find a ritual or a spell or an exorcism." I stared around the room, but no one would meet my eyes.

Meira dropped into the nearest chair with none of her usual grace. "It's too late." She shook her head when I tried to object. "Your soul is bonded to the demon." Meira looked up at me. "If we remove the demon, it will take your soul with it. You'll die."

"I have to get rid of him." I raked my fingernails across my chest, wishing I could dig him out with my bare hands.

"Stop." Craig reached for my hands before I could burrow my nails in deeper. Even when I stopped scratching, he kept my hands in his, stroking his thumbs across the inside of my wrists.

How could I become the thing I hate? "What does this make me?"

Meira stood and crossed the room until she stood shoulder to shoulder with Craig. "Now, you listen to me, Kali." She tapped a manicured finger against my chest. "The demon is not in control. You are. So, call yourself whatever you like because you are something new."

It didn't make me feel better.

"Have you considered the advantages?" Volkov cut into my pity party.

"Advantages?" I scoffed. I stepped away from Craig and toward Volkov. "What advantages? Bloodlust? The ability to vacation in hell?"

Volkov tilted his head to study me. "Physical strength, heightened senses, and the ability to compel for starters." He looked down at my French manicure that had miraculously survived a vampire and a witch attack. "Claws that actually serve a purpose in a fight."

"I don't have any of those things." I pointed to my eyes. "Do you see red-rimmed demon eyes?" My eyes were as brown today as they had been before the demon had taken up residence on my chest.

Volkov grimaced. "Have you tried to access any of those things, Ms. James? Or are you content to wallow in self-pity?" He had about as much compassion as a drill sergeant, but compassion wouldn't save me, anyway.

"I didn't ask for this."

"No one asks for this," Volkov countered. "No one gets to choose what they are."

Craig stiffened, and he glared at Volkov. "That's enough, Max."

"No. It's not enough." Volkov scanned all our faces. "Keep coddling her, and she'll wind up dead." He stalked over to the bookcase and pulled out a volume. Flipping to a page he must have bookmarked earlier, he slammed it on the table. We all moved closer. Volkov pointed to a sigil that bore a striking resemblance to the tree branches at the center of my tattoo. Next to it was a picture of a demon, half man and half crow.

"That's not some weak demon she's got in there. It's Raum,

and he may not be as strong as Zepar, but I guarantee you he's the strongest demon currently on this plane." Volkov picked the book up and shoved it at Celeste, who paled as she read the entry.

After scanning the page, she read it aloud. "According to this, Raum commands thirty legions of demons in hell. Unlike other demons, he doesn't mind taking human form—relishes it, even." She paused to stare at the tattoo peeking from beneath my tank top. "He's known to take the form of a crow, and he is said to be able to see past, present, and future."

Volkov snatched the book back, closing it and tossing it to the pile I'd dumped on the table earlier. He stepped closer, his wolf looking out at me from behind Volkov's eyes. "It's time for you to make a choice, Ms. James. You can live or die. It's that simple. If you want the demon out, I'll get him out, but you'll die in the process."

Craig moved to step in front of me, but I grabbed his arm and pulled him back. "And if I live but can't control this demon? Then what?"

"Then you become another rogue demon that needs to be put down." Volkov took a menacing step toward me, anger vibrating his chest. Craig did put himself in front of me, but Volkov talked around him. "If you want to live, there won't be any more of this toying around with your powers. No more half-assed training sessions. If you live, you need to learn to tap into that demon without allowing him to take over, so that you are strong enough to handle whatever is coming at us."

The crow ruffled its wings before settling against my skin. I stepped to the side, away from both men. "Aldea said a war was coming," I told them. "He called Claire and I weapons. He said that's why we had to be killed."

"Because of your potential to control vampires," Meira theorized.

"I don't think so," I said. "I think he wanted me dead because I could summon demons."

"With Kali under his control, Frederick Masterson could use her to raise an army of demons." Meira appeared thoughtful.

I nodded. "You've all said it. Vampires won't want demons here so they can subjugate them again. If I can raise demons, that makes me a weapon in Aldea's eyes."

"How does Aldea fit into all of this?" Meira asked.

"Everyone is working on the assumption that Aldea was here at Ratcliff's request. What if he wasn't, and this was his power grab?" Celeste ventured.

I sighed. "Frederick Masterson sent Aldea here."

"Why?" Meira asked.

I ran a finger over the tattoo. "Aldea was Masterson's way of guaranteeing I bonded with this demon. He knew I'd choose the demon if it meant taking out my sister's killer."

Meira looked at me thoughtfully. "And Ratcliff?"

None of them had seen Aldea as I had. "Aldea was a fanatic. He wasn't afraid of dying as long as he took me out with him." I tried unsuccessfully to block out the memory of his face when he went for Claire. "But Aldea was just an attack dog, and I'd bet everything he did was on Ratcliff's orders. I suspect Ratcliff has known about the threat Frederick Masterson poses for a long time." At Meira's questioning look, I explained. "Ratcliff made it clear that he saw me as a threat to be eliminated. I tried to control him when we met, and I failed. Ratcliff didn't seem afraid of my potential to control vampires. But I think he knew Masterson harbored a demon and intended to use me and that's why he saw me as a threat." It was clear Ratcliff hadn't wanted Masterson to get his hands on me.

Craig nodded. "That fits."

"Why was Masterson after fire elementals?" Meira voiced the question I'd wondered since we put the pattern together.

At the mention of fire, the image of Aldea and Xavier covered in flames flashed in my head—two vampires reduced to ash in a matter of minutes. My head snapped up. *Of course.* "Who has the most to lose if Masterson succeeds and summons his legions of demons?"

"Vampires." Meira said without hesitation.

Craig swore, piecing the last of the puzzle together. "If Masterson controls the fire elementals, he can decimate his most formidable opposition."

I nodded. "He's being strategic, trying to turn supernaturals who will be useful to him."

Celeste paled. "We need to keep the rest of the fire elementals under protection." She looked to Volkov. "Double the guard on Olivia. I'll take care of the others."

"Olivia is gone," Volkov said, looking at me. "She's somewhere safe where Masterson can't get to her."

I hoped that was true. As a Shadow, Olivia would be back at the Compound, but that wasn't the guarantee of safety it should be. Masterson had gotten to Naomi there. Olivia was better equipped to protect herself than Naomi had been, and I hoped it would be enough to keep her alive and out of Masterson's hands.

Celeste paced the floor. "If Masterson gets his hands on fire elementals, and Raum takes control of Kali to call demons to this plane..." Celeste trailed off.

"Masterson would be virtually unstoppable," Volkov

finished, glaring at me. "Do you understand what's at stake now?"

"Yes." I ran my fingertips across the crow's back. "I have to learn to control this demon."

Meira slipped into planning mode, slipping her reading glasses on and picking up the book about demons. "We'll start training tomorrow. You can work with Craig on the physical fighting and with me on spiritual warfare."

Craig's shoulders eased at the thought.

"It won't be enough," I argued.

"It has to be," Volkov snapped. "It's the only chance we've got."

I shook my head. "No. It's not." There was one place equipped to train me, and one man prepared to do whatever was necessary to help me master the predator bound to my soul.

While everyone continued debating what I needed, I pulled out the plain white business card Aleksei had tucked in my purse when he dropped me off at the airport. Craig was standing close enough to take the card from my hand. When I looked up at him, I saw the recognition on his face and read the objection before it passed his lips.

"Now, I'm asking you to trust me." I held my breath as I waited for his answer.

Craig's eyes turned a tumultuous gray as he battled his nature. Then he nodded, a slight tremor in his hands as he handed the card back to me.

The only thing printed on the front of the business card was a phone number. I flipped it over and read what Aleksei had written on the back. *Call when you're ready.*

And I did.

NOTE TO READERS

If you enjoyed this book, please consider leaving a review or rating on Amazon and/or GoodReads. Your reviews help new readers discover my books and are always appreciated!

If you'd like to be notified of new releases and exclusive content, you can sign up for my newsletter at lamcbride.com/newsletter/ and join my Facebook Readers Group at https://www.facebook.com/groups/lamcbridereaders

BOOKS BY L.A. MCBRIDE

KALI JAMES SERIES

Book 1: Fastening the Grave

Book 2: Threading the Bones

Book 3: Stitching the Talisman

Book 4: Gathering the Dead

RILEY CRUZ SERIES

Prequel Novella: Boneyard Thief

Book 1: Demon Relic Hunter

ACKNOWLEDGMENTS

Special thanks goes to my husband Chris, my fantastic editor Sara Lundberg who is more accommodating than I deserve, and to my amazing readers who laugh at my jokes and send me goat videos to brighten my day.

www.ingramcontent.com/pod-product-compliance
Lightning Source LLC
Chambersburg PA
CBHW061759190726

48289CB00007B/2002